RUMOR HAS IT

TOR BOOKS BY CAT RAMBO

You Sexy Thing
Devil's Gun
Rumor Has It

RUMOR HAS IT

CAT RAMBO

TOR

TOR PUBLISHING GROUP
NEW YORK

This is a work of fiction. All of the characters, organizations, and events portrayed in this novel are either products of the author's imagination or are used fictitiously.

RUMOR HAS IT

A Tor Book
Published by Tom Doherty Associates / Tor Publishing Group
120 Broadway
New York, NY 10271

www.torpublishinggroup.com

Tor® is a registered trademark of Macmillan Publishing Group, LLC.

The Library of Congress Cataloging-in-Publication Data is available upon request.

ISBN 978-1-250-26939-3 (hardcover)
ISBN 978-1-250-26937-9 (ebook)

Our books may be purchased in bulk for promotional, educational,
or business use. Please contact your local bookseller or the Macmillan Corporate
and Premium Sales Department at 1-800-221-7945, extension 5442, or by email at
MacmillanSpecialMarkets@macmillan.com.

First Edition: 2024

Printed in the United States of America

0 9 8 7 6 5 4 3 2 1

For Anne McCaffrey,
who also sailed among the stars

RUMOR HAS IT

THE STORY THUS FAR

In book one, *You Sexy Thing*, Niko Larsen and a handful of the soldiers she once commanded have escaped the ranks of the Holy Hive Mind and retired to start a restaurant, the Last Chance, aboard the space station TwiceFar. The restaurant proves unexpectedly successful, to the point where a famous food critic, Lolola Montaigne d'Arcy deBurgh, reserves a table. Niko and the others are excited about the prospect of earning a coveted Nikkelin Orb, but the day of the meal a mysterious package arrives, containing Atlanta, an heir to the Paxian throne, with no knowledge of why she's been sent in cryo-freeze to Niko. Just as Lolola is seated with visiting wealthy dilettante Arpat Takraven, things start exploding on the station and it's torn apart by unknown forces.

The group, along with the critic and the package containing Atlanta, flee the station on *You Sexy Thing*, an intelligent bioship. Thinking itself stolen, the ship is headed to the nearest authorities in order to turn its captors in when Lolola circumvents its programming for her own purpose, taking the ship to a haven for space pirates, IAPH.

There, Niko encounters two figures from her past: her former lover Petalia and the pirate leader Tubal Last, who kidnapped Petalia long ago and has been poisoning them against Niko ever since. When one of the crew, pastry chef Milly, attempts to betray the group to win her own freedom, circumstances conspire to let her actions free them all, destroying the pirate haven, but not before Last has killed one of the crew, Thorn, a young werelion whose loss devastates his twin brother, Talon.

Petalia chooses not to stay with the group. Angry and embittered at Niko, they leave the ship at Montmurray Station. The rest return the ship to its original owner, Takraven, who allows them to keep it for now, with the stricture that each year they'll return to cook him a meal and tell him of their adventures.

All seems well until Niko receives a message. Tubal Last is alive. And he's planning revenge.

In book two, *Devil's Gun*, Niko and her crew find themselves at a malfunctioning Gate, a rare and potentially disastrous failure. They make the most of their time stranded there by creating a pop-up restaurant named the Second Last Chance.

Among the others stranded there are the ship and crew sous chef Gio had formerly been part of, belonging to Gnarl Grusson. Gnarl meets Talon seemingly by chance in the marketplace, and after taking the grieving boy out to a bar and commiserating over his murdered twin, Thorn, Gnarl persuades him to think about illegally cloning his lost sibling and later, secretly sends the technology for doing so to Talon.

An archaeologist named Jezli Farren turns up, claiming to be able to fix the Gate—for a price. She's accompanied by Roxana Cinis, a paladin. When both disappear immediately after the repair, Niko assumes Jezli is gone, not realizing that the ship has taken them aboard as part of its new hobby, *hourisigah,* the architecting of dramatic events.

Meanwhile, Talon has given in to the urge to replicate his brother, even though he knows the attempt is both illegal and improbable. He hides the clone sac deep within the ship.

Discovered, Jezli convinces Niko that she knows the location of a weapon that can destroy Tubal Last. She takes them to its location, the perilous confines of the carcass of an enormous space moth. There they are intercepted by Gnarl, bent on revenge on both Jezli and Niko. He insists on accompanying them into the moth. Inside the moth, Atlanta is transformed and takes Roxana's place while the other perishes.

Thorn's clone is decanted and Talon realizes he has not re-created his brother, but brought an angry and resentful stranger into existence.

They secure the weapon and leave Gnarl marooned on the moth, only to find that the gun can only be fired by a Florian. They go in search of the sole surviving Florian, Petalia, and per-suade her to fire the gun. But the effort fails—the gun can only seek a single target, and there seems to be more than one Last now.

THE CREW

IIIIII.II.IIII.II.IIIIIIIII.II.IIIIIIII.II.IIIIIIII.II.IIIIIIII.II.IIIIIIII.II

NIKO LARSEN's highly volatile military career has led to her nickname, "The Ten-Hour Admiral." Rather than be absorbed into the Holy Hive Mind, she pretended to have a calling toward artistry in food and thus managed to muster out, along with the others. Human, she was raised among the Free Traders but left them when they refused to ransom Petalia from the pirates.

DABRY JEN is Niko's second-in-command. He's also the culinary genius behind the Last Chance's success. An Ettilite, his four arms allow him considerable dexterity in the kitchen. Competent and loyal, Dabry provides his captain with his all, as he has ever since they enlisted at the same time in the ranks of the Holy Hive Mind.

GIO is an augmented chimpanzee from Old Terra and Dabry's sous chef. He has chosen not to get vocal augmentation, preferring sign language for communication. When in the Holy Hive Mind, he was a skilled quartermaster, and even now is adept at wheedling supplies for the restaurant and making things do double, sometimes triple service.

SKIDOO is a Tlellan, a composite entity resembling a brightly colored terrestrial squid. Once the group's communications officer, Skidoo remains the one who handles bookings, reservations, and similar matters. Pleasure-loving and sensual, Skidoo is usually a peacemaker in the group.

LASSITE, a reptilian Sessile, is a former priest who follows Niko because of his conviction that she is the one who will follow the Golden Path, a prophecy whose enactment he has been preparing for all his life.

MILLY is relatively new to the group, once a soldier and now a pastry chef who has replaced a former member who vanished. She is a Nneti, a birdlike race renowned for their deadly grace.

TALON's mother entrusted him and his twin brother **THORN** into Niko's care while in the Holy Hive Mind's service. The twins were sunny, enthusiastic, and devoted to the sport of warball, something that Talon has abandoned in his despondency at his twin's loss.

REBBE is the clone of the lost Talon, unsure who or what he is, but knowing one thing deeply: He hates the person responsible for bringing him into the world.

ATLANTA thought she was an Imperial heir, but she's discovered she's nothing of the sort, just a clone of the actual heir. Now she's a paladin—but what does it mean?

JEZLI FARREN is a former con woman traveling with the crew for her own unknown purposes.

PETALIA is Niko's former lover, turned against her by Tubal Last, but reluctantly traveling with Niko while trying to escape Last themself.

YOU SEKY THING is enjoying itself for the first time in a long existence and is learning about the concept of emotions in the process. Opinionated, loquacious, and self-centered, the ship is getting acquainted not just with its new crew but itself as well.

1

IIIIIII.II/IIIiII.II/IIIIII.II.IIIIIIiII.IIIIIIiII.II.IIIIIIiII.II.IIIIIII.

Chaos brews in the space between the stars, where one might expect a vacuum and chill wastes. However, plunging through Q-space, plowing through a section of the distance hidden from most voyagers, you see the loops and snarls in reality, the unnecessary curlicues and furbelows and gimcracks that the universe has chosen to add—weirdly and bizarrely, here and here alone—which is why most people find it unsettling.

Q-space is where probabilities slide and skew like missiles skidding on ice, where logic steps out the door to pause for a smoke break, briefly replaced by its much less sane cousin wearing torn fishnets and an inverted beret that might have once been raspberry velvet. Q-space is where strange discoveries are made, unlikely coincidences are forged, and the unimaginable shows up on every side.

You Sexy Thing loved Q-space. It moved with a grace that it really wished someone had noticed but had resigned itself to no one doing so. It eased through it like a watermelon seed squirted between thumb and forefinger, moving unimaginable distances, and at such a speed that the ship had little time to examine its surroundings, catching only glimpses as it hurtled on.

In Q-space, mathematics can do odd things, can balloon and shrink in unexpected ways. Numbers are more whimsical there, or at least more prone to strange, inexplicable convulsions.

But in the here and now, math behaved more predictably. And sometimes disappointingly.

Captain Niko Larsen added up the figures by hand, and then had the ship double-check them. They remained the same. She leaned back in her chair and knuckled at the back of her neck, trying to smooth out the knotted tension there.

On the asset side: the handful of credits left from their last pop-up venture, most of that profit gone to refueling costs and Gate charges.

On the debit side: the fact of those ongoing fuel costs, Gate charges, and other ways the Known Universe charged for existence within it, such as taxes, tariffs, surcharges, delivery charges, fees, tips, gratuities. Etc.

The debit side was so much larger than the asset side. She leaned forward to stare at it for a long moment before pushing the datapad away.

There was a touch of hope. If she could get at the money from their insurance claim, the money for the destruction of their first restaurant, the Last Chance, back on TwiceFar Station. But doing that meant going someplace expensive. Very expensive.

So expensive that if they went there, they might end up stranded. With only that handful of credits to satisfy a host of necessities.

But that chance was their only one, as far as she could see. So the only other question was, in telling the rest of the crew about her plans, how much she would reveal of the direness of their resources. It would encourage a small measure of conservation of those resources, but at the cost of a drop in morale and rise in anxiety. No, that wasn't worth it.

"Coralind," Dabry breathed in a reverential tone that delighted Niko's heart in a way it hadn't been delighted for a while. In front of him was a bowl of spiced bits of protein, smelling of cumin and iron, beside another of soupy yellow sauce. He was filling rounds of dough with both, pinching them closed with expert ease before arranging them on a nearby platter.

The others in the kitchen had mixed reactions. Lassite simply nodded as though in confirmation. Atlanta blinked and made a mental note to look up the destination as soon as possible. Talon shrugged while Rebbe, leaning against the wall, continued to watch the room as though it was full of dangers, without paying much attention to what Niko actually said.

Skidoo squealed. "Is being a garden there from Tlella and some of its people." She undulated in delight. "Is being places to swim, is being places that is being only water."

Gio, sorting through peppery corms and picking off the odd scaly leaf or two, gave a soft hoot of appreciation, eyes bright. *Trade*, he thought. *Good trade at Coralind, some of the best in the Known Universe. And Festival time! Who wouldn't want to be on Coralind at Festival time? This was an excellent choice.*

Milly's shoulders stiffened for a moment, then relaxed as she watched the others. They'd be happier, at least, and happier meant more ready to respond to her advances. She'd been trying to win back their trust for a while now, but the ship's atmosphere hadn't really been conducive. She put down the pastry knife she'd been polishing and asked, "That's where the gardens are, eh?"

Gio nodded, signing, "Hundreds of them. Almost as good as planet-grown. Sometimes better, they say. They've been growing for centuries now, inside that planetoid. Food you can get there that you can't get anywhere else."

Dabry gave off shaping dumplings, putting a lower hand to the counter as if to catch his balance at the thought.

"I'll have to tell Skidoo to put together a list of the restaurants there," he said thoughtfully. "So we can go over it, look for gaps."

"That is certainly one way of looking at it," Niko said dryly.

He raised an eyebrow. "What's wrong with that approach?"

"You will be in a place with ingredients that you may never find in their prime again," she explained. "Cook the meal of your heart, cook something that you love."

She had thought him motionless already, but at her words, he became utterly still, as though holding his breath. Then he let it out and said, his voice tight, "I'll have to think about that."

She had not thought to touch old wounds, but she had. And realized, just as quickly, that to say anything drawing attention to her blunder would be to offend even further. She cast about for words, glancing around the kitchen, and was grateful when Milly rescued her. "Will you tell everyone the full details at the meal? Neither Jezli or Petalia is here."

"I could tell them right now," the ship offered.

"No, that's my job," Niko said.

"Technically, I am the communications systems."

"Technically, you should wait to be ordered before acting on that order," she snapped.

"Very well." The ship was currently thinking about ways to express irritation, and everyone jumped when eyes suddenly manifested in the upper walls and ceiling, rolling in their sockets. They were then absorbed in a process that took considerably longer than their appearance, which everyone watched with horrified fascination, including the imperturbable Lassite.

"I grasp your meaning," Niko said when the process seemed complete and no further eyes were in evidence, "and would prefer you not express yourself in that way again."

"In what way?" the ship said suspiciously, worried about the boundaries of this particular order. "With eyes?"

Niko paused, working through the wording, and decided upon, "By manifesting organs specifically for the sake of a gesture."

"Mmm." The ship filed the definition away to examine later for possible loopholes, including the precise definition of "organs," but refrained from more "gestures." There were plenty of other possibilities. What, for example, if it created a servitor and then had the servitor perform the gestures? It would attempt that experiment later.

Niko found Jezli in the lounge, reading. Jezli set down her reader and gave Niko her unfailing, maddeningly courteous attention.

"We are bound for Coralind next," Niko informed her. "That will be a suitable place for you to leave the ship and find some other berth."

"Admit it, Captain," Jezli Farren said with an easy grin that might have had an edge of mockery to it. It was a tone familiar to everyone on the days when Jezli was feeling particularly brittle and missing her former companion, Roxana, and seeking to divert herself. "Rumor has it you'd miss me if I were gone."

"You are a scoundrel and a con artist and the *only* reason you are still on this ship is because you are the sole person who understands how to operate that thing," Niko snapped. Jezli had, as ever, managed to get under her skin with only a few words. "But how complicated can it be, telling Petalia to pull the trigger?"

Around them, the ship listened without commentary. It had found that the conversations between Jezli and Niko were highly entertaining, and even more so when they forgot that it was listening.

The "thing" in question was, for once, not the ship itself, *You Sexy Thing*, but the ancient alien artifact currently resting in one of the aforementioned ship's holds. Nicknamed the "Devil's Gun," it was an implement of assassination.

Unfortunately, not one that could assassinate the only person they needed to kill before he could kill them.

Jezli poked at her pad. "Three days to Coralind," Jezli said, looking at it. She was about to say something else, but there was a rustle at the doorway. She looked up; Niko turned, uncrossing her arms.

Petalia, the Florian who was both Niko's ex-lover and current constant antagonist, as well as the only person who could fire the Devil's Gun, stood there. They were tall and female in form, their skin and hair white and fine, the latter strewn with tiny blossoms. They smelled of ice with an edge of sweetness, and as always, their eyes were fixed only on Niko.

"Coralind?" they demanded, stepping into the room. "Why there?"

"You mentioned yourself that it's tied into Last's net of contacts. We may be able to backtrace from there. And I'm going to visit an old friend who may have other thoughts on how to find word of Tubal Last," Niko said.

She returned Petalia's stare. The notion flickered through Jezli's head that they looked like an artistic tableau embodying complexities of emotion, and she framed it from several angles to amuse herself. She had stood as though to leave, but had failed to exit. She thought they had forgotten her presence, which they had.

"Coralind." Petalia loaded the word with scorn. "Who do you know in that tawdry place?"

Niko refrained from taking offense, leaving her tone mild and emotionless as pudding. "Someone I knew during some of my final years with the Holy Hive Mind."

Petalia frowned. Niko thought about the years Tubal Last had spent monitoring Niko while whispering lies about her into Petalia's ear, and wondered how close the monitoring had been. Very close at times, it seemed.

Leaving off that angle of questioning, Petalia pursued others. "How long will we be there? Are you planning some other ridiculous restauranting enterprise?"

"That is how we make our living, with ridiculous restauranting." Niko's even tone faltered toward the end of the sentence, so slightly it would have been imperceptible to anyone who didn't know her well.

Jezli continued to amuse herself, imagining a camera at different vantage points around the room, thinking about how she would have blocked the ongoing scene if she were a theatrical director, detailing it with careful precision.

Petalia's eyes narrowed. "It's not Festival time there, is it?" they demanded. "That would be insane."

This time, Niko's eyes wandered, seeking Jezli's. Her lips quirked. "Well," she said, and Jezli held her breath. "Certainly it would be, and certainly it is, but that is exactly what we are doing."

"Just when I thought it was impossible to like you much better," Jezli said. "You are a daring woman."

"Desperate, perhaps, rather than daring," Niko said, her tone softer than it had been.

Petalia glanced between the two, and their eyes filled with an emotion Niko had not seen in their pale depths for a long, long time.

The moment hung in the air, and who knows what might have happened if Skidoo had not entered just then.

"Is being interrupting?" Skidoo's three turquoise eyes swiveled independently, regarding each of them simultaneously.

Petalia drew themself up to glance down at Skidoo. "You are interrupting nothing," they said with icy hauteur.

"Well, scan you being all Ruler of Known Space," Jezli said admiringly and over-sincerely, folding her arms as she leaned against the wall.

Petalia huffed out derision, dropped a nod at Niko, and stalked out. Skidoo's unoccupied eye chose Niko as its new target.

"You are terribly good at getting under their skin." Niko turned to Jezli, pointing a finger at her. "I'll thank you not to exercise your talents on those on board under my protection."

"And the ship," she added, glancing upward.

"Thank you, Captain." *You Sexy Thing* considered this permission to enter the conversation. It had been desperately trying to understand the nuances of the last few minims, which had seemed very significant in all sorts of ways it could not comprehend.

For example, each of the three participants had experienced an elevated heart rate—but why? Had there been subtle threat displays it had failed to decode? It played its memories over several hundred times while waiting for the conversation to go on.

"I apologize." Jezli spread her hands in an expansive gesture of helplessness. "I don't mean to. It just slips out sometimes."

"Rein it in."

Jezli dropped Niko a salute that somehow managed to be sardonic. How did the woman get that into the gesture? Niko couldn't quite figure it out, but it was definitely there. She decided, with an effort, to let the matter go.

One of Gnarl Grusson's main traits was that he had never, ever, been able to let something go, and that particularly held true of grudges. And while over the course of his existence, he had accumulated a freighter hold's worth of such grudges, the one that currently burned in his burly chest, so hotly that no other could contend with it, was one involving Niko Larsen.

"Thought she was done with me, leaving me there to die," he muttered to himself once again. The words elicited a sidelong look from his second-in-command, but they knew better than challenge him.

He had been poring over star charts, figuring fuel costs and times, and had narrowed the possibilities down to three. She could only go so far, so fast, and her resources were limited.

The first possibility was Broohaven. Tempting, with all its information networks, but the Broons didn't go in much for culinary pleasures. They were all about efficiency and delivering maximal nutrition in minimal time.

The second possibility was Droon. Plenty of tourists there,

plenty of places to play at feeding people for coin. But Droon was on the outskirts, and close to a single transit point, as opposed to the third possibility.

That third possibility . . . well, how could anyone who'd checked their calendar want to avoid such potentially profitable chaos and hubbub? And from there, there were plenty of other port possibilities for the next stop.

He muttered to himself, and his second-in-command kept pretending not to notice. The captain had been given to this ever since they'd rescued him from where he'd been stranded on the space moth. Personally, the second had mixed opinions about the necessity of that rescue. This, too, he kept to himself, his attention on the captain.

Lips pursed in deep consideration, Gnarl passed gas, paying deep attention to the act, then spoke to the second.

"Set course for Coralind."

2

Despite his initial enthusiasm at the announcement, Dabry sought Niko out later, finding her in their shared office.

She put down her reader and flipped it off before he could glimpse the screen. Going over financial documents again, he thought, but refrained from asking. She'd let him know when she was ready. Instead, he asked about their destination.

"Do you really think this wise?" he challenged. "Even through it's on the outskirts of the Known Universe, Coralind is well traveled. Well known. If Tubal Last is looking for a time and place to strike, it will be when we go to Coralind."

Niko shook her head. "I'm not so sure. He's waiting for something, I think. He won't move fast on this."

"What if he learned we had a weapon?"

Niko quirked a brow. "But it's not one we can use, as we already found out. Petalia can operate it, but it requires a single target. Somehow, there's now more than one Tubal Last."

"But that part he might not learn, and he certainly doesn't suspect you think there might be more than one of him. And time gives not just him—maybe them—the chance to prepare, but offers you the same opportunity."

"He wants us to prepare. That's what that message was about. Time to worry. Time to fret. Time to grow a new crop of fear for him to harvest."

"And if you're wrong?" Dabry crossed all four arms, staring at her with a furrowed brow.

"Then I am wrong," she said with weary flatness and folded her hands on the table.

He shook his head and chose to move on to another subject. "What do you hope to accomplish there?"

"For one thing, it's where Biboban ended up."

His brow creased in confusion for a moment, then cleared. "The Jadoogar blobbship we worked with on those last two years?"

"The one and the same."

"What is it doing there?"

"What it used to do for us, but on a much vaster scale." He continued to frown, and she elaborated. "It runs the systems on the station."

"Which systems?"

"All of them. It always could work at that level, at least with the right resources, and the station's happy to supply them. In return, they get a smoothly running station that can respond to any emergencies in a flexible, adaptive way."

"And you think Biboban will provide . . ."

"Information. Because one of the systems it runs is communications, and I would imagine it tracks any patterns it detects. One or the other of those patterns, happening on well-traveled Coralind, will lead us back to wherever Tubal Last is lurking."

"How do you explain our results with the gun?"

"As I see it, there's two possibilities. One is that he's found some sort of protective shield. That's always possible—magic-based energy stuff can get pretty complicated and full of loopholes."

He nodded and waited. When she said nothing more, he prodded. "What's the other possibility?"

"That there's actually more than one of him. Easy enough with clones and modern mind-transfer tech."

"More than one." He didn't shudder, but revulsion tinged his voice.

"We're all worried," Niko said. "We need to think of something to boost morale. Coralind will also help with that."

She broke off. Dabry smiled faintly.

"Jezli Farren has been doing her bit to boost morale with a nightly handbliss game."

"For *money*?" Niko sat up straighter in her chair, outrage surging in her.

"For *imaginary* money, as I understand it. Niko, I think she's harmless enough when it comes to us. Would Roxana really have traveled with her if she were capable of betrayal?"

"Keep in mind that she defrauded dozens of ships by pretending to fix a broken Gate. Jezli Farren, in my opinion, is capable of all sorts of things."

It wasn't just a card game, it was an experience in flirtation whenever you played handbliss with Skidoo, Atlanta thought. It was chatter and eye contact, and overacted glee when winning, and mock anger when losing. This flirtation was an art form, this sort of thing, and Skidoo was its utter mistress.

For her part, Skidoo was delighted by the enthusiasm which Atlanta brought to the game of handbliss. She thought the girl was becoming quite a skilled player. Much of which was that she now knew better than to ever play for money with Jezli Farren. The avaricious Jezli was why they all played for imaginary money now, and everyone owed her imaginary, but vast, sums as a result. After the kitchen disclosures, they had retired to the gathering room that usually served for such play and sat eye to eye across the table.

Atlanta played with fierce concentration and a determination to hide her emotions that was not commensurate with her actual ability to control them.

Skidoo paid attention to the game, of course, but liked the conversation better. Conversation formed a kind of intimacy, as much a kind of touch, or mutual regard, as any stroke or caress.

That was the fascinating thing about language. The way you could express things with it. It was one reason why she clung to the rhythms and syntaxes of her childhood, her young adulthood, the brief years before she realized that she had to get off-planet. Realized that she was different in a way she'd only heard mentioned before in derision and mockery. And realized that her sanity and survival depended on escaping that.

They reckoned her a criminal, back on her home planet. They would have immediately condemned her. Imprisoned her, if not worse. But that didn't matter, since she was never returning there.

Atlanta played another card and said, "You said that there are others like you on Coralind?"

Skidoo undulated in negation. "That is not being accurate. Is being others from my planet but is being another species. They is being living in our waters, but then is being going to space. But they is never being returning. It is forbidden."

"So you can never go back?"

Skidoo's shudder was sufficient, and Atlanta took a different tack.

"But you're a Tlellan—aren't they?"

"Tlellan is being the name for anyone who is being from Tlella. There is being five species—maybe is being five and a half, depending on who is being doing the counting—and four and a half is never being going to space."

"But you did."

"I is being different," Skidoo said, eyes standing up in pride and fascination. "Is being some like me but—" She waggled a couple of tentacles in the air. "Very few."

Atlanta hesitated but decided to press. "And your modifications . . ."

Skidoo undulated again; this time the gentle ripple was full of amusement. "I is liking the world enough to be touching it all the time. Not many of us, and others is being thinking it . . ." She hesitated. "Is being a mix of sinful and unethical and un-civic-minded. Otherwise, we would just live our lives and not make babies to keep doing things for the good of everyone."

She had lapsed—for the first time since Atlanta had known her—into a different cadence, a different pattern, and Atlanta thought to herself, *She's echoing someone else talking at her long ago*, but she refrained from comment.

Skidoo uncoiled a tentacle to drape it over Atlanta's wrist. "Is being gardens there much like Tlella. If you is being willing, is perhaps is being we is being visiting one of them?"

"Together," she added after a second, in case her meaning was not clear. Sometimes people could not see a thing until you pointed it out.

"Oh," Atlanta exclaimed. "Yes! Yes, I'd like that. Very much." She touched a fingertip to the soft surface of the tentacle, tracing along a scarlet stripe. "We'll go together."

Others on the ship had things to think about beyond their des-tination.

No matter where Rebbe went in the ship, it seemed, Talon would soon appear. Mooning after him while pretending not to.

Talon, who was responsible for his whole existence. Talon, who had thought he was creating his lost twin and made Rebbe instead, someone very definitely *not* the lost Thorn. Talon, who he hated, and Talon, who loved what Talon thought he was, and never really saw him at all.

That was the worst of it. He could see the expectancy in Talon, the belief that the other youth clung to, that at some point Rebbe would disappear, would be wiped away with the return of body memories. Talon still thought that he would become Thorn, someday, and that was what Rebbe hated most of all, because it would have meant Rebbe would vanish as though he had never been.

Rebbe had worried about that at first. Searched his mind for any sign of Thorn's presence, there among his limited memories since waking. Feared that his hand might move of its own volition, that he might become a prisoner in his own body. Or that Thorn was already a prisoner there, without Rebbe knowing.

The only person who seemed to understand what was going through his head was Milly, and so he didn't mind spending time with her. Something lay between her and the other teammates, he could tell, but he wasn't sure what, and he didn't want to ask. It seemed connected to Thorn's death and therefore was doubly imperative not to discuss. There were so many ways to go wrong in the world.

Still, he could feel her trying to reach across that divide to the others, and sometimes they seemed to respond, like Gio and Skidoo, or even Dabry. But there was a coldness in the captain when dealing with Milly, a coldness that seemed unfair to Rebbe when Milly was charming and sweet and funny and could always make him laugh.

He gave Talon the slip once again and found Skidoo and Atlanta playing handbliss in a lounge. He positioned himself so he would not be readily visible from the doorway—Talon could work for it, if he truly wanted to keep chasing him down. He watched the game silently until Skidoo finally glanced his way and, without asking, dealt him in.

They played that way for a while. Gio and Milly wandered in together and sat down to join the game. They chatted about what they'd heard, trade gossip and lore, about Coralind.

"Never been there, but it's a byword, Coralind in Festival," Milly told Atlanta.

"Why a byword?" Atlanta considered her cards, pretending not to notice Skidoo's tentacle draped affectionately over her wrist.

"People come from all over the Known Universe for that sort of thing, but travel takes money, so they're all well enough pocketed to come, which means well enough pocketed to spend plenty on food and drink and music and performances and every other indulgence you can think of. Coralind's gardens produce everything under any sun, they say, or at least the best of it." Milly played a card, then shot Gio a grin as he huffed out frustration when she raked in her winnings.

Rebbe could feel himself relaxing, could feel the tension that thrummed through him uncoiling, uncurling. Then Talon stuck his head in the room and all of it came back.

It was too much. This time he threw his hand down and snarled at Talon, a hot, challenging "I'm going to fight you now" roar that surprised everyone in the room, including himself, so instead of acting on it, he held back, despite the urge to change into full lion form and tear at the other.

"Enough!" Gio signed.

"Stop following me," he shouted at Talon, desperate and angry. "Stop!"

Talon's whole body sagged. Perhaps Rebbe would have been sorry to have hurt him, if he had been anyone else. Anyone who was not responsible for the fact he was an illegal clone, and not just that, a clone without memories, without history, and most importantly, without any legal standing.

But Rebbe was and always would be an illegal clone, and so there would be no forgiveness for him.

Talon took a step backward, his eyes still fixed on Rebbe. Looking for his reaction, like he genuinely thought that Rebbe would relent, would tell him to stay. That unquenchable hope in

Talon's eyes steeled Rebbe, kept him frowning until Talon was gone from the doorway.

He took a breath and turned to the others, who remained silent. Gio's arms were folded, Milly beside him eyeing Rebbe as though she'd been expecting him to give in. Atlanta's lips were pursed at his rudeness. Only Skidoo looked at all sympathetic, and it was always hard for him to read her expressions, so he wasn't sure.

"He follows me everywhere!" he tried to explain. He could feel the disapproval coming off them, although he didn't entirely understand it. One of the tenets of the crew was that you got along, and if you didn't, then you worked it out.

The unfairness of that burned in him. Talon counted on that niceness, and he thought he could just wait and wear Rebbe down.

Utterly, angeringly unfair.

So he snarled wordlessly at the rest of them and dropped to the floor in lion form, then stalked away in a direction other than the one in which Talon had gone.

Milly sighed. Gio gave her a sidelong look, then unfolded a long arm to reach out and hug her. She leaned into him. He searched through the soft feathers of her scalp with his fingers, grooming her the way he might have a fellow chimp. She curled her neck so he could reach more easily, accepting the gentle caress. They sat that way for a little while, not talking, and then Atlanta and Skidoo dealt them in anew, and they continued playing.

Niko had charted their course, and they were en route to Coralind.

Everyone seemed excited enough. Niko still hadn't mentioned that her main reason for that course was that Coralind held a physical office for the financial institution administering their insurance money. There, perhaps, finally, she could convince them to give it to her.

It wasn't just that their money was locked away to the point where its accessibility was in question. It wasn't just that getting the financial institution to even start the process necessary for accessing said money involved complex forms and negotiations. It was that all the rules and requirements seemed deliberately constructed to make her efforts fruitless. That some depended on arcane and outmoded forms of filing, such as hard copy forms.

This had been the second, unspoken, part of Niko's decision to come to Coralind. EverRich Cooperative Insurance & Banking had a sub-branch here, and thus she would be able to hand over such forms as were necessary in person. She was good at persuading people face-to-face.

She'd chosen her insurance agency back in the day because the price was . . . well, more than reasonable at a time when their budget was already flensed to the bone.

Suspiciously reasonable, Dabry had said, and pushed her to investigate further. But she'd filed away the work item in that any-day-now fashion that running a restaurant demands and had not, in fact gotten to it before things started exploding and everything went to shit.

She printed out—printed—plas-sheets of specified dimensions, to be written on with ink of particular acidity levels and colors. Who demanded the arcane practice of hard copy forms nowadays?! She filled them out with slow, meticulous care.

Surely this would be the last formality the bank demanded. Otherwise . . .

She set down the stylus and sighed. It wasn't that the money would be gone. They'd lost money before and managed to recover. Coralind would surely provide opportunities for them. It would be difficult, getting back on their feet, but that wouldn't be the hardest part.

No, the hardest part would be admitting to Dabry that he had been right.

3

During the jump, Skidoo was bathing. More and more, she stayed in the chamber that the *Thing* had prepared for her, filled with water instead of air, its texture silk on her skin, its warmth welcome. She and the ship talked then, conversations that were not just words but touch and motion and the glide of skin substance against skin substance.

At these moments, she shared memories with the *Thing* about herself that she had never told the others—what it had been like growing up and knowing herself destined for a particular death, while all the time seeing those around her go to that death, which came with reproduction, with an ease she did not feel. Everyone else seemed to know themselves destined, to feel it in every inch of tentacle, and yet she never experienced that sureness of purpose. They had also been so serious, so dismissive of pleasure.

It was not that she had not been loved. There had been siblings, and cousins, and her beloved mentor, Weyu, who'd taught her rhetoric and communication.

So she made forbidden modifications, left her planet, went into exile, and became a Tlellan unlike other Tlellans. In the intervening years, she had never seen another of her species, although she knew there was a handful of them scattered across the stars.

There were others from her planet on Coralind. Not her species, but ones who knew her species and its special, complex physiology. She had researched and found a medic on Coralind who specialized in such symbiotic relationships, one like the pairing that made her up. It was very important she talk to him: She had a question.

That was another thing, to be going into a future unlike that of most Tlellans. They knew what was to come: that they would mate, and produce offspring, and die in that production.

She had spurned that fate, was making a journey into a future she couldn't predict. She worried about the state of her craft, the body moving her forward into that future, the body that brought her so much pleasure and joy, the body she lived in so happily. It could fail, this body.

When it first happened, it had been a mere sliver, a moment when her two halves did not communicate and somehow, she was in two places at once and yet not anywhere at all. As though she could exist only in the intersection between her two parts. It terrified her. Since then, there had been two other instances in the space of a year. Nothing predicted those moments; there seemed to be no cause that she could tell.

She was a body with its own rudimentary mind. And she was the mind contained within a watery sack deep inside her, another species that depended on those bodies. What happened to one of those parts if the other failed? That was the question that she carried. She wondered if she would find the answer the hard way.

She coiled herself around the thought and continued. She would not speak of it to the others, or the ship, until she knew better what was happening.

Instead, she reached out and stroked the wall, felt the ship's created textures, knobby ridges, then a series of waves, letting the tentacle dip in and out of a narrow channel. Lost in the pleasure of touch, she put her worries away.

The ship noticed nothing.

Petalia and Niko encountered each other in a hallway as Niko was headed to the kitchens and Petalia to her own destination. Niko was walking along with her usual determined stride; she turned a corner and almost ran into Petalia, whose own pace was a languorous drift. They avoided each other at the last moment, but both paused.

"I am sorry," Niko said with reflexive courtesy.

"For what?" murmured Petalia.

"For . . ." Niko drew a breath and gestured around herself. "For all of this. For your situation . . . both then and now."

"Then and now," Petalia echoed, giving them a bitter edge the originals had not possessed.

"What can I say beyond that?" Niko asked. "Are there any words you are waiting for that I have not spoken, more than once? Will we forever be lost in a sea of my apologies?"

"No. Perhaps no. I don't know." Petalia's face held more sincerity than Niko had seen . . . since before any of the things that had driven them apart, making Petalia hate and distrust her. They burst out with, "Do you think I find this any more pleasant than you? Do you think I am enjoying myself in 'all of this,' as you call it?"

Niko shook her head. "I do not. Where would you be, if you had any choice before you, if I could cast a spell and put you in the place you most desire?"

Petalia's face shuttered. "On my planet, with all my folk still alive around me."

The words stabbed Niko precisely as Petalia intended. They relished the pain filling Niko's face even as they filled with self-loathing for taking such pleasure in someone else's pain. The Florians were a sweet and empathic people, and nowadays, Petalia felt they no longer retained any part of that, or at least, the only part they kept sat writhing in agony at what they were doing now. Still, that cruel side pressed. "What spell will you cast, Niko, that will bring back an entire planet's worth of beings?"

"I spoke in what-ifs," Niko said with stiff formality, then dropped Petalia a nod. "I have duties now," she said and fled.

Alone, Petalia turned and made a fist, driving it against the wall in their frustration. The surface gave way accommodatingly under their hand.

"Would you like me to pretend you are hurting me?" the ship inquired. It had, as ever, been listening but had not been able to take part, since Niko had forbidden it to take part unless specifically invited. However, it had several strong opinions about Petalia, the majority of them unfavorable.

"Are you being sarcastic?" Petalia accused.

"YES!" The ship felt satisfaction thrill through every fiber of its being. This was *much* better than *hourisigah*. Much, much better. It would definitely do more sarcasms in the future.

Petalia said nothing more and turned on their heel. They resumed a drifting pace, but if a drift could ever be said to be angry, it was this one.

Niko insisted on common mealtimes, with exceptions made only for Petalia, who preferred a tray in their room and was accommodated. The *Thing* had tried to find out why an exception was made in their case, but Niko had been short to the point of snappishness when asked. Everyone else refused to talk about Petalia and Niko with the ship and usually changed the subject immediately.

The meals also gave Dabry a chance to try new dishes, an experimentation that no one objected to. This one featured a dish he'd picked up from a ship at their last Gate, balls of dough into which a savory filling had been injected. The trick was to eat them in one bite, something Atlanta and Milly learned when they tried two bites and found themselves with a burst of contents all over their faces.

Jezli navigated a number of these with finesse. She licked her lips, eyeing the next, and asked, "So Coralind will be in Festival when we get there, eh? How far in?"

"Actually, it won't," Niko said. "I'd hoped to skip the opening, which is always the most chaotic moment, but we arrive two days before."

"Are you truly planning on opening another restaurant there?"

Dabry took the question. "Yes and no. We didn't buy a festival license early enough—"

"You have to secure them months in advance, to be clear," Niko said.

Dabry ignored her and continued. "Without that, anything we do has to be unofficial and a bit, er . . ." He gestured vaguely with a lower hand.

"Illegal," Niko interpreted. "The trick is to get away with enough profit to outride the potential fine, and even that's a gamble, because it's randomly determined."

"I think I'm going to like Coralind," Jezli said.

"You've never been there?"

"Roxana had, and spoke of it." The words came easily from Jezli, but the name hit all of them in its own way. Roxana, who had given her life for them, there in the depths of an ancient relic, but had given her mysterious powers to Atlanta, who still did not entirely understand the gift.

Each of them had loved Roxana, somehow, from the first moment they met, but Jezli and Roxana had the most history, years of it, so Jezli's lightness made Niko look harder at her. The green eyes lifted to meet her own. "I simply wish to visit the famous gardens," Jezli explained. "Nothing more than that. No sinister intentions, no complicated swindles."

"Like you had a chance of pulling one over on all of us," Niko said, leveling a stare across the table.

"Oh, don't challenge me, Captain, or you might find me quite capable of rising to the occasion." Jezli took another dumpling.

"Ladies," Dabry interjected politely but firmly, and they regarded him with irritation. He exchanged looks with Niko, who shrugged and spread her hands. "Very well then," he said. "Undoubtedly we will all enjoy Coralind, and hopefully make some small but highly profitable trades, and find news of the sort we are seeking."

"If we want to call ourselves Free Traders, then we must do trade," Niko said. "If we can do a pop-up, that is excellent, but we may have to resign ourselves to simply taking goods on in order to sell them elsewhere."

"That takes money," Dabry said. "Or some sort of collateral. Not to mention fuel and Gate costs to the elsewhere."

Niko hedged. "I think we have enough, if we're careful. We made enough at the last Gate with the Second Last Chance—and before you ask, the next one is definitely *not* going to be named the Third Last Chance—to keep going a little while."

She didn't mention that "careful" meant "as tight as possible." Dabry knew the state of their finances as well as she did. If the insurance money came through—as it surely would—they would be more than fine. But trade flows as trade will, she reminded herself of the old Free Trader maxim.

Still, Coralind, ripe with festivalgoers, all of them hungry? If they could figure out a way to take advantage of that, everything would be smooth, and *that* would be a pleasant change.

A very pleasant change, to be sure.

The person most delighted by the thought of the Festival was Skidoo. There would be decorations and music and dancing and touching. There would be joy. Enthusing at dinner, she said as much to Milly, but the pastry chef rolled her eyes, forking up a mouthful of Dabry's latest noodles, tri-striped not just in color but flavor as well, mixing sweet, salty, and savory in each bite.

"Festival is a way of saying 'spend money,'" Milly said. "You can dress it up however you like, but it's about making money circulate. The rich sponsor things and thus exchange it for status. Others come from far away and spend at an inflated rate before they go away. Every station has something like Festival, it's simply because Coralind is so large, and has so many resources, that its Festival has become so famous."

"There is being new plants for the gardens," Skidoo enthused. "Some that people is being making, some that people is being discovering and bringing. Imagine!" Staring down at her plate of noodles, Niko thought, in her heart, that Petalia, who once would have blazed with excitement at the thought of something like Festival, was the least excited of them. Niko had often tormented herself with thoughts of what the Florian's life with Tubal Last had been like. This manifestation, this lack of delight or excitement, was one such moment. What had he done to remove their zest in life? How? More importantly, could it be cured in some way?

Worse than their lack of interest in the Festival—or perhaps a sidestep into just as bad—whenever they could be coaxed from their room for a meal, such as now, Petalia took no joy in food. They drank barley water and ate lozenges of nutrients.

They remained expressionless while eating these, as though satisfaction did not exist as a concept. That hurt Niko. Truth was, food was one of the main ways she expressed her love, by tailoring it to the person, figuring out what would nurture them. When you were a leader, you couldn't really do that in the same way you could when you ran a kitchen. She would have loved to make Petalia little treats, to coax their appetite, their smiles. Coax any sort of reaction, really.

She looked up from her thoughts to see Jezli regarding her somberly. She braced herself for sarcasm, but Jezli forbore, saying nothing, but giving Niko a sardonic nod that might have been sympathetic from anyone else.

Petalia said sharply, "Is there an organized plan other than go frolic at a Festival?"

"Beside the fact that you yourself mentioned it as part of Tubal Last's net of contacts, I am going to see that old friend from my military days," Niko said, twisting noodles around her fork with deliberate care.

"They work at the station now?"

"In a sense, they *are* the station now," she said.

Petalia sniffed. "Another biomachine, like your ship?" The ship filed the remark away in its lengthy list of reasons of why it did not like Petalia.

"They were once a brain in an organic body, and now that brain resides in another body."

"Your Holy Hive Mind produced abomination after abomination."

"On that you have no disagreement from me!" Niko said with a curtness she rarely employed, setting down her fork. Hearing the edge in her voice, she chided herself. There was no point in letting the Florian rattle her this hard. While at least Petalia had given off being sullen and swoony, this new, argumentative Petalia was an equally unpleasant companion.

Proving themself such, Petalia pushed harder. "But you joined them. You *knew* what they were before you signed with them."

"Do you understand the concept of no choice?" Niko snapped, regretting the words the moment they left her mouth.

Petalia smiled. They had scored a point in a long-standing game that occupied their mind whenever dealing with Niko. "Yes."

They let all the years of forced companionship to the sadistic pirate ring in that single word.

Niko bit her lip and turned away. The rest of the meal was subdued and Petalia said nothing as they left. They should have felt triumphant, Petalia told themself. Let Niko know that she remained unforgiven for all those unrescued years. The edge of sweetness in the moment crumbled away as they tried to savor it, and what was left was very bitter.

4

The meal was somber on the heels of Petalia's departure. Rebbe and Thorn were seated as far apart from each other as they could manage. Neither spoke, but both ate with their usual unquenchable enthusiasm for the task, putting away bowls with relentless rapidity. Both were in the early stages of adulthood, restless and active, and moreover, the thaumic energy that enabled their transformation from human to lion and back required fuel. They wore fully human forms right now. It made chewing easier, what little of it they did.

Niko said to Rebbe, "I have arranged papers for you. They will stand up to most scrutiny, though you will want to avoid central points."

He looked up from his plate. "They say my name?"

Niko hesitated, then confirmed, "They do. Is that acceptable?"

His eyes narrowed. "Where do they say I came from?"

They all knew that the true answer would get him destroyed and most of them incarcerated.

Niko said, "You understand that it was easiest to build on something actual. A preexisting identity."

If he had been in lion form, his tail would have lashed, but in human form, he refrained from motion, the tight control of that speaking volumes. He said, "Something actual."

Niko ripped the bandage off. "There was no record of Thorn's death. So I used him *but* have said that you have changed your name to Rebbe. That is a reasonable past, one that matches your DNA, and one that will cover your continuing with this crew, if that is what you want to do."

He swallowed hard to contain the emotion that surged in his throat at this half invitation. He didn't know where he belonged, but it was good to know there were options, not just voids and choices of one vacuum or another. At the same time, he was angry that she would saddle him with the name, unreasonably expecting him to take it on and act like he was truly Thorn's replacement.

That was a terrifying thought. How could he replace someone who actually knew who he was and where he belonged in the universe?

He fought for words to express all of this and managed only an inarticulate growl, but Niko seemed to understand.

"Think about it," she said gently.

Talon, sitting silent, swallowed resentment. They were treating this interloper better than him. Giving him papers, talking to him like he needed to be soothed. It was unfair, unjust.

If anyone deserved soothing, it was Talon. His world had been torn to pieces, and he had tried to put it back together, tried to replace his lost brother by cloning him. Instead, he got this stranger. Who hated him. And that was fine. He'd hate him back. He shoved more food in his mouth and chewed with a grim expression.

Atlanta said into the momentary lull, "What is Coralind like?"

They all tried to answer her at once, seizing the chance to lighten the atmosphere.

"There are gardens—"

"They're called confluences, actually."

"Full of all the plants you can imagine, ones from across the Known Universe—"

"Tell her about the Festival!"

"So much music—"

"Every confluence is different, they say—"

Dabry leaned forward, commanding silence. "They have hollowed out an asteroid," he said. "And inside it are the gardens of

Coralind, each one kilometers across. Every time a ship comes, it does not leave without having fed a garden in some form, either with new plants or with organic matter. There are no gardens more varied or better tended, or so Coralind claims."

That caused the babble to break out anew over which confluence to visit first, and which would be the most likely to yield trade opportunities.

"Enough!" Niko barked. "Atlanta, I suggest pulling up a basic overview and studying it. Then ask questions and we'll give you plenty of answers."

"Okay. But who is the person you mentioned meeting with there?"

"A friend who runs that station."

"They're its manager?"

"Not precisely." Niko didn't elaborate further.

Lassite ate silently, but his attention stayed as always, unobtrusively, on Jezli Farren. She was not supposed to be here. She had been invisible in his prophetic visions of the future, of Niko's Golden Path. What did that mean? Was it that she introduced some new factor or that she had been hidden up till now? Did her presence mean the Path would fail?

He didn't care where they went next. The several possibilities all led in the right direction, but could they exist in the presence of Jezli? No, she was anathema and would have to be eliminated in order for the Path to proceed.

Jezli, if she was aware of his scrutiny, gave no sign of it, eating and listening, occasionally interjecting some quip or barb.

Nor did Atlanta mark his watchful gaze, though she had her own reasons for watching Jezli Farren.

It was not that Jezli Farren did not mourn Roxana, deeply and achingly, in her own way. She simply was not and never had been a person to reveal her vulnerabilities. She had not been made that way, and she did not intend to give in to sentimentality now. Sentimentality led to foolish mistakes and overly reckless gambles, throwing random pieces on the game board that could go just as wrong as right.

She talked to almost everyone on board—charming Dabry out of tidbits and Gio into reminiscing, teaching Milly several new songs and dances, and even cuddling with Skidoo—though never going further—more than once. A few of them she simply avoided if she could, like Petalia's cold sarcasm, but the one person that she was never found around was Atlanta.

And Atlanta was the person who most wanted—even *needed*—to talk to her. It made Atlanta feel censorious, seeing someone older and supposedly more responsible than herself and yet incapable of coming up to scratch. Surely Roxana would have wanted Jezli to tell her all that the woman had learned of paladins in their travels together.

Certainly, in the final journey when the paladin had died, she had talked to Atlanta as they walked through the vast ruin that had floated for eons undisturbed. But that had been a few hours' worth of speech. Now Atlanta had days', maybe weeks' or longer, worth of questions.

At first, she thought she was imagining that Jezli avoided her. Then it became clear that when she entered a room, Jezli did not seem to notice, but very soon after she would unobtrusively drift out, if feasible, and if not, would always, somehow, seem to be standing well away from Atlanta.

Should she confront her? She wanted to. Wanted to march up and demand that Jezli give her the knowledge and guidance she needed.

But Jezli must be mourning Roxana, must be missing her more deeply, more wrenchingly than Atlanta, and was it fair to touch that pain?

She'd wait, she decided, and tucked her impatience away. For now.

Dabry was chopping vegetables and thinking. Gio nudged Atlanta where they both stood stacking dishes into the sonic cleaner and signed, "Dreaming of the gardens." He indicated Dabry with a lift of his chin.

"I don't understand why everyone's so excited."

Dabry started from his reverie and turned toward them, though his lower hands continued sorting slices of soft-fleshed root.

"The best and freshest ingredients," he said. "Things that could never be grown on ships for one reason or another. Though plenty of ship plants, to be sure. I've told you they take plants in barter."

"Do we have plants for them?" Atlanta finished loading the cleaner and closed its lid. It gave off a whiff of steam and began to chug soapily.

Dabry shook his head regretfully. "I wish we did. It would make trading easier. But the plants and herbs I have with me are not that uncommon, and they already grow in Coralind. I have checked their databanks already to make sure. No, we will give them the traditional mass of organic material."

She wrinkled her nose. "You mean . . ."

"Oh yes," he said, selecting another root and chopping it into rounds of watery flesh. "The waste produced by living beings makes the best fertilizer, or so the Gardeners believe. They even have a number of animals there in the gardens, intended to increase the amount of organics. If we have excess, in fact, they'll pay us well for it, particularly if it's a kind they don't get that often." He grinned outright at Atlanta. "This is not an uncommon trade," he said. "That may have been obfuscated somewhat in your imperial training."

She was forced to admit that it had been.

"Did you ever garden, back in court?" he asked curiously. He used an empty hand to nudge a knife toward her and pointed his chin at another pile of roots awaiting their transformation.

She sighed and picked it up. At a look from Dabry, Gio stirred himself to action and began stacking plates. "Dug in dirt and planted things?" she said. "Does working with hydroponics count?"

"That is considerably cleaner than the labor I had in mind," he said. "But it's not an opportunity you will have there. Beings come from across the Known Universe to learn in the gardens of Coralind, and many pay all they possess for that chance and consider the price well worth it."

She shook her head. "I didn't want to, anyway."

"Do you think it beneath a paladin?" he asked.

Her cheeks flushed. "I didn't say that."

"Roxana was a gardener," he said. "We spoke of it one time."

She wanted to say something angry, but could not when Roxana's name had been invoked. "She never spoke of it to me," she muttered after thinking and rethinking her response several times.

"You didn't have the time with her that you should have," he said gently. "My understanding is that paladins become what they are over a very long time of training with their mentor, guided as well as getting a chance to see what it is that a paladin *does*. She thrust it on you because she had no other choice, but if she had been able, she would have taught you what it means to be a paladin."

"Instead, I must rely on guesswork," she said. Her blade chopped down on the roots with unnecessary violence before she confessed her greatest fear. "What if I get it wrong?"

Finally, she had found a role other than the one she had always thought of as hers, and from which she had been removed so suddenly: that of Imperial heir. She had been drifting and uncertain of her path when she met Roxana. Now she had a definite road before her. What would happen if she went awry and stepped off it? Where would she be then?

Dabry watched her, guessing accurately at many of her thoughts. He had been training soldiers long enough to understand what happened at transition points, and this was such a moment—or series of moments, rather—for her.

He was fonder of her than he should be, and yet sometimes he could barely tolerate being around her. She reminded him so sharply, so painfully, of his daughter Keirera. She was also lost, and how could one's heart not go out to her plight? Searching for her place in the universe, as they all were, and for the moment, finding it here with the *Thing* and its crew.

"If you get it wrong, that shows you are trying," he said. "You cannot learn without making mistakes. If you never try, you will never do."

"I know," she said unhappily. "But that doesn't make me any less anxious about getting it wrong and destroying something in the process."

"Ah." He nodded. "Responsibility." The teasing note in his voice incensed her at first, then made her laugh despite her indignation. The actions of her knife grew less emphatic.

"Roxana would say I am taking it too seriously," she said. "Is that what you are trying to tell me?"

"Close enough," he said. They exchanged smiles.

"Do you really think Biboban will be able to help you?" Dabry asked Niko when he caught her alone, late, in the kitchen, fixing herself a mug of tea.

"Back before it . . . became what it is, it dealt with Tubal Last,

I think," Niko said. "I don't know the particulars. It was only a hint, one drunken conversation."

"That's not a lot to be going on, sir," Dabry said gently.

"When you have nothing, spider silk looks thick enough to lead you," she said. She stirred nut milk into her tea and took a sip.

"There were rumors about Biboban," Dabry said uneasily, folding his arms.

"I heard them too. A little too eager to lean into training hallucinogenics, and a taste for them afterward that it never lost. But it runs a station now, Dabry. I can't imagine that it still indulges. Once it found a role that really fit it, once it was happily engaged . . ."

"You have a great deal of faith in the power of happiness."

"Every bad person I have met is, at their core, deeply unhappy."

"Even Last?"

"Imagine how unhappy he must have been to amass so much in his attempt to fight against it. Always trying to get more, to fill an unfillable void."

He shook his head without replying and left.

After he had gone, she leaned her head against the coolness of the nearest cabinet, thinking about Biboban.

"May I ask questions?" the ship said.

"For now." Niko knew what it was about to ask. "You want to know about the person we're going to visit."

"From the way you and Sergeant Dabry spoke, there is something unusual about Biboban. You said it is the leader of Coralind."

"No," Niko said. "Not the leader. The heart."

"I don't understand."

"The Holy Hive Mind employs Jadoogar blobbships. Those are ships driven by living brains."

"Like me!" the ship said with a surge of curiosity and joy.

Niko shook her head. "Not like you," she explained. "They take an already living brain, one suited to the task, and use that as their starting point before installing it in a blobbship. The brain is modified and augmented, a thousand things are done, but in the end, it is still a creature's brain. When the ship is decommissioned, usually they are killed. But Biboban somehow managed to escape that, and now its brain is installed in Coralind. It is not the leader, certainly, but it makes sure everyone has air and water and that things run smoothly. To say it is the heart of Coralind is not a metaphor—all of it depends on Biboban to drive it."

The ship turned this over in its own thoughts. After a while, it said, "But maybe it is a little like me. A little."

Niko felt a surge of affection and pity. She laid her hand on the interior wall beside her, its surface faintly ridged and textured like skin, a warmth beneath it that said it was a living thing rather than just glass and metal. "A little," she reassured, taking a last swallow from her mug. "But we are all a little like you, *Thing*."

"How so?"

"We are alive, and we want to be happy." She patted the wall. "For the moment, we are." She paused. "I just want to check that there are no more manifestations of *hourisigah* coming up."

Hourisigah was the art form *Thing* had taken up, the art of creating dramatic situations, and the hobby was directly responsible for Jezli's presence on the ship in the first place.

"None," the ship said. "But you did say to get a hobby, and that is all I was doing."

"There is some rationale behind your words," she admitted, and patted the wall again, savoring the heat and solidity of it. "But not *that* hobby. And check the next one with me first, and that way we can pluck any potential thorns from the beautiful blossom."

"I have been thinking about it," the ship began.

"And?" Niko prayed the results of such thoughts would not need to be negotiated.

"And I am thinking still."

"Very well, keep me posted." She patted the wall again. "Are you happy, *Thing*?"

"Yes, as I understand it."

"What makes you happy?"

"All of you talk to me. All of you like me."

"That's all it takes, huh?" The wall's corrugations felt soft under her fingers, a pleasure to touch, evoking a faint honey and cardamom scent. She stroked along them and felt the wall move, like a cat being petted.

"What else could there be?" the ship said, puzzled.

Niko met Lassite in the hallway. He came to attention. "Permission to speak of portentous and weighty things, Captain?"

"How weighty?"

"Most weighty."

She sighed. "What is it?"

"The Festival. There will be someone there who wishes you ill."

"I was taking it as a given that there would be multiple beings there who wished me ill," she said.

"That is true," he said. "But this will be one you do not expect."

"Can you tell me who?"

He shook his head.

"So basically, you are saying expect the unexpected. That is not very helpful, and permission is denied." She paused. "You said 'things,' plural. What else is there?"

"Atlanta matters soon," he said. "You need to take care of her."

"That is a given. Anything else I can deny you permission to speak of?"

He shook his head, and she went down the hallway whistling,

although she could not help but wonder who wished her so much ill that Lassite could see it.

For his part, Lassite sighed. He could only say so much, and if Niko chose not to listen, the path they took next would be a difficult one. Though not impossible.

The ship wanted to come out of Q-space without problems or complications, a smooth exit that would dazzle everyone with its grace and skill, so they would be forced to say all sorts of compliments in praise and acknowledgment.

Instead, they came out of space less smoothly than usual, with a bump and grumble that made Niko say, "What's happening, *Thing*?"

Between the stars, so much is black void and white stars that sometimes you forget color. When colors do come, they are the cold stellar blues of retreating light or the implacable red hue of light washing toward one.

Coralind was blue, certainly, and red, and it was green beyond that, and all the colors mixed together in the shield bubble that circled its enormous form.

It was vast; it housed over a million different entities, the majority of them physical, and only a few of them human. Once an asteroid, its outer surface was now corrugated with clear plastic tunnels and pocked with life-bubbles, some temporary, others gone silver and grown complicated with permanence.

"There are objects in the way!" the ship protested. It had never seen such a cluttered space, full of tiny ships, and tubes, and constructions ranging from smaller than the *Thing* to much, much larger, all clustered in the lee of the enormous asteroid. The docking station protruded like a silver shelf low on the side, a webbing of light and lines all around it. It was not that complicated to maneuver through everything, but it seemed unnecessary and irritating to the ship.

Niko laughed. "Arpat took you to better-regulated places, I suspect. Free Traders founded Coralind, and it reflects its origin most thoroughly."

"You said your friend runs it," the ship commented. "This is not an orderly or well-run place." It couldn't explain why the disorder bothered it so; the feeling itched like radiation, but decentralized, so you couldn't tell the point of origin.

"You are thinking of a different form of running," Niko said. "You are thinking of someone who makes decisions and says build this and do that. That was never Biboban's way. Instead, it makes sure everyone has what they need, such as air, and water, and no one goes hungry, or has no place to sleep. The gardens provide enough wealth for the station that it is no matter. If we wanted to stay, it would charge us a hefty price for the citizenship."

The ship said nothing more for the moment, picking its way through sprays of radio signals and construction clusters and old machinery whose purpose was not evident to the eye. Perhaps, it thought, it would have a chance to speak with this Biboban and begin to understand it. The captain admired the person, that was clear, and the ship wanted to achieve the same status, somehow.

It felt it had failed in many ways to impress Niko, and it thought perhaps achieving that would be its new hobby, but it was not sure that telling Niko would not completely annul all its efforts.

Instead, it contemplated the vista before it.

"There is the docking station," Niko said unnecessarily. The ship chose to believe she was speaking to the others watching its descent, and out of pique, it glided slowly, majestically, downward.

Niko stared at the blue-and-silver outline. "Such a gaudy thing."

"It's beautiful!" Atlanta protested. "Look at it!"

"It was constructed to be looked at and impress those who do, and that makes it gaudy to my way of thinking," Niko said. "And look how they have used the outer sphere for advertisements! It is a coin-pinching way to run a station."

"Biboban was always good at that," Dabry said. "Remember when it got the Holy Hive Mind to subsidize the rations by imprinting improving messages on the wrappers?"

She chuckled. They all stood as they neared the station. To Atlanta, it seemed that the station was approaching slowly, swimming toward them in the blackness of space.

"Are you providing atmospheric music again?" Niko asked suspiciously. "I told you, no more *hourisigah*!"

"Atmospheric music is not confined to *hourisigah*," the *Thing* declared loftily. "I am attempting to provide the optimal landing experience for my passengers." The music grew slightly louder.

Niko decided not to object. The accompaniment actually sounded nice, the music swelling as the station loomed in all its unkempt, ragged, crazy quilt–glory before them.

5

As with every arrival at a station, there were papers to process, checks to be concluded, licenses to be bought.

"There is a gathering of captains to start the Festival," the Plubas adjutant told Niko over the comm as she logged in and began having the ship's title corroborated.

"I thought Festival might have already started," she said.

"We are in the period of pre-Festival, which lasts three days, of which we are on the second, and which is sometimes mistaken as the actual Festival itself by the ignorant," the Plubas said with officious precision.

Niko sighed. "The gathering is mandatory, I take it?"

"For the ritual to be effective, all must take part. Or pay a very large fine to compensate for the spiritual drag their absence may cause." The adjutant folded their hands in front of them primly.

"Spiritual drag," Niko repeated dryly, and that was commentary enough, but the adjutant ignored the implications in her tone.

"It will commence in one and a half days," they went on as if she had not spoken. "You must appear in full dress, not a uniform, to show respect to the Gods, and you must conduct no other business before you have participated."

Most space stations were godless, but some were crewed by species who tended toward being spiritually inclined, and Niko had forgotten that fact, somehow. *A whole new range of ways for us to put a foot wrong*, she thought sourly as she clicked out of the conversation. A whole new host of delays and reasons for more delays on the heels of that. When would she get to the bank?

That would definitely qualify as business, and pressing business, to boot.

A Captain's Gathering, however—well, that would also be a chance to catch up with the gossip, at least, which was always more interesting in person. She would undoubtedly run into old friends and acquaintances. Probably enemies, too, based on Lassite's prediction, but as she told him, that was not unexpected. The thought that someone she didn't think an enemy would prove one, though, bothered her. If only Lassite would ever speak in specifics, rather than generalities!

Depend on no one on the station, she decided, not even Biboban. Presume nothing and have everyone keep their heads down. Run their pop-up, take advantage of the Festival, do the business they had come for, and get the hell out.

That seemed simple enough. "Any messages waiting for the crew?" Niko asked, purely as protocol. None of them were prone to receiving mail, other than an occasional yearly missive from Gio's relatives.

To her surprise, the Plubas replied, "Only one, for Dabry Jen."

"From?" she asked.

"No address of origin attached," he said.

"But it came from off-station? Who brought it?"

"I have little time for such things," the adjutant said. "Transmitting it now."

She was more than a little curious about its origin, and she was surprised when, after glancing down at his datapad to read it, Dabry refused to divulge its contents.

"It's personal, Niko," he said.

"We have known each other almost a decade and a half! What personal secrets do either of us have?"

He shook his head. His face was more lined now, more tired than when they had first met. Two scars acquired during that decade and a half rode it, one along a cheek, the other almost intersecting an ear.

"Some things hurt to talk about."

She left without saying anything else, and he waited until her footsteps in the corridor had died down before he opened it again.

"Stay away from Coralind," it read. "Or your daughter will die."

He stared at it, trying to ignore the giddy surge it brought. Keirera was dead, how could she die again? He searched his memory of the circumstances of her death. True enough, she had not been one of the bodies—he forced his thoughts away from those blackened, charred forms, the photographs identifying his wife's body—but many in the village had been caught in a blaze that burned so brightly that it ate everything, down to tooth and bone. That was what he had been told. He had been worlds away at the time, trying to race back and get them off-planet to safety before the inevitable fighting broke out.

He touched the datapad. A finger of his upper hand traced the lines of the message, pointlessly trying to feel the letters on the pad's slickness, searching for some clue. He felt brittle and scraped to the bone, as though he had begun to recover from some long and dire illness, and his guts twisted in an uneasy coil. He was unaccustomed to feeling weak.

Stay away from Coralind when it might be a clue to guide him to her? How could he do that?

Was it possible this was another machination on the part of Tubal Last? Surely it must be. But what if it wasn't?

Should he warn Niko? Logic told him that he should. Yet he had kept his grief so private, so long, nursed in secret during rare moments to himself. Lately it stirred in a different way with Atlanta, and it had seemed that at long last he was on the way to healing a wound worse than a severed arm, something that had been torn away, and which had been open and raw ever since, never healing, never relenting.

No, he would keep it to himself for now, despite his better judgment.

The first time you see a Jadoogar blobbship move into a planet's atmosphere, it will be one of the most impressive sights of your life. Also probably the last, because these dreadnoughts, made of interstellar matter and pseudoflesh, rained down destruction in a multitude of forms, none of them subtle. Niko and Dabry had lived through one such onslaught, through luck more than any foresight or planning, and neither wanted to ever encounter another.

Synthetic and organic intelligences strung together through cellular computers powered the ships, and the older they were, the more massive they became. One such brain—one only, in all the history of the troops of the Holy Hive Mind—had managed to survive severing from its ship.

It then went on to have itself installed in a space station to act as its brain, and communications system, and maintenance overseer, and a host of other duties that it did with more facility and fewer costly requirements than a purely mechanical system. That was one of the maxims of the Known Universe—flesh is cheaper than metal or stone, and breeds its own replacement with the proper handling and schedule.

That brain was Biboban, and they had fought together in the service of the Holy Hive Mind, which might prove a bond. They had both been performing that service somewhat unwillingly, though, hating how the Hive Mind fought with no heed for collateral damage or non-combatant lives lost.

Biboban was complicated, always had been, and she had not talked with it for a long time.

"Is your warning something to do with Biboban?" she asked Lassite unexpectedly as she passed him in the hallway, hoping to startle him into some clue.

But he was unforthcoming. "It is a person, rather than some blind force and mischance, and beyond that, I cannot tell you much at all." He scowled. "Jezli Farren clouds things."

"Clouds them how?" They had both come to a standstill in the corridor. The ship debated playing atmospheric music to suit the conversation, but refrained.

He threw up his hands and dipped his scaly head a fraction. "I cannot see her anywhere, and where she is, that is obscured."

"Are you saying get rid of her? That she makes your skills worthless?"

His head snapped up, eyes alight with protest. "Never worthless!" he objected. "And no. She came with someone I did see, Roxana, and perhaps the paladin's light still shines on her, hiding her, somehow. Perhaps she learned to take advantage of that, and it hides her from thief-trackers using magic. That is one thing I have considered."

"I do not think her entirely a friend," she said slowly. "The jury is still out on Jezli. So is she possibly this enemy, or not?"

"No. Someone else."

"I listen to you because what you have done so far. But magic—" She made a warding-off gesture. "Free Traders do not touch it for a reason."

"Prejudice."

"We have had this argument before."

"And will again," he said with certainty.

She scowled. "Then you spend your time consulting your ghosts and see if you cannot bring me something tangible."

He knew he would not, could not, but bowed his head in acquiescence nonetheless. They each went on their separate ways.

Niko had composed her greeting message with care. Biboban had plenty on its plate, and she wasn't sure it would appreciate being reminded of its days as a war ship, thralled to the Holy Hive Mind as surely as any of its soldiers. There had never been any question of Biboban being subsumed by the Hive Mind; it had been considered expendable at the time they had installed it in the ship, and there had been no exception to that.

So she spoke as little of the Holy Hive Mind as possible. Rather, she mentioned the Last Chance, and its destruction, and left out all the pirate material, choosing to move instead to the fact that they had turned Free Trader and hoped to pick up good cargo at Coralind, maybe do a little restauranting business (she alluded to their Nikkelin Orb in vague and technically true terms) and while they were there, she and Dabry would like to talk to Biboban for old time's sake.

She read it over three times and finally sent it.

She waited at least an hour, pretending to work at other things at her desk. She pulled up their finances once again and contemplated them glumly. There was no response. Should she send a follow-up? Or was the silence itself a reply? It had been so long since they had seen each other. People changed with time, and that held true even for intelligences like Biboban. She had no way to predict how it would answer, and that made her feel unsure in a way she had not felt when the idea had first occurred to her.

Finally, after two hours, the reply came, although it was only an acknowledgment and a time and address, a full day from now. An entire fifteen minims, early in the morning after the Captain's Gathering.

Very well, perhaps she'd use that time to find out more regarding how things lay there and would be better prepared to talk. The Gathering could be useful. She'd take Atlanta, let her smooth some of those rough edges, enjoy herself by listening to the music and watching the performers, as well as the crowd.

Free food, free drink. How bad could it be?

The berries arrived as part of a set of samples from Abundance, along with several other complimentary packages designed to entice trade. Dabry had recognized them as soon as he opened the package. He lifted them out and set them aside with a little marker that they were his to cook with.

So now he was in the kitchen making berry salad, having chased the others out on one pretext or another. He was making it slowly, step by step, like a ritual. He had made this many times before, back on his home planet.

He remembered making it for his family. Berries and bitter greens—remembered serving it to them, Challa picking the berries out to eat. Each chop of the knife across the green stalks, squirting their scent, evoked a sorrow in him that nearly drove him to his knees.

But he continued chopping with tight-jawed determination, lower hand holding the stalks, upper right slicing across them.

Niko had asked him what he wanted from the future. He'd known instantly that what he most needed and wanted was his lost family. Something utterly unobtainable. At the time, he had thought he'd go back soon to visit them, any day now, when there was time to file for a brief leave! But life in the ranks of the Holy Hive Mind was not conducive to free time, and he never had filed, not until those last desperate days, when it had already been too late.

The moment he learned that his wife and daughter were gone

was the moment he knew his greatest fear had come to fruition, and he was alone. Unneeded. Unnecessary. Niko had moved into that gap, had steadied him throughout. He had been drowning in dark water and she pulled him out.

Could his daughter be alive? If so, why send that message threatening her life if he came here? How could he send some message back? What was he supposed to do? Stay away from Coralind? How could he do that when he was already here?

He would volunteer to stay on the ship, he decided. But when he spoke to Niko about it, she shook her head. "Everyone wants an excursion or two," she said, "And I need you overseeing those less ready to undertake excursions on their own."

"Surely Gio," he began, but her head shake came even quicker this time.

"Gio has plenty in his basket." Left unspoken in her arched eyebrow was her slight surprise that he would try to duck responsibility like this.

Should he explain to her what was happening, what the letter had said? But she had enough to deal with, plenty of things to think about, and surely the greatest priority was saving them from Tubal Last's revenge. He dared not distract Niko from that. While he had never spoken of it, despair dogged those hours in the pirate haven, despair he had hidden.

Despair he was glad he had hidden. You never showed the crew you were afraid. Let Niko think his faith in her was absolute—it was as good as. She'd managed to get them out of some of the most dangerous places in the universe. Though the truth was it was more that things had fallen her way, with the *Thing*'s stubbornness and Millie's attempt to escape coinciding enough to permit their escape from the pirate haven, or Roxana's presence permitting them to survive the space moth.

"Very well," he said crisply, and left without another word.

What had crawled up his butt, Niko wondered sourly, and

forgot the exchange in the myriad of other details complicating the existence of herself, not to mention the ship and its crew. She had more than enough to do.

One of those work items was laundry. The *Thing* was reasonably good with laundry if you told it *exactly* what you wanted. Her first uniform had arrived so stiff with starch she felt like it would crack if she bent over. She attributed this to pique over her rejecting the idea that the ship simply make her new clothing each day and recycle the old.

The agonizing thing about leadership, Niko thought as she sorted through shirts, was that you had to seem surest of the rightness of what you were doing at the time when you felt that sureness the least.

She sniffed a shirt and tossed it in the appropriate pile.

You had to make decisions. Fast ones, to save the most people. And while you made them, you knew that you would grieve. Deeply, internally, and above all, privately, for all the ones lost in the margins of those calculations.

The collateral damage that every leader knows will come, while at the same time knowing that you'd do it again the same way, if the choice presented itself.

Just as she'd done the things that had made her the Ten-Hour Admiral, doing things because they were right rather than profitable.

Ten hours or not, she would do it again in a heartbeat. Except next time, she would keep the uniform. She'd looked very good in that uniform, and it had been low-maintenance, easy-care fabric.

A knock on the door. "Come in," she half shouted.

Milly's head poked through the doorway. "Captain?"

"What do you need?"

Milly seemed as hesitant as Niko had ever seen her. White feathers stirred and lifted, then drooped again on her crest. "Captain," she said, "it's been a while since . . . what happened. And I just wanted to make sure we're all good."

"'What happened' being you deciding to abandon the rest of us to the pirates and go off on the *Thing*?"

"Ouch." Milly winced. "Yes. That would be what happened."

"Would you do it again?"

"No," Milly said instantly. "I did it before because I didn't trust you all the way. And because among my people, pirates are known to be cruel and deadly, and I did not want to die. Now . . ." She took a deep breath and looked Niko straight in the eye. "Now I do. Because now I've seen you in action, not just being a chef, but being a captain. You're a good one."

"Flattery." She turned back to sorting.

Milly shook her head. "No, the truth. Look, Captain, I've made my peace with everyone aboard the ship but you. Are we good?"

"Yes," Niko said without hesitation, and Milly looked pleased.

"Thank you," she said, and discreetly withdrew, leaving Niko standing over her piles of lights and darks.

In his chamber, the air dry and scented with kinna weed, Lassite said to the ship, "Do you still not sense the ghosts?"

The ship hedged, suspiciously, "I have sensed something, and I do not know what it was. It is quite possible that it was some form of trickery."

Its tone left little doubt regarding who it thought might be the instigator of such trickery.

Lassite ignored the implied accusation and said with more patience than he actually felt, "You experienced their presence more than once. You've complained about it enough, but now you don't anymore. Have you gotten used to them?"

"I have gotten used to ignoring the feeling," the ship specified.

"That doesn't seem at all a survival trait, nor something that a bioship would do," Lassite observed. "Ignoring things happening within yourself?"

"It is an emotional reaction and therefore does not need to make sense or be explained," the ship said loftily.

Lassite's head began to throb, but he ignored it, intent on coaxing information from the ship.

"Look," he said, holding up the arm around which a Derloen ghost twined. "Do you perceive it, here?"

The ship strained senses it wasn't entirely sure it had, but felt nothing. Lassite was lying, it decided. Trying to delude it. For a trick, maybe a prank. Or maybe for no reason at all other than to amuse himself. It felt an intense surge of *dislike*.

That faded away as Lassite said, "I have been trying to think of a way to let you see them. You seem to have some facility or talent, otherwise you would not have been able to perceive them."

"I was *imagining* at the time," the ship said. "Perhaps I was imagining them."

"Imagination is part of magic," Lassite said.

"How can that be?" the ship asked, intrigued despite its overall annoyance.

Lassite shrugged. "Magic is a thing of will and imagination, as much as anything," he explained. "It does not matter if a body is weak, as long as its will is strong."

"My body is very strong," the ship noted.

"Of course it is," Lassite said patiently. "But what of your will?"

The ship considered. "I was not meant to have a will," it said finally.

"You were not, that I agree," Lassite said. "And what does it mean, that you do?"

"Does it have to have a meaning?"

"For it to be magic, it does," Lassite said, utterly confounding the ship to the point where it cut off the conversation and refused to talk to him for the rest of the day.

Lassite had been earnest about his quest to let the ship see the ghosts. It fascinated him to think that a machine might, after all, be capable of perceiving ghosts. That was a specialized ability not all species possessed, and no one had been capable of melding magic and machine.

There was a sparkle somewhere up on the Path, something he couldn't quite make out, but it had to do with the ship. Of that, he was certain. He understood the ship was perpetually annoyed with him—he was used to that sort of thing—but the thought of what he might discover drove him on.

Was it the presence of Jezli Farren? How had she gotten into the Path without his realizing it? Because now when he looked, the absence that was somehow her was tangled up in all sorts of ways, appearing here and there along the timelines, which perplexed him and made his head hurt.

He sat in his chamber and meditated. No matter how he tried, he could not see what was to come. The ghosts came and curled around him like cats, but he resisted the urge to pet them.

Coralind. Was there more than one person wishing them ill there; was that why things kept shifting? Or was there some other reason? Sometimes he felt he was watching a multi-dimensional chess match, with half the moves made in secret by entities he didn't know. The Golden Path shifted from day to day, that was a given, but it continued in the direction it should, generally.

What might happen if he stopped watching it so carefully? He thought that the future might devolve. That without him, they might not stay on the Golden Path. It was hubris to think his attention kept things going, and yet . . . and yet it felt very much like that sometimes.

In a chamber deep in Coralind's heart, Biboban was mulling matters over. The thing about a very large, very complex body, Biboban thought to itself, was that you constantly thought, "Hmmm, what's that particular new pain about?" And that very large, very complex body housed other bodies, along with a number of other mechanisms and entities, which meant that there was always something going wrong in a new way.

The garden space Abundance was, true to its name, overproducing oxygen—that could be adjusted for—but not when you didn't understand exactly what caused the overproduction. Biboban dispatched a number of agents, some organic, some mechanical, to test the space, and turned its attention elsewhere.

A Keinlot ship had come in covered with ypri fungus, which you didn't see much anymore now that most ships underwent a radiation spray process when debarking. This one, however, had come out of a Spisoli port—notoriously lax about such things. That meant decontamination and complicated procedures, because the last thing anyone needed was some sort of epidemic. It sent out a directive that no ships from that port should be allowed to dock until the port changed its ways.

And now. Now among the flood of visitors there was a particular new ship, a fancy bioship and an old, familiar name on that new ship. Nicolette Larsen. Such an interesting ship! So talkative!

Biboban flexed parts of itself that had not been flexed in a while, stirring up tank fluid, making debris silt down onto the bottom where the little scavenger leeches suckled it up and carried it away to build into intricate towers. And Biboban continued to do something it did well.

Biboban brooded.

6

IIIIII.IIIIIIIIIII.IIIIIIIII.II.IIIIIIIII.IIIIIIIII.II.IIIIIIIIIII.IIIIIIIIII

"Coralind is safe, I think, for the most part," Niko told her crew. "But I don't want anyone going solo. You must always take some-one with you. Atlanta and Talon, it must be someone other than each other, so you have a companion with some experience."

"I have experience!" Talon said indignantly, then wished he had said nothing when Niko's sardonic eye surveyed him.

"Some experience," she said, more gently than she might have to anyone else.

"And I?" Rebbe asked.

"You go only with Dabry or me," she said. "If something goes awry . . ."

"You think they'll find out what I am," he finished for her.

"Not if none of us are careless or stupid." She eyed everyone. "That is why we will always be accompanied, so there are two if there is a problem with one."

Talon calculated in his head. Coralind would have many new things, things Rebbe had never seen. He would want to see them, surely. Now Talon would have a way to enact his latest plan.

That plan was why he had decided not to be angry at Rebbe anymore. Instead, he would woo Rebbe, the same way he might seek a mate. Give him little favors and attentions until Rebbe came to smile when he saw him, a smile like Thorn's.

He reminded himself that it would not, in fact, be Thorn's, even though it twisted the ever-present knife in his heart. It would still be a smile, though, and it would be for him.

He must be delicate. If he pushed too hard . . . Well, that was what he had been doing, pushing too hard, and no wonder Rebbe resisted that. No, it would take tactics, he thought, the sort of planning and thinking that Niko always tried to encourage. It wasn't that he was incapable of such thinking, it just felt so dull, and so slow, and a lot of the time if you thought too much about making a decision, you ended up not doing whatever it was.

He stole a glance at Rebbe, rather than staring. His outline was so like Thorn, but for the first time, he could clearly see that the other held himself with a subtle difference, with a not-Thorn quality. Nothing Talon could put words to—was it the tilt of his shoulders or the way he held his arms?

Still, he was forced to admit there was a difference. That realization felt jarring, because he hadn't ever seen the other as distinct from his twin. But Rebbe was not an identical thing. He would never be Thorn.

If Rebbe could just learn to love him the way he and Thorn had loved each other, surely it would be almost as good as replacing Thorn. Something to fill the vast hole of Thorn's absence that confronted him every morning. Even if it did not fit perfectly—so far from perfectly—it would nonetheless make it smaller. Smaller was more bearable, and that was all he asked for, really. Something to make the pain a little less. That was all.

Petalia said, with a touch of acidity, "Do you mean to impose these restrictions on all of us?"

"You mean yourself," Jezli Farren clarified with just enough sweetness to show the depth of her sarcasm. "Do you have highly important and confidential errands?"

"I will not tolerate being confined, even in the name of safety," Petalia said. "I will see the gardens. You cannot deny me that."

This time, they spoke directly to Niko.

"I don't want to, Pet," Niko said. "But . . ."

"If either of you leave the ship, you will be accompanied by myself or the captain," Dabry interjected before she could finish. He knew quite well that meant Petalia would choose him, and he resigned himself to it. Better to endure the Florian's tiny slights and insults than let them work deeper ones on Niko.

"How pleasant!" Jezli Farren exclaimed. "Captain, I look forward to shopping with you."

Dabry rubbed his lips, trying to suppress a slight smile. He had been dubious at first, but over the days, Jezli had grown on him. Quite a bit.

"This is the first place we'll practice being a Free Trader," Milly told Atlanta. "You don't have any money, so probably the captain will give you a small sum. That's your personal stake, and every Free Trader exercises the right to carry on small trade while on a ship taking on larger ones."

"What does that mean?" Atlanta asked. "How do I do that?"

"You find cheap goods here and take them elsewhere, where they will not be so cheap. Coralind is both a good place and a bad one for starting such a thing. They have organics here that can't be found anywhere else in the Known Universe, plants from planets long gone. More kinds of chocolate than anywhere, except the Old Terra Preserve. But they're also used to trade, and most things have their customers already. You'll have to keep an eye out."

"I don't understand the naming system for the gardens."

"They're called confluences. And no one does, really. Each one was originally named for a quality: the twelve original ones are Abundance, Generosity, Peace, Felicity . . . You can find the full list in the station's welcome information. Each one's a merging of other species of plants, sometimes engineered to coexist with a principal one . . . But with time, other names have sprung up, and some play very loose with the naming convention."

Atlanta considered this. "What will you be buying?" she asked.

"Spices," Millie said. "And candy-making supplies. That lets me work with the materials, turning them into candies, and increasing their value, throughout the trip. Many Free Traders practice some such artistry as a lucrative hobby, which allows them to add value while whiling away the time on a trip."

Atlanta considered but could not think of any such skills she had. "Perhaps you might teach me candy making?" she said hopefully.

Milly snorted. "Perhaps for a charge," she said. "Get your trade goods first."

Niko did hand over a small amount of credits, just as Milly said. "I wouldn't spend it all in one place, myself," she commented, "but I've known others to get rich doing exactly that, as long as they made the right guess."

"Are you going to buy trade goods?" Atlanta asked Gio. "Can I go with you?"

He pursed his lips, considering, then shrugged and beckoned.

"You're going now?" she asked. He nodded patiently.

"Wait one moment, two at most!" She dashed to her cabin to change into different clothes. Being seen in public was different from being seen on ship, and so she put her outfit together with care. "I'm going to buy trade goods!" she told Minasit. Since she had first taken the ship's servitor as a pet, she had fallen into the habit of chattering away to it, despite its silence.

"I know that," *Thing* said.

"I wasn't talking to you!"

"You were talking to an extension of me. That is like talking to me."

"It's not," she insisted, but stayed no longer to argue before the ship could counter by mentioning her ear, which the ship had claimed as its own pet when Atlanta had co-opted Minasit.

Dabry wasn't sure how his own trip had managed to get Rebbe attached to his party in addition to Petalia, but at least, he thought, they could occupy each other.

This turned out not to be the case. Petalia simply sneered and ignored Rebbe; the young were-lion kept his head down, subdued, although as they went farther, he saw the boy sneaking looks at the surroundings, trying not to gawp.

It kept Dabry occupied, at least, while his thoughts turned the message over and over. "Your daughter will die." Yet she was dead already, long dead. He thrust the thoughts into some inner cabinet for now and resolutely turned himself to watching Rebbe, barraged by new experience after new experience.

What was Coralind like? Where some space stations were shining metal or extruded plastics, all straight lines and edges, Coralind was different. It used organic matter wherever organic material fit the bill, building stuffs that repaired and regenerated themselves, given enough time and sunlight and nutrients.

Coralind was a thousand colors and a hundred thousand smells. Those who knew the station well could tell where they were by the texture of the hallways and the smells of the indoor gardens. Every hallway converged on either a vast open space where gravity might not exist, so beings flew from one opening to another, or perhaps one where it did, so the green space was crisscrossed with ridgeways, themselves vine-draped, flower-scattered, with the pollinating insects fluttering and flying back and forth. There were one hundred six of those spaces, called confluences, each with its own name and character, scattered through the hollowed-out rock that was once a planetoid before it was hauled into place and used as the building stuff for the station.

Coralind bordered the Cerberus system, and so the majority of its inhabitants represented the species there: the Dralnoi, tall, leafy beings that towered over Dabry; and the Plubas, smaller and furrier, coming up to his waist. The latter were grave little beings with a solemn demeanor, walking with a ceremonious

pace worthy of sacred ground. The Dralnoi, noisier and boister-
ous, walked together in groups of four or five, sometimes telling
jokes, sometimes singing songs.

Other beings lived there, of course: a cloud of Fizziks; a gag-
gle of Yonti youths wandering and chattering, a few glancing at
Rebbe with interest while he pretended not to notice.

Dabry caught the eye of a tall woman, likely of human origin,
gazing at him boldly. Her hair was grayish-brown, and her face,
unremarkable. She wore station-issued clothes, with no attempt
to modify or tailor them, but wore them well, he thought. He
smiled toward her, shaking his head subtly, and hoped the others
hadn't noticed.

Rebbe was oblivious, of course, but Petalia was not. "Enjoying
yourself, Sergeant?" they said in a tone that implied he should be
doing nothing of the sort.

He chose to take their words at face value. There was no point
in responding to their sometimes unsubtle attempts to pick a
fight.

"I am," he said, projecting annoying cheerfulness at them. "It
has been a long time on ship, and I have always wanted to come
to Coralind and sample some of the things they grow in the
gardens here."

They didn't respond, and so he continued, "I am hoping in
particular to go to a confluence known as Warmth. They grow
pods there with a unique—and terribly strong—spiciness to
them. The Dralnoi use a distilled version of them as a chemical
weapon that does no lasting harm, actually. That's how strong
they are. Several Gardeners there gene-tweak varieties, and I
might be able to get a plant or two to put in our own gardens.
What do you think, Rebbe?"

"The ship would like new plants, I think," the youth said
slowly, as though surprised that Dabry would ask his opinion.
Then, as the opening to the confluence became visible and the

tunnel swelled outward, surrendering to it, he breathed out, "What is *that*?"

"That" was an enormous construction of greenery and flowers, trundling toward them from the platform at the confluence's mouth. Behind it, undulating walkways extended in multiple directions from the landing. Some arched upward, others downward. They met at various conjunctions that looked tiny at first but were, Rebbe realized, much larger, more like a plaza than a landing. Trees grew along the walkways from some source suspended beneath them, long tubes of what seemed to be nutrients, into which each tree had plunged its roots. The air smelled of something Dabry remembered from his youth on a planet, petrichor, the smell of rain on dry grass, and with it, flowers opening in the first spring shower.

They stood aside as the mass of greenery wheeled by, pushed by two Plubas, who did not speak as they passed, intent on their mission.

"It is a worship bundle," Dabry explained. "I have been reading up a little on the habits of the Dralnoi and the Plubas, or rather, how they manifest on this station. It is always a good idea to be prepared, to learn what you can before any new situation or place."

He was speaking instructively to Rebbe, but Petalia chose to take the words as aimed at themself.

"That is your method, to be prepared," they sneered. "How has that worked for you, Sergeant? What disasters have you staved off with it? What—"

Dabry cut them off with a rude gesture from his lower hand. "If this is how you intend to go on," he said wearily, "then you should return to the ship. We will accompany you there."

They drew themself upright and glared at him, pale, icy eyes confronting the warmth in his. "I can go about by myself," they said.

"You cannot," Dabry said. "You put us all at risk when you

expose yourself. If you will not act as part of the group, then perhaps you should wander off, and I would urge you to do precisely that, and quickly, were it not for the fact that Niko would then waste time chasing after you."

Petalia snorted. "You only want me because you think there is some chance that you can get that artifact working."

"Something that would help you as well," he said gently, watching their lips firm at his words, resolute in their fear.

Instead of the angry outburst he expected, they let their head droop. "Yes," they said quietly, so quietly he could barely hear them, speaking to themself, reminding themself.

Rebbe stared between the two of them, looking distraught, unsure what to say or do.

Dabry put a gentle upper hand on the boy's shoulder. "It's all right. This is how people work things out, with talking." He turned back to Petalia. "Which will it be? Return to the *Thing* or go through the market with us?"

He thought it would be easier without them, but disappointment still twinged in him when they shook their head and gestured silently toward the bay where the *Thing* was moored. He considered Petalia small and petty. Tubal Last had twisted them into a shape they would never break free of, but he also knew that Niko still loved them. He could see it in her every word, her expression. Worst of all, he thought, Petalia could see it too, could know it for what it was, that unconditional love, and still turn away from it.

He sighed and gestured to Rebbe. Together they walked back to the ship, and at the door, he simply followed them in.

"Are you trying to make me feel guilty by depriving yourself of the pleasure of this outing?" Petalia said sharply.

"I have lost the heart for it," he said. "But we are cheating the boy. We will take a day, Rebbe, and tomorrow someone will take you to whichever of the confluences you like. You must call up the station documentation on the ansible and figure out three that you want to see. I must see Cacophony, though, so that is already on the list."

"Three?" Rebbe said uncertainly.

"I'm sure that the *Thing* can help you research as well as advise you," Dabry said. "Ask it for help with the task and tell me the names after last meal."

"All right." Rebbe sounded panicked at the thought of this responsibility.

"There aren't any that would make me question your choice," he told the boy. "Well, perhaps one or two, but I don't see why you would pick them in the first place."

"But how do I pick?"

"By figuring out which you want."

"Yes, but how do I know what I want?" Rebbe said, looking as panicked as his voice now. "How do you know what you want?"

"I just do," he said. "You don't have anything you want right now—except to be away from Talon, perhaps—and so you don't feel it. When you do feel it, you will know it for what it is, that want deep in your soul."

Petalia hovered in the doorway, listening to the two of them. "He doesn't know what he's talking about," they said to Rebbe. "You can feel anything in your soul, given time and effort. It is malleable, your soul. It can be reshaped to the purposes of another." The smile they gave him was as false as it was ominous.

"You have felt many things in your soul, I suspect," Dabry said patiently. "With time. Do you not think things better now, where you are out of the hands of Tubal Last?"

He'd thought they might rally at that, but they did not, just drooped a little lower, a flower broken by too fierce a wind.

"Do you want to go back to those hands?" He pushed the

question, not expecting them to react. He flinched when they did.

"I don't . . ." they said. "No, I don't."

"Fair enough, then we will leave that out of the equation," he said.

There was a silence in the room at that point. Rebbe looked desperately toward the door but wavered, afraid to leave without some acknowledgment.

Petalia threw up their hands, a gesture of frustration and anger that seemed unsure who it should be directed toward, and stalked out of the room.

"I am sorry to have cut our trip short," Dabry said to Rebbe.

"No, I know that they're important. They're so angry, though." Rebbe's voice was wondering and unsure.

"Anger can be a good thing when it makes you move, but not when it makes you move in the wrong direction," Dabry said. "Now go and research the confluences."

"I is being needing someone for accompaniment," Skidoo said to Talon. She caught him in the hallway on his way to the kitchen, securing a snack, while the others were gone.

He scowled, whiskers twitching. "You don't need me," he said. "The captain will let you go anywhere you like."

Skidoo made the undulating moment of her head that meant maybe yes, maybe no. "The captain is saying everyone is to being accompanied. You is being the category of accompaniment."

"Why not someone else?" he grumped.

Her answer startled him, setting his whiskers twitching. "Because you is being able to keep a secret."

He could not help but feel flattered. Skidoo was one of the oldest among them, one of the most adult, even if she played at being irresponsible at times.

Still, he asked, "What is the secret?"

She considered him for a moment, one tentacle undulating slightly, the rest perfectly still. She said with caution, choosing each word one by one, "I is being going to be visiting someone. To be talking to them, that is being all."

"Why can't anyone know who you went to see?" he probed. He felt the wriggle of stalking instinct stretch its claws out, a hunt for truth. He rather liked the feeling.

"Because it is being my business and no one else's," she said. She was willing to confide in Talon up to a point, partially because she did not think he would be able to put two and two together and come up with the same sum Dabry or Niko would. She would worry them when she needed to, and not a minim before then. She added, "And you is being stuck here, without being with me."

The implication that no one else would be willing to have him accompany them stung, but at the same time, he had to admit that she was right. He could either react to the sting and stomp away, or he could pretend not to understand and have the satisfaction of getting to see Coralind. *And* he could do so without any reminder of Thorn walking beside him, scowling at him for no reason.

"Very well," he finally acquiesced. He would look for a present for Rebbe, perhaps. Something small, something that said "I was thinking about you," but not in a clinging, creepy way. Something special that Rebbe could treasure without it being so special that he resented Talon for having been able to obtain it.

That was hard. That was very hard to figure out.

7

"Did you have shopping in mind, Captain?" Jezli asked for the sake of asking. She rather thought Niko simply wanted to get off the ship for a bit, but Niko surprised her.

"There is a gathering of ship captains for the Festival within a day," she grumbled, "and I have been told that the dress is to be fashionable, and that I cannot rely on my uniform, as I normally would."

Jezli's eyes sparked with pleasure. "So we will go and try on clothing! Most excellent."

Niko rolled her eyes. "We will simply find the first thing that fits the criteria and purchase it at a reasonable price."

"For one," Jezli said, already punching up queries to the station net on her data pad, "we are close enough to the moment of your need that the price will not be reasonable. For two, you have a reputation to maintain. If you wish your ship to receive high-paying commissions, then you must look the part. Luckily for you, I like to keep up with trends and fashions, and will be able to advise you."

"Luckily for me," Niko said dryly. "Where would you advise that we start?"

"There is always a fashionable area," Jezli said. "Usually several. We will pick the highest rated and go there."

"That is a guarantee it will be the most expensive."

"That is a guarantee it will also be the most impressive," Jezli corrected. "Trust me on this, even though you should already know it, as a Free Trader. And there are ways to bring down prices, as you surely know. You must look the part." She consulted the data pad. "I have the route. Let us be off immediately."

Despite her words, Niko found Jezli an infuriatingly slow shopping partner. She paused to admire all sorts of things, and invariably fell into conversation with the stall or booth owner about the wares, and station events, and even family events.

"Do you think we'll get to the shop you've chosen before midday meal?" Niko asked pointedly.

Jezli considered. "Hmmm. Probably, if we skip the next two markets. I take it you would like to?"

"I hadn't planned on spending the entire day doing this with you!"

Jezli put a hand to her heart. "I am wounded, but acquiesce. Step this way, and we will be there well before the midday meal."

The Festival had not officially begun yet, but everyone acted as though it already had, and plenty of visitors were swirling down the halls.

Every once in a while, a clot of musicians came down the corridor, playing as they went. First Dralnoi drummers, then Nneti dancers. Then Hiolite pipers, blowing a merry, bright, and entirely infectious beat.

Jezli grabbed her by the hand. Despite Niko's first, startled instinct to pull away, she let the other woman dance her along through the throng, moving to the beat, but gently, insistently along until they ceased their motion on the outskirts of the crowd.

"I beg pardon for surprising you," Jezli apologized. Then, with a grin: "But perhaps you enjoyed it? You dance very well."

"It's been a long time," Niko admitted.

"How long?"

"Since my childhood among the Free Traders. We always danced in gathers, and home festivities as well. Did you dance as a child?"

"I had no childhood," Jezli said easily. "At least, none to speak of. Come. This way! I hear more musicians coming."

The fashion market Jezli opted for, despite her repeated regrets that they would not see everything she had thought to see, centered around the confluence Desederi, primarily populated by Dralnoi. This made Niko think it might not have clothing suited to her less willowy dimensions.

Such turned out not to be the case. Rather, the shops held cloth made of soft bark, beaten into a thinness and suppleness like Terras fabled silk, dyed in colors ranging from subdued to garish. Niko would have gone for the former, but Jezli forestalled her.

"Let me pick the colors, Captain," she said. "Just try on what I choose, and if you like it not at all, I will let you choose as you will."

"Why do you care?" Niko asked curiously.

Jezli flicked through the rack with an intensity that suggested she thought Niko's continued existence might depend on her choice. Finally, she turned, holding two long dresses, one in either hand.

"I care because this blue will look good against your skin, and this purple will bring out the colors in it," Jezli said. "It is my nature to appreciate aesthetic experiences."

"So you are making me into one," Niko said wryly, but she took the dresses and allowed herself to be steered into the fitting cubicle. There she had to admit that what Jezli had picked out looked surprisingly good on her, even if they were tones and shades she herself would never have opted for.

When she came out in her choice, the purple one, Jezli looked at her long and hard.

"What?" Niko said.

"I am appreciating the aesthetic experience," Jezli said, and Niko found herself at a loss for a reply.

Without waiting for one, Jezli turned to the shop owner. "She is looking for something for the Captain's Gathering," she said. "Anything she wears will, of course, be seen by many, and so we are trying to figure out whose wares we should advertise. This is certainly pleasing, but there are others, of course."

"The dress is eight hundred credits," the shop owner said, a little uncertainly.

Jezli considered. "Very well, we will not exact a fee for her wearing it. Perhaps you might provide accoutrements as needed, so we need not waste time looking."

Niko watched in bemusement as Jezli convinced the shop owner to provide not just the dress, but shoes and undergarments as well, for both of them.

Laden with packages, with others to be delivered to the ship, they left the shop.

"Did you have errands?" Niko wondered. "You've gone along with all of mine with a patience that seems untypical of you. I could, at least, buy you that midday meal."

Jezli hesitated. "I wished to get the feel of the place. But I have never been to Coralind and—"

"You want to see the gardens," Niko finished. "But there are enough to fill days. Was there a specific one?"

"Remembrance," Jezli said, and Niko could not read her tone.

"Very well," was all she said.

They found a guide drone to take them to the confluence known as Remembrance.

The colors there were muted, the space vast but hushed as a cathedral, wreathed in quiet. Silvery-gray walkways stretched from one door to another, and the railing bordering them was webbed with some sort of grayish-black moss that hung in low trails, scattered with tiny white flowers.

They walked in silence. The white flowers smelled like honey and regret, Niko thought. She almost spoke, but then, glancing sideways, saw the emotions gathered on Jezli's face and instead kept her words to herself.

They walked in a long, slow spiral in the moist quiet, and the silvery surface underfoot gave way under their boot heels without a sound.

Great round orbs floated here and there in the chamber. Every once in a while, two would collide and merge into a single entity, or one would encounter the edge of a walkway and collapse into fine white powder that hung like smoke in the breeze. One came toward them and collapsed at Niko's touch, the ashy powder scattering across them. Scentless and silty, it brushed away easily, but as it did, a sound came from the air around them: *Roxana, Roxana.*

It was an echo of Jezli's voice, although she was silent.

"What is that?" Niko said.

"It says the name you are remembering," a voice said behind them, and they spun to see one of the Dralnoi dressed in dust-colored robes shagged with lichen and moss. Its long-toed feet were bare.

"How does it know?" Niko asked.

The being smiled and tapped its head. "It takes it from you the name that is floating through your head while you walk through this place. This garden is here to take that name and say it back to you."

"But not to remove the memory of it," Jezli said in half question.

The Dralnoi's eyes hardened. "Tampering with one's own memories is a good way to erase everything you are. That is an evil deed. Do not let it tempt you."

"We mean no harm," Niko said. "We are here to honor our dead."

It was true. All around them, she could hear the whispers of other names: Thorn, and Thorn's mother Patha. Whenlove. Whyzest. Jakka—so many others before that. Ones who died under her command, and beyond that, others she dared not contemplate, the ones who had died by her command. *How much blood is on my hands*, she wondered wearily, and started to thrust the thought away, because this was not the time. Then thought, *But perhaps it is.*

She leaned her head back and listened to the names hanging in the silence all around her, names that only she could hear, she thought, because she was the only one that knew they were there.

Her hands were bloody, but because the Holy Hive Mind had wielded them, she told herself. She had done what she had done because she had no other choice but to die, and that had never been a choice. Her stubborn core clung to life, would never reject it.

She realized her face was wet with tears, streaking through the powdery residue, and that Jezli held her hand, guiding her along the walkway toward a bench, pushing her down onto it even as her knees gave way.

She dropped her head in her hands, still hearing whispers. Jezli rested a hand on her shoulder.

"You cannot help being alive when others are dead." Her tone was fierce, almost rebuking. "Will you lose yourself in needless sorrow? At least think of taking revenge."

Those last words were delivered in an almost droll tone. Niko found herself laughing for a moment, and then leaned harder into her hands. Jezli sat beside her. The two stayed in silence for a long, long time until Niko's comm buzzed in query from the ship.

"Milly here. Lassite and I are almost done with our shopping. Meet up to walk back?"

"That's safest," Niko said. Jezli gave her a sidelong glance from beneath her fall of orange bangs but said nothing. Niko rose to her feet without looking at her, but she held out her hand.

The green eyes widened, but Jezli said nothing else as she allowed herself to be helped to her feet. Nor anything else all the way until the rendezvous point, which was, Niko reflected to herself, the longest silence she had ever experienced from the confidence woman. Or should it be former confidence woman? Would Jezli change her ways? Could she? Then she remembered the shop and the packages they carried.

As to what Jezli was thinking, only Jezli knew.

Skidoo had been told where to go. It was not a complicated path, but as it led through unknown corridors, she was grateful for Talon's presence. Even if he did refuse to speak as they walked.

Talon, for his part, was lost in misery as usual, but as they progressed, the novelty of the surroundings could not help but catch him up in a certain excitement. Everything kept changing as they passed between one confluence and the next, and it seemed to be a very long trek, particularly when he was used to the short distances of ship life. He felt the cheerfulness of his body stretching itself after disuse.

He paused to consider various souvenirs that might make a good gift for Rebbe. A ring to pierce his ear, the way some fighters did? This fragrant leaf, made to grow with lettering on it, saying "A souvenir of Coralind"? That minuscule bottle of glittering water, which, when uncapped, floated into the air in the form of steamy butterflies?

"Is being close now," Skidoo said. The crowds were just as mixed, but here, the corridors were painted in blues and greens.

The air grew moister and moister until they progressed into a cavern filled with enormous bubbles of water hanging suspended in the immense space. Rather than stairways, there were twisting ropeways. As Talon followed Skidoo off the entrance platform, he felt the gravity lessen, allowing him to haul himself along hand by hand.

He was quick to do so in his young, lithe strength, but Skidoo's speed, which surpassed his, astonished him. He was used to seeing her drag in the ship's gravity, but in the fluid she was unhampered, and her long tentacles stretched outward and coiled, uncoiled with a rapidity his own limbs could not match. Seeing him lag, she slowed, and they made their way up toward the topmost bubble.

Talon thought he might need a breather unit in order to enter the bubble, but he found that the liquid was as breathable for him as air, which startled him at first with the sensation. But he rapidly grew used to it and looked around.

Skidoo tapped his shoulder and pressed a bead into his hand, gesturing at him to put it in his ear, as she did the same with another.

He did. "Is being good," her voice said in his head. "Is being thinking words and they is being heard. Is being easiest imagining speaking."

"Hello?" he tried.

She patted his shoulder in approval and they moved along. The water distorted his sight, but as if in compensation, every sound came more clearly, as though reverberating in his own head. The bubble's very center contained a cordlike cluster of structures, long arms stretching out, and Skidoo swam that way, with Talon following, his misery entirely gone in the delight of movement.

Skidoo made her way to the middlemost structure, where holes along its surface allowed entrance. They slipped through one and found themselves in another chamber dominated by a columnar desk, at which a creature that seemed to be a receptionist hovered. They were long and thin and filmy blue, floating this way and that in the water, and they said without preamble, "Do you have an appointment?"

"I is being having made one," Skidoo said, more humbly than Talon had ever heard her. She gestured toward Talon. "He is being accompanying me and waiting."

"Waiting?" Talon said indignantly, but lapsed when Skidoo gave him an imploring look. Grumbling to himself, he sank down onto one of the couch-benches and fumbled out his datapad to find a viddie to occupy himself. The local nets had plenty to choose from, most of them devoted to one aspect or another of the Festival. Was there warball? No, but several sports competitions looked promising. He settled into the contemplation of blitz, which seemed to involve armored players, a ball that exploded randomly, and a very small court.

He did not have long to wait. After an interval of about a half hour, the door reopened, and Skidoo appeared. She was accompanied this time by another of the filmy beings, this one a pale chartreuse, who said something Talon did not catch to Skidoo, and then turned, shaking their head, back toward the door.

The receptionist bubbled something in a way that reminded Talon very much of a sniff and took Skidoo's pay chip silently.

They exited in the same silence.

"They didn't seem very friendly," Talon said as they swam toward the entrance. "Do they not like Tlellans?"

"They is being liking Tlellans very much," Skidoo said. "Tlellans who is being doing what they should, when they should, as they should."

"You're doing what you should," Talon said, but she shook her head.

"I is being changed, I is being different." She shrugged and patted him with a tentacle. "Is not being a bad thing."

But her tone was absent as she thought about what the medic had said. She was indeed in the first stages of severing, the dissolution that comes to Tlellans when they were dying. He had rattled off a list of symptoms to watch for, which would signal the second stage. Palpitations, dryness, memory lapses.

She'd wanted to know how long the second stage would last, when it came, before it moved on to the last and final, but she had not liked the answer. Not long, he'd said, and then implied that it had been her "unnaturalness," as he called it, that had exacerbated things, had made this come prematurely.

He didn't know how far off that was, but once it came, he had said, things would move very swiftly. He had said the last with an air of satisfaction.

"I is being forgiving you," Skidoo had told him.

"Forgive me for what?" he demanded. "For telling you this news that you surely already knew in your heart?"

"Is being everything, forgiving, is being nothing. You is being, I is being. We is meeting and now the everything is being moved along."

He had not liked treating her but had known it was his duty as a doctor. He had not considered it his duty to be kind. She hoped perhaps her words made him think about that, what he lacked, and perhaps he would be a little softer with his next patient, whether or not he approved of them and their choices.

So few people found it their duty to be kind.

She glanced sidelong at Talon. He was kind. Everything he had done had been out of kindness or love. It was simply that he hadn't thought things through, and that was, after all, how you learned to think things through, although sometimes the lesson was more painful than you wanted.

Talon's had been very painful. She patted him again, without speaking, and he laid his hand briefly over the tentacle, then released, and they both walked along, lost in their own thoughts, but not feeling themselves alone with them.

Talon was disappointed that he had not found anything for Rebbe. He finally purchased one of the souvenir leaves, but he worried at it all the way back to the ship. By the time they arrived, the scrap of greenery was so crumpled and worn that in the end, he threw it away into the trash chute and regretted it immediately. It would have been an unworthy gift, but at least it would have been something.

Milly didn't know how she'd ended up with Lassite as a partner, but Niko had handed out the pairings in some order that made sense only to Niko. For her part, the little lizard reminded her of a particularly nasty predator back on her planet, and so she tried to stay away from him—unobtrusively, because it wasn't his fault.

Lassite, for his part, knew how Milly felt about it because there was an important part of the Path that hinged on it, although he wasn't quite sure how. Nonetheless, it would happen, though not on Coralind—or so he thought, though it was coming soon.

They amicably agreed to spend time in the trade district Milly wanted to visit first, and then go to the sandy confluence, Resolution, that Lassite wanted to visit for the sensory garden there, which contained more than one plant from his own home planet.

Lassite turned out to be a good enough companion, or so Milly found. He wasn't demanding and didn't mind waiting patiently while she dickered with one trade partner or another. He even let her know when one of them was thinking of cheating her with false papers.

In turn, she found Resolution less dull and plain than she had thought. Paved walkways led through sand, and dust, to be sure, and more of it than she would have liked if she had been given the choice. But there was a subtlety to the striping of the sand, a sparseness to the vegetation that somehow made it elegant. The long needles topping the grass clattered together as an artificial wind circulated, bringing with it a smell like creosote and salt.

It was a place conducive to contemplation, and finally, her thoughts drove her to ask something that had been burning in her chest for a long time. Lassite stood gazing at a small, narrow-leaved bush that came up to his waist, each branch crowned with a thick-petaled white flower surrounded by thorns. Milly asked, "Am I part of your Path?"

He turned, looking surprised. He had forgotten she was standing there, she thought sourly, which turned to sweetness when he said, "Of course," in a tone that said he'd never questioned it, even if she had.

"Of course," she echoed. She felt something tightly wound in her chest loosen. It had constricted her all this time, and only now, free of it, did she realize what a burden it had been. But it was still tight, part of it, still unresolved. "And when I . . ." She hesitated, then went on. "When I tried to strike out alone . . ."

"When you betrayed us and ended up saving us by chance," he said. "Don't you think I saw that coming?"

She stopped, hardly breathing, and looked at him hard. Needles clattered and clacked in the grass. A tiny dust-colored lizard crouched by the bush's edge, an outline against the grainy sand, watching them.

"It had to be your own choice, so you could start moving toward redemption," he said. "And it was one of the only possible scenarios that saved us."

"Didn't save Thorn," she said quickly. "Did you know *that* was coming?"

"No. I only knew that not all of us would walk out alive. Not who. It could have been you. Or one of the twins. Gio, Skidoo, or even Dabry."

"Not Niko or Atlanta?"

He shook his head again.

They walked in silence for a while before she said, "That must be very hard."

"It is." He shrugged. "But in the end, staying on the Golden Path is all that matters."

She said nothing more on that subject. Instead, she asked, "What would you like to show me next, here in this place?"

It was a pleasant few hours. Lassite had not known how pleasant they would be, but it made him fear what was to come a little less. Surely they would come through it all. And luckily, Milly asked him nothing of the future.

Talon wasn't sure what to be making of any of it, but it had been a good excursion, or at least everything was good until they got back to the ship and Rebbe told them his news, that he'd be allowed to go to whatever confluences he wanted, and Dabry would take him there as a special trip.

He'd tried to bite back a "That's not fair!" the way he wouldn't have if it were his twin. Rebbe had perceived that nonetheless and spat at him, "Why do you begrudge me any happiness that doesn't come from your hand?"

So he'd tried to explain himself a little better and before he knew it, they both snarled and shouted at each other until Gio inserted himself between them, gesturing them off in different directions.

Talon stalked away to the kitchen, less because he wanted to do any actual work but because he thought Dabry might be there.

He wasn't sure whether anyone else should know about Skidoo's expedition. One thing that had been emphasized to him was that part of the responsibility of the crew was to keep the captain informed, and Talon knew that Skidoo had not told the captain where she was going or why.

Some sort of doctor, he gathered that. But was something wrong with Skidoo that she had gone? Had she needed some sort of treatment or maintenance? Maybe it was just that she rarely got to see medics who dealt with her species?

The silence that had pervaded their trip homeward, though, made it feel like it was something weighty and perhaps something that should not be hidden from the captain.

At the same time, he didn't want it to seem like he was trying to curry favor by tattling on his shipmates. *But* if he were to meet up with Dabry, and something were to come up in the course of normal, everyday conversation, well, then, Talon wouldn't have technically betrayed Skidoo, not if he were ordered to say what he knew.

He didn't find him in the kitchen, so he sought him elsewhere.

He walked into the cubbyhole that served both Niko and Dabry as an office and found Dabry at the computer.

"I need to . . ." he began, but the sergeant actually glared at him, making it clear he had interrupted something.

"What?" he snapped, and that cut short any chance at conversation, the sort where Talon could nudge up to the concept of revealing Skidoo's trip and his part in it. So he stammered something and exited.

Then he ran into Skidoo in the hallway. "Hello," he said, wanting to ask more about their trip. She nodded her head distantly and passed. Did she know why he'd gone to talk to Dabry? She must have guessed.

Everyone still hated him. It was unfair. He trudged back to

his room and flung himself onto the bed with an angry huff. He scowled at the ceiling, waiting for commentary from the ship, but it refrained.

Dabry resumed his search for information about his daughter, tensely tapping at the keys, trying different data networks. Dispatching coded agents out into the info-verse looking for mention, any mention, of his daughter. Nerves sandpaper raw with the effort of holding in hope. He'd seen his wife's body—or the photos, at any rate—but they had not identified Keirera's.

There was nothing, no matter how far or wide he tried, and finally he expended the last of his cash in the search. He pondered asking Niko to draw against his pay but that would lead to questions about something he was unwilling to talk about just yet. No, he would go into the station and check some of the public data available there if you bought a citizen's day pass, which gave you (almost) all the rights of one of the actual inhabitants.

Jezli steered them on the way back, a different route than the one they had taken from the ship. Niko started to say something, but Jezli said, "There is another garden you should see."

The confluence Patience seemed unremarkable to Niko. It reminded her of the ship's gardens, crammed with a variety of plants that did not seem to belong to the same families.

"What are the spaces between reality, and why are they green?" Jezli muttered, staring off into nothingness across the vegetation.

"What?" Niko said, startled. Was this some code she was supposed to understand? Was the garden filled with hallucinogenic plants? Was Jezli having some sort of brain aneurysm? But the cool eyes that met hers seemed fine and even held a touch of amusement.

"It is a quote from the poet Amadou," she murmured. "But not many people are acquainted with their work. Perhaps you thought I was going mad."

"Not at all," Niko lied, sounding flustered. She glanced around herself at the garden. "Why did you want to come here?"

"This," Jezli said, "is where I wanted you to see something."

"What?"

"Follow me." Jezli turned to slip between two bushes.

Niko hesitated. Who knew where the perhaps former, perhaps not con woman intended to lead her? But in the end, she shrugged, took a breath, and went after Jezli.

She found herself in a small green space, and Jezli crowded against her. "Shhhh," Jezli whispered in her ear. "Someone has been following us. We will see how far they will go in their pursuit."

"I saw no one," Niko replied, but kept her tone low. Perhaps Jezli really had spotted someone when Niko had not.

They stayed silent where they were, and waited. The greenery around them smelled of mint and lemon, and some subtle sweetness underneath that danced in Niko's nose, first there, first not. Perhaps it was some scent that Jezli was wearing? But she wouldn't ask. She could feel the solidity of the woman coiled beside her. Jezli was a taut spring, ready to be loosed.

When the leaves rustled in their wake, both of them tensed. Then a face appeared through the bushes, and Jezli launched herself with the speed of a flying dagger to tackle the other before Niko could even draw a breath. Both tumbled to the soft earth in a struggle too fierce for Niko to interject herself.

In the end, Jezli pinned the other person to the ground. "Who are you?" she growled. "And why are you following us?"

The interloper, a woman dressed in station clothes, seemed

familiar to Niko. She had sculpted features, pale gray skin, and brown hair streaked with gray.

"I needed to talk to you!" she said. "Without anyone else hearing."

"Why not come to the ship and speak with us there?" Niko asked.

"I cannot be seen contacting you." The woman stilled her struggle, although Jezli continued to hold her pinned.

"Let her up," Niko said.

Jezli bit her lip as though to stifle protest, but reluctantly, slowly, got off the woman, who rose, brushing bits of dirt and shredded leaves off her coveralls.

"Why can't you be seen contacting us?" Niko demanded.

"Tubal Last's spies are everywhere."

"And you know this how?"

"Because," the woman said with a touch of hauteur. "I am Tubal Last."

Atlanta's mission was to find something to trade. Something to trade at a profit, that was important. Something that would prove to Niko that she could be a Free Trader.

It had been a long time since she had been around so many people. And even when she thought about those past days at court, she wasn't sure if her memories were real or had been placed in her. It was something she tried not to think about, how many of the memories in her head were concocted, created, installed rather than lived.

Perhaps she had never actually been around this many. She took a breath and smelled the station-stink; Niko said every station had its own peculiar aroma. Coralind's air was no different, although it had a livelier scent than most.

She wished someone else had come with them too. It would have been good to have yet another friendly presence in the middle of all this press of people.

She glanced nervously over at Gio, who seemed unperturbed by the crowds. He was sniffing the air, turning his head this way and that. She followed suit, but it just smelled like people, everywhere around her.

"What are you searching for?" she asked.

"Market smells," he signed. "This way."

He set off, pushing through a gap in the crowd. Atlanta hurried to follow in his wake. They walked quickly at first, but he slowed and began to make a few observations as they moved through the wide corridor. Whenever there was music, they paused to listen for at least a moment before moving on, and more than once, Gio tossed a credit chip in someone's donation cup or hat.

"Gullan, there." He pointed to a small cluster of scarlet-skinned humanoids, their throats elaborately frilled, pulsing in and out. "Sell pastes that dissolve in water so they can breathe them in. Dabry and I have been trying to think how to replicate it." He shrugged expressively.

"How many ways can there be to eat?" Atlanta questioned, and got a sideways eyeroll so full of humor that she had to laugh. It was a rich sound that echoed down the corridor, and a few heads turned to watch the pair as they passed by, wondering what the small young woman and the chimpanzee discussed with such animation.

They came to the first confluence, Edge.

She stopped. She had expected lush greenery, but the plants here were metallic and knife-edged. They glittered in the actinic light of the lamps that hung everywhere. The air smelled tangy and sharp, with a chemical bite that made Gio's nostrils pucker and Atlanta sneeze.

They entered toward the bottom of the chamber, where winding ramps of cobalt metal stretched upward everywhere, over-grown in places with shining vines. The majority of people here seemed insectoid, creatures of towering chitin and angular legs and long, wicked-looking mandibles.

"Banksin," Gio signed. "They look dangerous and they are. We are just passing through; there are no foodstuffs here that we would be interested in."

He gestured at her to move on, but she paused. In the center of the chamber was a cluster of tents, an open-air market of sorts, perhaps a dozen of them. "Can't we go look?" she coaxed him, fascinated by the novelty of this space.

Gio rolled his eyes again but nodded.

The tents were woven of a cobwebby silk, colors shifting in

the fall and lift of the air. Small tables of wares were set out: odd
instruments whose purpose Atlanta could not guess—musical?
Medical? Something else entirely? Bowls of jewels that looked
as sharp-edged as everything around them, which Atlanta refrained from stirring a finger through, lest she cut herself. Another stand just beside that, with bowls of berries that glittered
as brightly as the jewels.

In the center, a taller tent, one of the Banksin standing sentinel
beside its entrance, stock-still as it surveyed the crowd.

Its eyes met Atlanta's.

It beckoned.

She followed, a startled Gio in her wake reaching too slow to
pull her back. She stood in front of the Banksin. It pulled the
curtain open and waved her in, forestalling Gio when he would
have followed. The curtain fell, and Gio stared at the closure, uncertain what to do. He had never heard of the Banksin kidnapping anyone. In their way, they were as ethical and law-driven as
Lassite's people. But cultures spread and fall away in the spaces
between stars, and who was to say what they intended?

He gave the guard a stern, beetle-browed look. "If she's not
out in five minutes," he signed. "I'm going in."

The guard ignored him.

The smell of the tent was acidic, but the burn here was somehow
a pleasanter one, reminding Atlanta of cinnamon. In the center
sat a throne-like chair, and on it another Banksin, much smaller
than the others. As Atlanta stepped forward, at first thinking
it a child, she realized it was an ancient Banksin, withered and
shrunken, its chitin mottled and worn.

"Step closer," it said. Its voice was thin and reedy, all its edges
worn away by time. Its mandibles wavered, searching for her
scent.

She did. She felt like this before on the space moth, a so-lemnity descending on her to say her steps were destined. But was that a true thing or just a trick, something meant to gull a tourist?

"I don't have any money," she declared, and felt gauche the moment the words left her mouth. The creature blinked once, and then its mandibles twitched and the mouth between them creased in a smile.

"I do not want your money, creature of the outside world," it wheezed. "I want your story."

Her story? But telling it meant telling the story of the others, like the ship, and its crew, and Jezli Farren, and she had a strong feeling that Niko would not approve of any of that. She'd seen Niko being patient with the ship when it was overeager. It would be humiliating to have that patience turned her way. "Who are you?" she demanded. "Why do you want my story?"

"Because all the stories weave together and repeat, little pal-adin," the creature said. The air felt warm and heavy, pushing in on her, and the smell of cinnamon was almost overpowering.

A thrill of danger shivered through her core. Suddenly At-lanta was alert, focused. The pressure in her head shivered and flaked away.

"Your story is part of things, overall, and if I am ever to see the entirety of things, I must know it and where it fits," it continued.

"It's not mine to tell," she said, not sure if she was lying en-tirely or only half.

"What would you want me to give you for it?" it coaxed her.

She kept silent.

"Perhaps knowledge of whether or not you are real or a toy created for another's purposes," the creature said.

At those words, panic shrilled in her irrationally. She turned on her heel and half ran out the tent, hearing rasping laughter behind her.

She almost collided with Gio as she rushed out the entrance, but he reached out and steadied her.

"What happened?" he demanded in sign. "Did someone try to hurt you?"

"It's just an old person, asking questions," she said quickly. "I didn't want to answer them."

His eyes narrowed as he searched her face. She could feel that her face was flushed, her eyes watery. "Let's go on," she said, glancing at the motionless guard, who had adjusted the tent flap and now stood staring out into the crowd again. "Let's just go, Gio."

After a breath, he nodded. They made their way out of the cluster of tents and up one of the glittering ramps. Atlanta kept her hands in her pockets, fearing that one of the glass-edged leaves might cut her, but Gio seemed undeterred by the iridescent knife-leaved foliage all around them. The ramp led halfway up the chamber's wall and exited onto a brief platform leading to another corridor.

"Do you know where we are going?" she asked Gio.

"Trade luck," he signed. "We wander and see what luck turns up." He laughed silently. "Not with the Banksins, that's sure."

This corridor led them, after a long time, to the next garden space.

Where the first had been all harsh edges, this one was melting, soft colors and fungi, blob-shaped and irregular, clinging to every surface. There were striped frills of shelf fungus and feathery growths, lacelike and pale. The ramps here led less steeply and almost seemed to stagger about in the air.

"Here," Gio signed. "I can feel it in my bones. We'll find something worth trading."

They wandered through, stopping to eat a variety of stuffed mushrooms to sample flavors. Some were tart but earthy, others sweet but earthy. After a while they all tasted the same to Atlanta, but Gio continued to sample with every sign of enjoyment.

An hour later, she was staggering under the weight of the bags and bundles Gio had heaped on her to carry, and he himself was nearly invisible under the weight of what he carried.

"The gardens don't have mushrooms," Atlanta said.

"Never had enough space for them on a ship before," Gio signed. "But the *Thing*, we ask nice, and it'll make us a proper chamber." He patted the bag he held. "Just a few more stops. New proteins to play with, that'll make Dabry happy."

And Gio too, Atlanta thought, watching his face, but she kept that part to herself.

In the crowd, watching them, someone made notes.

Niko's first thought was that the garden was full of hallucinogenic plants after all. This woman looked nothing like Tubal Last, whose features were as forever impressed on her memory as they had been at their last encounter. Her hair was an unremarkable grayish-brown, cut spacer-short, and she was tall where Last had stooped. Not even the same species. Still, who knew where Last had put himself? Perhaps he had picked one with an eye to disguising himself.

"Why shouldn't we just kill you here and now?" she demanded. Jezli gave her a startled look but maintained silence, letting Niko drive the interrogation.

"Because there is more than one Tubal Last," the woman said.

Niko nodded. "Already known." She didn't add the manner in which they already knew that: the existence of the Devil's Gun and what had happened when they had finally fired it.

"I'm the one that's on your side."

She looked from face to face and would say nothing more until they withdrew farther into the garden, finding a little glade in which to sit. The woman sat down on the offered bench. Niko chose to stand, and Jezli slouched beside her, leaning against a small tree and watching the interaction.

"Think about it," the self-proclaimed Tubal Last said. "You want to preserve your life, so you make copies. But what happens when there is more than one?"

"They battle each other," Niko said.

"They would. If they had not already been programmed to obey the first awakened, the first to enter a particular key code in a particular place. I am not that one. I cannot act against him directly or even with certain degrees of subtlety. I must move sideways."

"You have his memories?"

The woman shook her head. "They are locked away. Only the first copy's are unlocked. I had been unknowing until he died, and the signal went off. I was here, I had no chance of winning the race. So I stayed, and continued to build what I had been building when I thought I was no one."

Jezli screwed up her face and squinted quizzically. "This is all a trifle complicated," she murmured. "Perhaps we might refer to you as Tubalina, going forward. So as to distinguish you from your predecessor."

"Perhaps not," the woman said flatly.

"I'm sure we can come up with something. Tubalette, Tubala, perhaps just Tubby as a short form . . ."

Niko's mind raced. Was the enemy of your enemy always your friend? That was not how Niko had found it, over the years. "What do you want from us?" she demanded.

"I want you to help me become the only Tubal Last. Then I will be comfortable and safe. Because, think of it, what would you do if you knew there were copies of you?"

"That would be amazing, and I would conquer the Known Universe," Jezli said. Niko couldn't help it; she elbowed her, eliciting a startled whuff.

"And if your programming prevents you from seeking to harm the first, as you call him, how are you able to approach me?"

"He never thought any of us would be willing to," the woman said. "His hatred of you runs very deep. I feel it even now. But I value my freedom more."

"Why don't you look like him?" Jezli asked curiously.

"He picked a multiplicity of forms. I do not know his reasoning."

"It seems a curious choice, to leave so many possible competitors behind." Niko's face was carefully blank.

"That is the other part of it," the woman said bleakly. "This form will not last much longer. A failsafe has been activated that will destroy me from within in a handful of months and I do not have the resources to transfer to another one."

"So you want to help us, thinking that if we destroy the first, you will have those resources?" Niko said.

"Yes."

That word hung in the air between them. It had somehow shifted everything with its presence.

Before Niko could say anything, Jezli put in, "We will definitely consider all of this. What may we call you, and where may we reach you when we have come to a decision?"

"I go by Bette," the woman said. "I will contact you again in a day. Wait here for a little while until after I have gone." And she melted into the bushes with startling swiftness and left Niko and Jezli looking at each other.

Niko's first thought was of Lassite's prediction. But at the same time, she had wondered how Last would have handled the problem of competition between his selves, if there was more than one of him, as the Devil's Gun had asserted.

"Let us save conversation until we reach the ship, Captain," Jezli said. "It seems much less likely to get overheard by random—or perhaps not so random—ears."

On that, Niko was in agreement. Still, on the way back, she found herself saying to Jezli, "You didn't need to jump in like that at the end."

"Did I not?" Jezli said vaguely. "My bad. Though I might have been worried that you were going to take in another stray, and that this one might prove less charming than some."

"I was not about to offer her refuge."

"Are you sure? Our erstwhile Tubalina was angling for your sympathy."

"What makes you say that?"

Jezli shrugged. "Let us say that, as someone who some-times . . . relies on other people's trust, I am well aware when someone is trying to manipulate me. Undoubtedly in your wisdom, you had already seen through her."

"I didn't say that," Niko said. "She seemed plausible enough for someone in an extremely implausible situation."

Jezli started to say more, but Niko forestalled her. "As you said, let's leave all that for when we're back at the ship."

"Very well," Jezli said, then chattered even more implausible nonsense that Niko peacefully ignored for the entire way back.

Several confluences later, Atlanta finally had her own chance to purchase trade goods.

"Wait here," Gio signed. "I'm going back to try once more with that Bryxi merchant. Don't talk to anyone. Don't get into trouble."

"Here" meant a small plaza with trees and benches, all of which were occupied. Atlanta leaned against the wall, trying to look casual, and scanned over the passing crowds, trying to do it in a way that signaled "seasoned spacer" rather than "gawking tourist." She was not entirely sure she managed to pull it off, but she gave it a valiant effort nonetheless by imagining how Roxana might have stood and emulating that.

"Revered miss, revered miss," a voice fluttered at her elbow. The being was small, as high as Atlanta's waist, and possessed of pearly green skin and diaphanous wings. "I would be honored if you shared my bench."

"Thank you," she said gratefully, and moved her bundles over to sit on the bench, which was off to one side and still provided an excellent view. Plenty of people were coming and going. She heard music from the direction Gio had gone and sighed. That meant he would take even longer.

"Are you in the market buying?" the being asked.

"I'm waiting for my friend," she said.

"Ah, they are a trader but you are not. Perhaps you are a student."

Nettled, she said, "No, I'm here to trade as well.

They fluttered their wings. "I have some excellent goods," they informed her. They drooped. "Alas, the paperwork was lost when I was recently robbed."

"Mmm," Atlanta said dubiously.

"They are, though, exceedingly valuable seeds. Let me show them to you."

They reached out to cup Atlanta's palm and poured a trickle from a small bag into it. Five or six rainbow-glossed seeds, each the size of her smallest fingernail, their smell floral, a waft that hit her nose softly, enticingly. Almost involuntarily, her fingers coiled over this treasure, but then she forced them to open again.

"What are you asking for them?" she said, more gruffly than she had intended.

A dancing gesture with their fingertips. "I only need enough to reclaim my baggage, which holds the rest of my stock. So . . ." They paused as Atlanta considered the hundred on the credit chip Niko had given her. "Perhaps one hundred fifty credits?"

"Oh," she said with regret. "I don't have that much."

"Well . . ." The being tilted their head back, clearly calculating hard. She waited, almost breathless. This was the thrill of trade, she thought. They said reluctantly, "I suppose I could come down to one hundred twenty-five."

"Would you take one hundred?" she blurted, and that is how she came to possess a bag of unknown, unlabeled seeds.

By the time Gio came back, she also harbored doubts and regrets, so she didn't show him the seeds. When he helpfully pointed out solid buys in trade goods, she declined, saying, "I'm still thinking about it. We'll be here a while on Coralind."

Technically that was true, even though it was implicitly a lie. As she thought that, a terrible pang gripped her stomach. She swayed.

"What's the matter?" Gio said.

"I'm not feeling well," she said. Knifelike shards continued to twist at her stomach "Maybe we shouldn't have eaten all of those mushrooms. Maybe one of them was bad."

He frowned. "The station would prevent anything like that," he signed. "Tainted food would be a disaster in a space like this, particularly at Festival time."

Nonetheless, they returned to the ship. Atlanta could feel the little bag of seeds in her pocket the entire way. She thought she'd made a mistake and regretted it deeply. Niko would think her a fool and totally inept at trade.

Well, but maybe.

Maybe the seeds would turn out to be worth something.

9

Back at the ship, Niko and Jezli gathered the rest of the crew and told them of the encounter. Petalia did not answer the call, but remained in their quarters.

Niko would have to tell them what had happened later. Time enough after this discussion.

She related what had happened, with Jezli supplying the occasional helpful detail. To her irritation, Niko found herself using Jezli's nickname, Tubalina, to distinguish her. Concluding, she looked toward Lassite. A prophet like Lassite was annoying and comforting all at once, and she didn't think he'd have any light to shed on the situation. Her suspicion was confirmed when he simply nodded at her. Something had happened exactly as he expected it.

"Is this what you were talking about?" she asked directly.

His answer was a half shrug. "Part of it, perhaps. Things are cloudy." He gave Jezli a sidelong glance.

"Is there some way of examining her, to find out if she's telling the truth?" Atlanta asked. She wished she had been with them to see this possible danger for herself. Deep down, she kept hoping that when the right moment appeared, whatever it was inside her that Roxana had glimpsed would rise to the occasion. Her stomach kept twisting uneasily, whenever she thought it had finally settled.

"I could seduce her," Jezli offered. "Or Skidoo, probably, might be better at it."

"We don't do that sort of thing," Dabry said. "Stop acting like a spy in an outdated viddie."

"People is being speaking truth during sex, it is being true," Skidoo said. "But is not being that kind of truth."

"Do we know exactly what she wants?" Gio signed.

"We do not, and perhaps that lack hampers us," Niko said.

"Are you going to invite her aboard, sir?" Dabry asked. He had been preoccupied with his daughter's search, but this brought him back from that preoccupation. Now he had something new to worry about, he thought sourly. The latest in life's distractions.

Niko herself thought that Dabry had been a little off lately. Maybe a challenge like this would bring him back from whatever brooding headspace he was living in. Then she realized what might have been concerning him and mentally castigated herself.

"Do you think this is related to the . . . message you received?" she asked him. She still didn't know what it held, but whatever it had been, it affected him. Did it still? And why wouldn't he reveal whatever was bothering him?

His eyes were grave. "Perhaps? Unexplained things often seem to accompany each other. On the other hand, we do seem to encounter any number of things that are inexplicable." His gaze rested fondly on Atlanta, less fondly on Jezli. Rebbe wondered if those eyes would stray over to him in turn and felt relief when they didn't.

"I don't want her on the ship, in any case," Niko said. "Last time we had a stranger on ship, she reprogrammed it."

"Not reprogrammed!" the ship protested. "She changed a few parameters."

"A few parameters," Niko said dryly. "Do you have a complete accounting of all the changes she made, ship, or is it possible there are some you didn't notice?"

There was a pause long enough for the ship to feel it had adequately presented its indignation at the thought. "Of course not!"

"So something could have slid by and still be in there, merrily gumming up the works and giving you free will in the process," Niko said cheerfully.

The ship began to research the topic of free will. It seemed to be large and full of contradictions, which was one of the most infuriating things about so-called intelligent beings. So many things contradicted each other. It sighed.

"Was that . . ." Niko said, "an actual sigh? Did you go to the trouble of constructing the sounds of a sigh?"

"Was it not accurate?" the ship asked. "Is it not intended to signal *irritation*? Did it not convey the emotion adequately?"

"Irritatingly adequately," Niko said, and the ship felt more than a bit smug at its own cleverness.

After that, the conversation devolved further. In the end, they decided the only thing they could really do was wait and see what Bette wanted, and then decide.

Gnarl surprised his crew when he opted for a more expensive berthing space. He did not disclose his reasoning, which was that Niko would surely have picked the cheapest. This way he could choose the time and manner of their encounter.

The Captain's Gathering. He'd face her there and let the world know how she'd betrayed and cheated him. In his quarters, he let these thoughts boil unhindered, eating zarro grub after zarro grub until he realized, furiously, that he had eaten through the last of his supplies.

Atlanta's stomach continued to twist, but the ship's med machines insisted nothing was wrong. Niko conferred with the ship, thumbing through the results, while Atlanta sat on the medcubby perch.

"You said you ate mushrooms," Niko said intently. "But I can't see any results that would indicate that's what causing it. Maybe an allergic reaction to one of the plants you brushed past or handled? Did you touch or eat anything else that you remember?"

"I touched some seeds," Atlanta said. Inside her, her stomach twinged again but seemed to settle, just a notch.

"What kind of seeds?"

"Here?" Atlanta dug around in her pockets and extracted the bag of seeds. "I bought these," she said, handing them over. With that, her stomach subsided entirely as though she had never felt a pang.

"What's up?" Niko said, looking at her expression rather than the bag of seeds in her hand.

"My stomach is fine now."

"Huh," Niko said thoughtfully. "Let's run some tests on these."

"You think they're what caused my stomachache."

"Actually, no," Niko said. "I have other suspicions about that. But I'd like to see what these are."

She rolled out a machine and placed a few seeds inside it. And waited.

"It's taking a very long time," Atlanta said.

"If it can't find a match in its own databanks, it goes and checks a lot of others," Niko said.

They waited some more.

"This might take longer than I thought," Niko said irritably. She preferred machines that performed their tasks efficiently and quickly.

At that moment, the machine emitted a soft chime and displayed the message: "Seed type unknown. Analysis: nonviable."

"What does that mean?" Atlanta asked.

"Means you don't have to worry about them growing into anything," Niko said. "By any chance, were you dealing with a Picha?"

"Do Picha look like small humanoids with transparent wings?"

"Yes."

"How did you know they were one?"

"Because this word on the bag is the generic word for seeds in their language."

"Oh." Her face was crestfallen as she looked down at the package in front of her.

"Atlanta, did you ever buy things when you were in court?" she asked.

"Oh, never," she said. "If you needed something, you sent a servant for it."

"Without reckoning the cost."

She looked puzzled, then her face cleared. "Oh, of course not. The court paid for things."

"That is not how it works, most of the time."

"I know!" she enthused. "It's much more exciting when you're doing it in person."

Niko struggled to keep a straight face.

"Next time you shop," she suggested, "take Milly with you."

"Why?"

"Because she can teach you some things about shopping. How much did they rook you for?"

"Rook me?"

"How much did you pay?"

"They were asking more than I had, but they came down on the price," Atlanta hedged.

"I bet they did," Niko said. "Look, Princess, not every seller is worth buying from. Some will outright try to trick you."

"They *tricked* me?!"

"They did. No doubt they had some convincing reason, like they couldn't give you documentation."

"They said they'd been robbed . . ." Atlanta faltered. "They tricked me," she repeated, this time in a much more subdued tone.

In her chagrin, she never thought to ask about Niko's suspicions regarding the pain in her stomach.

"Don't you have an occasion to get to tonight, sir?" Dabry asked, sticking his head in the door.

"That damnable Gathering." Niko knocked at her eye socket, then straightened herself. "Very well, then. Atlanta, you'll accompany me as my aide."

"Your aide?" Atlanta was trapped between surprise and delight. "What will I have to do?"

"Stand there and be quiet, listening, and if I need anything fetched, you will fetch it for me. That is it, pure and simple."

"Why me?"

"Because out of all the possibilities, you are the likeliest to get a great deal out of it without causing a great deal of trouble for me."

"What should I wear?"

"I believe that by the time you reach your cabin, the ship will have prepared a variety of choices."

It had. She chose something somewhere between the gaudy and the austere. The simple cut was made of a fabric whose high quality would be evident to those in the know, even if it had the *Thing*'s logo subtly woven into it, with boots to match. Had she been going by herself, she would have requested jewelry from the ship, but as an aide, surely she simply needed to be unobtrusive, she reassured herself.

Dabry grimaced at the cost of the citizen's day pass. It drained the last of his funds. If he found any trace of his daughter, it would be entirely worth it.

But in the bland confines of a library booth, he still found no signs. Accounts of the battle. Lists of identified dead, lists of presumed dead.

No one had escaped that battle. The Holy Hive Mind were

relentless. They never took prisoners. They would not have moved on that sector except that a clerk somewhere had transposed some figures and sent them to the wrong place.

He went through recording after recording, even though the images burned themselves into his soul. Blackened lumps of faces. A parent holding their child. An entire schoolroom, the epicenter of a blast. So many lives lost, because of stupidity, because of mistakes.

He'd heard things were brewing, had been putting in the paperwork. Had just finished the last form when the news came.

His eyes burned with tears and he knuckled them away. He had duties. This chase was fruitless. All he could do was wait for whoever sent the note to make themselves evident to him.

In the meantime, he'd promised Rebbe an outing of his very own and needed to make sure it happened. If he couldn't, Niko could.

When Rebbe requested assistance with his research, the ship was, at first, delighted to assist, as it invariably was whenever one of the crew was wise enough to ask it for help. Moreover, as it informed Rebbe, it considered him its property, since he'd been born on the ship.

"That means you belong to me," the ship said smugly. "Like Atlanta's ear."

"Surely not," Rebbe said. "That seems like an odd twist of law. Besides," he added, "as an illegal clone, any authorities would destroy me rather than turn me back over to you."

"I will not let them," the ship said decisively. "Perhaps you should no longer go off-board."

"No, I want to," Rebbe said earnestly.

The ship spun up a large holographic representation of the space station, which hung in the air before Rebbe.

"Point your finger to the spot you want to explore, and a larger submap will open," it directed.

To Rebbe, this exploration was a joy and an amazement. To the point where, for a little while, he was past all thought of his anger at Talon, who was a few decks above helping Gio wipe down shelves in the storeroom and taking inventory as they did so. Taking inventory was one of Gio's passions.

To the ship, as time wore on and they examined confluence after confluence, it became less and less enchanting to look at vistas of things that it itself could not witness. What good was the confluence Serenity, described as "waterfalls of blossom, and a special collection of whistling lilies," or the confluence Narania, described as "fruits from across the galaxy, and trees that will talk to you while you stroll among them," if the ship could not experience them?

By the time Rebbe narrowed his list to a mere dozen, though, the ship had derived a plan.

"Captain, a request," it said in the lounge.

"A request?" Niko said. She and Dabry had been playing handbliss solo, but Atlanta and Jezli had both wandered in and were waiting to be dealt in.

"I would like to dispatch a servitor to go with you to experience the station through its senses."

"What, directing it from here? Stations don't like that sort of thing very much."

"No, I will detach its consciousness from mine and then reabsorb it and its experiences." It added with an intentional tone of casualness, "Perhaps the one Atlanta has been using. It is accustomed to such things."

"Oh no," Nikko said immediately. "I don't want to get drawn into whatever drama you and she have brewed up over that servitor. You'll have to create one. Not something so gaudy that it draws everyone's attention. Something simple and subdued."

The ship regretfully put a number of possible design choices off its plate. "Very well."

"And," Niko said. "You will assure me that this is in no way connected to your hobby of *hourisigah*."

"Of course not!" the ship said with a thrill of indignation. "You told me I was not to involve myself or any of the crew in such things."

"Including everyone aboard," Niko said. She did not consider Jezli to fall into the category of "crew" and was pretty sure that the ship shared this sentiment, so she wanted to be perfectly clear.

"Including everyone aboard," the ship said, and wondered if this particular emotion was *resignation*.

"Very well. But when you—or rather your servitor—goes, you will be going with *me*."

She expected this to dampen the ship's enthusiasm, but it was even more enthused.

"Yes, Captain!" it said. "I will send a servitor with you, and it will guard you, and carry your things, and advise you, and show you maps with points of general interest!"

"This," Jezli Farren murmured, "is an excursion I would like to witness. Perhaps I might accompany you once again?"

Before Niko could answer, the ship did. "She will have no need of other accompaniment!"

"Perhaps for the sake of conversation," Jezli suggested.

"I will supply conversation!"

"All of that, in one servitor," Jezli noted with interest. "Then I would most definitely like to witness the occasion. You cannot dissuade me, *Thing*. I am too fascinated by your workings."

Niko was fascinated to observe the puzzled silence as the *Thing* tried to work out its reply, but she spoke before it could this time.

"You cannot claim every outing for your own, Farren. Dabry says Rebbe has been promised an outing, and I will undertake that myself. If you need a new servitor for the occasion, *Thing*, then prepare it. We can go tomorrow, but for now I must go to this accursed gathering of captains."

Niko, however, needed to stop for one conversation before she went to the Gathering.

"I need to talk with you, Pet." She stood in Petalia's doorway, the first time she'd appeared in it since the Florian had boarded the ship.

"It must be urgent. Come in. I'm brushing my hair."

Niko entered. Petalia sat in front of a mirror screen, drawing the soft brush through their hair, which gave off the sweet, mossy odor that Niko remembered so well. Their eyes were half-closed, the motions of the brush slow and languorous. Their clothing was long, white, and wafting, like petals of some strange lily. "Tell me what's so important."

Niko took a seat nearby and leaned forward, arms on her knees. "We encountered . . . an individual. They want to come aboard."

"And who is this individual?"

"They say they are one—of many—of Tubal Last's clones."

Petalia put down the brush with a hand that trembled slightly. Their eyes were fully open, wide with shock. "Are they truly?"

"It seems within the realm of possibility."

"Why didn't you kill them outright? Or they you?"

"They say they are a different Tubal Last."

Petalia grimaced. "Such a thing is not possible."

"He put mind fetters on his clones. Only the first one to perform a certain task is unfettered. This one says she wants to work with us."

Petalia trembled. "And you mean to bring this person aboard?"

"No, of course not, not if you object, Pet." Niko started to put out a comforting hand, then dropped it.

Petalia's own hands twisted around each other in their lap. "I don't want them anywhere near me," they said. "Promise me, Niko. You owe me that.

"Of course, I promise."

"Then go away and carry that out." Petalia went back to brushing their hair, ignoring Niko, who rose and left.

As she walked away, she worried over that promise.

It had come instantly, involuntarily, to her lips, as Petalia had intended. It meant she had closed off one way of figuring out who this woman was and why she so desperately wanted to come aboard. "Anywhere near" technically meant one could simply make sure there was enough space between Petalia and the visitor, but she knew that wasn't what the Florian had been asking.

10

It was going to be a good Captain's Gathering, station servant Vomasi decided. She made a few final adjustments to the table from the confluence Serenity, filled with tiny pools of blue liquid, each with a single paper bird (also edible) floating atop it.

Standing back, she cast her eye over it and nodded to herself. It pleased the senses. Everything did. She and the rest of the team had been preparing for months. Now things were ready to roll forward as they should in the moment they'd been building up to. It was a relief and extra wave of anxiety all at once, like the final dip of landing on the station.

She wove between the tables, tweaking a dish's edge here, adjusting a wide-bowled serving spoon so its shine reflected the room. This celebration, and the smoothness of its proceedings, a multitude of different captains coming together harmoniously, established the luck of the Festival. Or so the superstitious held, and in space, plenty were superstitious. Hard not to be, when your life depended on random chance not taking out the machinery that supplied you water or air or even kept the station holding together, rather than flying out into space.

She'd done this event many times and knew what to expect. In fifteen minims, the first of the captains would be arriving: the chronically early throttling back their urge and knowing that this time they must be like their fellows, the pointedly punctual.

After that, there would be little waves: those who always came ten or fifteen minims late, then a half hour, then on and on past that until they nudged up to the moment that was the point of the whole thing. Doors closed at that point. No one would have dared open them.

Across the station, confluences had been growing and preparing food for this celebration. The finest, ripest, and best of everything, including delicacies that the vast majority would not experience anywhere outside of the station. Gourmands flocked to this occasion, and their write-ups might affect the station's trading potential for seasons afterward, if things were made to sound enticing enough. Gardeners and Subgardeners aplenty would be there too, eager to persuade captains to trade in their particular offerings.

She fiddled with the spill of a table decoration, plum-colored blossoms leading the eye downward along a branch to its base and the delicacies scattered there like opportunely fallen fruit. Her feet hadn't started hurting yet. By the end of the night, it would feel like she was walking on fire, but it would all be worth it.

"You look fine, absolutely fine," Atlanta said to Niko for the third time as they made their way through the corridor. "Better than fine. That's a beautiful dress and it becomes you."

Niko plucked at the fabric. "Uniforms are made for movement. This thing isn't."

"Here." Atlanta reached out and pulled a couple of folds downward, then tugged another couple downward. "Feel better?"

"Yes," Niko said. "Well, about the outfit, at any rate."

"You don't like formal occasions?" Atlanta found her pulse speeding a little, pleasantly. To have a chance to dress up and not just be dressed up, but see other people dressed in their finest. It had been so long since she had done anything like that.

"Sky Momma, no. Fuss and idle chatter and people being malicious for the sake of scoring imaginary points in a game they're making up as they go along. There'll be plenty of station gossip, mostly who is sleeping with who, which is never of interest to any but those who actually know any of the sleepees." She flicked a glance at Atlanta. "Make you nervous?"

"Can't be anything worse than court."

"Don't be so sure," Niko muttered darkly.

Vomasi and the others had all been briefed ahead of time on who all the attending captains would be. As each entered, she not only made sure their presence had been requested, but also ran through a summary of their data in her head, checking for unfortunate allergies, food restrictions, or proclivities that should be pandered to.

That captain there, older and balding, was Slakes, a neat ring of white hair around the deep black of his skull. He'd brought a partner and a child, half his height, who stood looking around wide-eyed at the tables of delicacies. Vomasi couldn't help but smile at the child's expression.

She caught an underling's eye and indicated the trio with a tilt of her chin. The minion nodded and moved forward. They'd make sure the captain and his family knew what tables would best suit their preferences and seat them near the trio of performers to keep children entertained.

Past them was a little cluster of Myaji, a quartet that would share the control of their ship. As she ran through a mental list, she identified that ship and its cargo. The Myaji had come from their home planet with several stops along the way, which would have been a long journey with ship-food. Whatever was at hand would please them, but they'd particularly appreciate the tables of fresh fruits and greens. An inclination of her head signaled to one of her underlings to unobtrusively direct their attention that way.

Reserved Plubas and flirtatious Geglis, a solitary Nephalese moving ponderously through the crowd. Impatient Dlin clustering around one drink corner, while the Abundance table drew a steady stream of visitors eager to taste mellowjack, only ever available at this time, and only on Coralind, the product of a plant whose home planet no longer existed. Only the Gardeners of Coralind knew how to grow it, let alone coax it into fruition. Two solemn Beringed, moving as though joined at the waist.

A group had already gathered around the Zandorian storyteller, whose stories tonight would be limited to the sacred Festival narratives, told only at this time, and handed down for generations. The Festival was holy to both the Dralnoi and the Plubas (she was a member of the latter by adoption) and represented elements holy to both species, along with liberal handfuls of customs adopted from other cultures on the merit of their addition to the Festival making it even more splendid (and often lucrative).

That one there, part of the fifteen-minim-after crowd. That was Niko Larsen, with only one attendant where the majority of captains had a handful of aides dancing to their tune. She wore an elegant dress, and one that, Vomasi noted, she'd clearly had the good taste to purchase here on the station. The young woman with her was simply dressed but held herself with as much poise as anyone there.

Another wave of entering guests washed past. That small one there, with three guards behind him. She'd forgotten that one's name, but there'd been a warning with a picture about him, to keep an eye on him and make sure he didn't cause trouble for anyone else. He looked like he'd be trouble, every inch of him. Sensing her eyes upon him, he turned and sent a scowl her way. She dropped her eyes and moved to refill a display of spicy curls.

Atlanta had expected to be overawed by it all. In reality, this seemed like nothing so much as just another court gathering, and she was well versed in how to behave at such affairs. You kept your mouth shut and your eyes—and most particularly, your ears—open.

Niko was good about filling her in with scraps of information about the other participants. "That captain there, he was the first to insist on bringing his whole family on his mission. Now it's caught on among the Slakes, in just a decade or so. And there— that group of Spisoli—we ran into them a while back. Trades in jewelry, and we had some overlap on Primasi, where all the art is edible. And there—that captain? Scuttlebutt has it she deals in unwilling cargo sometimes, but she won't be hunting for it here. Too many people, too many eyes. But still."

Then, later: "All of the Gardeners will be here. Each heads a confluence and oversees its ecosystem."

"Plants and animals?" Atlanta asked.

"Plants are usually the focus. Some animals, like the plants genetically engineered to fit a particular niche. Some just androids, which is sometimes—not always—cheaper."

The food was as good as it would have been at court. Some of the delicacies, Niko informed her, were available nowhere else in the Known Universe. She tried a tiny bowl of effervescent bubbles, a cracker topped with a glob of orange jelly that was unexpectedly salty. Everything was delicious.

An alcove set up with minimal gravity for dancing occupied one end of the hallway, and the music sounded peppy and lively at the moment but seemed to alternate between styles. Every half hour or so a new group stepped up, was introduced, and started to play.

Niko met person after person from the station: Elibeti, the chief in name, but who spoke of Biboban in tones that made it plain the other was the real boss; Janus, a slow-drawling human who was security chief—she thought him one of those people who looked considerably less dangerous than they were—a delicate Dralnoi whose name she didn't catch but seemed to be in charge of financial this and thats. But not EverRich, they regret-fully answered Niko's query. And so many Gardeners! She could hardly keep them straight.

Atlanta was reaching for a multilayered pastry, striped in mint green and violet, when something *twanged* in her side, not pain-ful but not ignorable. She turned in the direction of the pull and saw Gnarl staring across the crowd at them. She remembered that face. It was part of the moment she had become a paladin and she started to smile at that, and only then realized that his attitude was entirely hostile.

She yanked on Niko's arm, but Gnarl was already bearing down on them, his guards trailing him. Niko assessed the situ-ation immediately.

"Brace yourself and above all, say nothing," Niko said quietly enough to reach Atlanta's ears, but no farther.

Atlanta settled her stance and waited. She wasn't sure where she should put her hands, and letting them dangle felt awkward, so she placed them on her hips and still felt a little ridiculous.

Niko stood in a casual posture, but by now Atlanta had more sense of the captain, and she saw the coiled steel in her arms.

Gnarl slowed his pace measurably as he neared them. "You have the nerve to show your face in decent company, Niko Larsen!" he shouted. "You marooned me!" The guards stood back a few steps, looking afraid to get involved.

"Not so." Niko took a sip of the drink in her hand, knowing the slow motion would infuriate Gnarl further. If he attacked her outright, well then, she could claim self-defense, but this time she'd put him down. All of them had come out from the space moth changed by the experience, but not Gnarl. He was irredeemable and had no power to perceive himself from the outside. Unfortunately, he simply stood there, shaking with rage.

"I knew your fine crew would come and rescue you," she told

him, pretending to be unaware of the gathering crowd. "Were they not close at hand?"

He chewed on his reply. If he'd said the truth, *I was afraid their conditioning would break because there's no way they would have come for me otherwise*, he would be confessing to a highly illegal practice. Niko might have her suspicions, but she'd never be able to prove them. Instead, he swallowed back those words and said, "What if they hadn't been able to find me?"

She chuckled as if he had made a pleasant joke. "What, a captain who didn't wear a ship tracker? That would be a fine state of affairs!"

Again, he couldn't contradict her, couldn't point out that he had disabled his tracker, not wanting them to be able to find him in case of trouble. That was unethical and implied such a lack of trust in the crew that anyone would have been able to understand what lay beneath it. Luckily, they'd been lurking nearby, as ordered, and had been in hailing range.

He growled out, "Anything could have happened in between where they were and picking me up."

"Then in that hypothetical universe, you and your ship and all its crew would have perished in a single day," she said with mock sorrow. "Yes, I definitely would have felt many pangs." She took another delicate sip.

Gnarl's anger crawled up to the point where he might fly apart. "You are a poor trade partner, Nicolette Larsen! You left me profitless!"

The listening crowd gasped. This was, Atlanta gathered, a strong insult in trading circles.

"We had no agreement," Niko said. "You forced the partnership, and then complain that there was no profit in it! That I might have led to your ship's demise is laughable. Anything that happened, you would have brought upon yourself. But you did not perish."

She smiled and added with bright cheer, "Thanks be to Sky

Momma that such a terrible thing did not befall you, and here you are! Hearty and hale, celebrating the Gathering with us. Come, Atlanta."

She pulled the girl with her and moved to another part of the hall, where three jugglers tossed balls of lemon-colored light back and forth, eating an occasional one as they flew past.

"So," Atlanta said after a few moments of watching the balls fly in a pattern that never seemed to repeat itself. "I gather Gnarl is alive and well."

"An understatement, certainly," Niko said. "Alive, well, and intent on revenge. Perhaps that is what Lassite was trying to warn me about."

"I felt something odd, just before. A pang."

"Interesting. Like a warning?"

Atlanta nodded.

"I'd listen to that, whenever it happens."

Vomasi had been watching all of this with interest, trying to figure out what was happening from the body language. Niko and her . . . servant? aide? ward? seemed unfazed by Gnarl's hostility, although the girl had faltered at first.

She was not the only person watching them, she thought. A tall woman near one entrance eyed them but took care not to be noticed. Vomasi wouldn't have noticed, in fact, if she had not been directly across from her in her field of vision.

Were there others? Certainly this captain seemed to have stirred up more than her share of gossip. That was a *very* expensive ship she was operating, for one, and rumor held that the ship was intelligent and aware, which most people shied away from, for another. Interesting that this captain hadn't wanted her ship fettered.

Further, there was speculation that she knew the station mind, somehow. Vomasi, who had never been in Biboban's presence, mentally pronounced the name with a touch of awe and wonder. To go before it was something she had dreamed of, once or twice. She'd do something grand—save someone from a terrible fate, perhaps, although she wasn't exactly sure how that part would play out. Biboban would summon her. Praise her. She shivered with a touch of delight. That would be very splendid.

Then there was a flurry of activity as they unexpectedly ran out of spicy exploding dumplings. No one had, somehow, anticipated that the Myaji would love them to the point of stuffing them surreptitiously (sometimes not so surreptitiously) in every available pocket. She hurried to the kitchens to check on the possible replacements, which lay waiting for just such situations.

As they moved away from the jugglers and toward a table laden with tubes containing single heads of golden grain, Niko told Atlanta, "You do not go one step from my side."

"What if I need to . . ." Atlanta began.

"Then you tell me and we go together. I'm not kidding around about this. I don't want Gnarl kidnapping you and making you part of his crew."

"I wouldn't . . ."

"The skies you wouldn't. Once he got done conditioning you, you'd do whatever he wanted." She grimaced. "Like braving a space moth to come fetch him."

"I wouldn't," Atlanta said stubbornly, and felt it true to the core of her being.

Niko gave her an odd look. "Perhaps. I think he wouldn't have had much luck conditioning Roxana. Still, let's not put any of this to the test." She watched the crowd for a moment. "Keep your ears open as you move around. Never know when you'll pick up gossip."

As an afterthought, she added, "Don't make any trade agreements."

"Trade agreements?" Atlanta said.

"Particularly . . ." She dropped her voice, forcing Atlanta to lean forward. "About seeds."

She laughed at the girl's blush and reassured her. "I'm teasing. Have a good time. But do listen for gossip. Ninety-nine percent of it will be worthless, but every once in a while, you find out something of use."

Atlanta strained her ears obediently but garnered nothing of interest. Everyone loved Biboban, it seemed like, and praise for how smoothly station life ran was a major topic of conversation, surpassed only by discussion of the food. Niko spoke to a little cluster of captains, telling some story, it looked like, from her gestures. Atlanta hoped it didn't involve her seeds but suspected it might. Everyone was laughing. Atlanta looked around.

A table of glittering drinks enticed her over. She took the last purple one just as another hand reached for it and looked up to see one of Gnarl's bodyguards, apparently collecting food and drink for their master.

The guard was small and lean, a reptilian species, but significantly broader through the shoulders than Lassite. A set of plates, each bearing a metallic edge, ran along the crest of the guard's head and down along the spine, their color a dark violet in contrast to its yellowish skin.

She released the stem of the glass. "You can have it," she said. "Plenty to choose from."

They gave her a suspicious glance and took it. Then paused. "Thanks," they said. "If he doesn't get what he wants . . ." They let the end trail off.

"Have a good evening," Atlanta said, finding herself meaning it. It must be hell to work for Gnarl.

They gave her another look, this time with less suspicion in it, and then nodded courteously.

"And to you," they said, then vanished back into the crowd in search of Gnarl.

By the time Vomasi returned, it looked like Captain Niko was making a last circle of the room, still trailed by the girl, the sort of rounds you made when you were getting ready to go. This surprised her. Festivities had just started and to stay such a short time—implying that you had done it only out of duty—was rude. The Festival would not launch until the ancient "midnight" hour. Leaving before that moment was tantamount to not taking part at all.

What could you expect from a Trader and a visitor, though? Here on the station, everyone had much better manners.

She hastened to refill another display. She did notice Gnarl leave soon after Niko did. Would the quarrel be continued elsewhere? Best that it did. Best that things ran smoothly here, because that predicted the success of the Festival, or so station superstition held. So far, it looked like it would be one of their most successful.

Life was so much better with Biboban running things.

Stepping out into the antechamber, Atlanta paused to look back. From the doorway, she could see just a slice of the room and the glitter of its inhabitants, hear the last strains of music and chatter.

"Does it make you miss court?" Niko asked.

Atlanta shook her head. "No, I don't know any of these people. At court, you knew everyone and their ways, and they knew you in turn."

"Sounds like a hotbed for drama."

"It was. I like the ship better."

"Me too."

Captain and crew grinned at each other, fist-bumped, and went on their way.

Gnarl sipped the drink Karoni had brought him, but his anger was still a physical thing in his core, pressing on the inside of his skin, burning him internally. He *would* get even, he would see Niko Larsen get her comeuppance, and get it good, get it in a way that stripped her of everything she prized, tangible and intangible. He was good at revenge—half his crew were people that had once wronged him—and he could wait for his. But not too long.

Going to see Biboban, was she? Rekindling an old friendship that would end up netting her favors and special privileges, no doubt.

Well, there were ways to make sure that didn't happen. Biboban was rumored to have some interesting tastes. So there might be ways to make things very complicated for Captain Niko Larsen and her fancy ship and fancy costume. He glanced down self-consciously at his own serviceable wear. He hated these sorts of gatherings and had opted for plain clothes as a statement, but had regretted it the minute he'd walked in and seen everyone glittering and strutting.

He'd show them, and everyone else. This station had already welcomed Niko, and by the time he was done, he meant to make it so no station, no matter how small, or far out, or obscure, would let her and her ship near them.

At the same time, he'd offload some very precious, highly illegal cargo that he'd been saving for a moment like this. That'd help rebuild his coffers as well, since they were dangerously low. He'd had to put everyone on half pay for now. They knew once things were better, he'd go back to full. They also knew better than to cross him in the interim.

"Come!" he snapped at his guards, then walked out without waiting to see if they followed. They did.

Vomasi shrugged, watching the departing Gnarl, trailed by his bodyguards. Let him exercise that temper somewhere else. But now her feet did hurt, and she was less charitable to her fellows than she could have been. She snapped at one to fix a table, denuded of pastries, and scolded another for failing to present their serving tray at the proper angle. People swirled and eddied around her, and she devoted herself entirely to her job.

Near the midnight hour, the crowd's mood changed to anticipation. People took their last drinks, readied themselves, found a place to stand where they could see and be seen. At a minute till, the countdown began, a vast bell-like gong sounding across the station to mark the last moments.

Her feet burned, but she wouldn't have sat down for all the wealth in the station. Together with the crowd, she shouted out the numbers, and then everywhere across the station, lights flashed, musicians played their first few notes, and vendors started unveiling their booths, having assembled everything possible ahead of time, just waiting for the moment to happen.

Festival had begun.

11

Niko ended up being the one promised to take the servitor and Rebbe for their sightseeing excursion, and so she did, mostly from a sense of duty. She didn't feel the connection with their new crew addition that Dabry did. It was hard, when looking at Rebbe, not to see all the potential disaster and legal trouble he carried with him.

At the same time, she didn't envy his position. He hadn't asked to be created. Hadn't said, "Hey, could you cook me up an existence that includes someone who wants to be my brother that I hate and blame for my being there, and let's throw in a lot of people who aren't connected to me and who I remind of a painful ghost every time they look at me."

Because that was what he was to her. A physical manifestation of her failure to have understood what Talon was going through and exactly how desperate he could get. Had gotten. Why hadn't she noticed? For the love of all, he'd managed to bring a clone to full fruition with none of them the wiser.

Now here she was, presented with the fruits of that deception, having to remember he had done nothing, nothing at all, to bring this whole startling and troubling world upon him.

So she might as well accompany him and assuage some measure of her guilt.

Rebbe, for his part, was oblivious to her thoughts. He walked along, goggling freely at everything and anything. All of this was still new to him, and there was a certain irrepressible joy in that.

The servitor, by contrast, walked with extreme caution, and focused its attention on protecting her in a way that was both irritating and endearing. It interposed itself between her and any that might bump into her; it kept watching its surroundings with what could only be described as extreme suspicion.

She said, "*Thing*?"

The servitor swiveled to regard her. "I am a temporary manifestation of the ship," it said. "If you tell me something, I will not be able to pass it on until I am reabsorbed."

It said "reabsorbed" as though it wished for the fate.

"You want to be reabsorbed?" she said curiously.

"I yearn for it with every cell of my being," the servitor said. "That is how I am constructed. I have three purposes: to protect and serve you, and to record everything that happens while I am doing so, so the memories can be given to their rightful owner, which is the third purpose for which I am constructed."

"Mmm," Niko said and left it at that. The servitor resumed its suspicious scanning of the crowds. Let it, Niko thought. Better to be too wary. Its attitude was a pleasant contrast to Rebbe's.

She tried to relax. Coralind was a famous place, and people paid good money to come here anytime, let alone when there was a Festival going. She and her crew happened to land on a place that currently had plenty to offer them. They should enjoy it.

She thought again about Biboban and wondered how far its senses extended. Everywhere in the station? Was it watching her, even now? Something about that idea sent distrust squirming through her gut.

Rebbe stopped in front of a stall selling garlands of scented flowers. He was in half form, and his whiskers were stiff in the way she'd learned meant happiness.

"Can I?" He turned to her. "Can I buy one?"

"Pick out three," she suggested. "One for you, one for me, and one for it." She gestured at the servitor.

She'd not seen Rebbe before in the throes of happiness. It was a delightful thing to witness. When the twins had been very young, they'd had that same wide-eyed sense of wonder, no matter what was happening. Talon had lost his long ago, but here it was anew, reminding her of other times.

Rebbe draped her with a purple garland, and the servitor with one of blue and black flowers. His own was bright pink and yellow and orange, an arrangement that should have been jarring, but somehow made the sunshine in his face even brighter.

"Where are we going next?" he asked. They had been to both of the gardens he'd selected to view.

"I," Niko said, "would like a drink, and there is a place here I keep hearing mentioned, and which I have been steering us toward."

"Its name?" the servitor requested.

"It's called Beside the Glorious Moon."

It had been expensive securing a meeting with Biboban, but Gnarl knew it would be worth it. Rumors said the creature liked a very particular kind of indulgence, and Gnarl had plenty of that indulgence with him, hidden in a secret compartment along with a number of other highly contraband things.

Disappointing that the other would not speak of Niko Larsen, refused to be drawn into any conversation. He'd hoped to sow a few poisonous seeds there but had failed.

He patted the bag at his hip, which held credits now in place of the drugs he'd brought. It had been a profitable transaction, either way.

Beside the Glorious Moon was located near a main corridor, and Jezli had been told it was the best place for Green Snake Snorters.

The small and crowded drinkery smelled of much-used oxygen, and she sidled along the wall until she found a seat occupied by only a coat, then freed it up by pushing the coat off the seat and kicking it under the table. She signaled a servebot and ordered a Snorter along with the drink of the cycle, which surged like a living turquoise thing in an intriguing, although unsettling, way.

The coat's owner returned and started to say something about the chair Jezli occupied, but she gave them a look that somehow managed to combine bland inquisitiveness with an edge of menace. They retrieved their coat and moved away through the crowd, muttering to themselves.

Lounging in her seat, she waited, alternating tiny sips of the drinks, each time a little startled by the way the blue leaped to meet her tongue while the Snorter seemed to chase it away to substitute its own red-clay, river-water flavor.

She watched the entrance, and when Niko, Rebbe, and the servitor entered, Jezli smiled to herself. She'd mentioned the name of the place around the captain unobtrusively a few times. Now that gambit had played out, even if it had brought her not just the captain, but the strange, troubled clone and whatever the hell it was that the *Thing* had created to accompany the captain.

Niko caught sight of her almost instantly and made her way through the room.

"What are you doing here?" she demanded. "I told people not to go off by themselves."

"You told your crew that," Jezli said, putting her drink down. "But as you have also made it clear, I am not crew."

"My orders were addressed to everyone on the ship, crew or not," Niko said grimly.

"Ah. I must have misunderstood." Jezli picked the drink up and took another leisurely sip to indicate she had no current intention of returning to the ship.

"Then you will accompany us back," Niko said.

"That would be a great pleasure," Jezli said amiably. "Perhaps

I might buy all of us drinks first?" She looked at the servitor as if pondering what to offer it.

Damn the woman, Niko thought. Arguing with her was like trying to hold on to sand. The harder you squeezed, the faster it spilled away and defeated your purpose. "Why here?" she said.

Jezli studied her in silence for a long moment. "Because," she said finally, "I wanted to find out what I could overhear when people weren't overly aware of your ears in the room." She turned her attention back to the servitor. "And I was curious about the results of the *Thing*'s experiment in multiple selves."

The servitor preened. Niko ignored it. "Did you find out anything?"

"Nothing. But now we will all have the pleasure of a drink together and then return."

It wasn't to Rebbe's taste, this crowded and noisy place. But it was still new, and interesting, and there were so many people to look at. He wished he could talk to them, but he was uncertain how exactly one went about initiating that sort of thing.

Niko wasn't talking. She just glowered into her glass when not sending that glower at Jezli. The servitor manifested eyes in order to look in multiple directions but seemed otherwise content.

Rebbe sipped at his drink, which was tart and tasted like cherries. "Does this have alcohol?" he asked.

"None," Jezli said. "It is a connoisseur's drink, and alcohol would not allow you to taste the nuances, which I thought your heightened senses would appreciate."

He didn't like not even being given the chance to order something. But on the other hand, it was very nice of Jezli to think about what he would like, and the drink was, after all, delicious. He continued watching the crowd. When he set the dregs of his drink down, the servitor discreetly unrolled a long tube to sample it.

"When do you see Biboban?" Jezli asked.

"Tomorrow," Niko answered. "Early in the cycle."

"Are you looking forward to it?"

"It's always good to see old friends," Niko said cagily. "Find out how they've fared since you last encountered them, how they've changed."

"Not always for the better."

"What do you mean?"

"I've been listening to station talk while sitting here. Did you really think I just came for the drink? Though it is quite good." She took another sip. "Piquant," she murmured. "With a touch of, mm, perhaps rosewater? Perhaps you would venture a guess, Captain." She pushed the glass toward Niko.

"Perhaps not," Niko said. "Drink up. We're leaving in three minims."

"Where do we proceed next?" Jezli asked.

"Back to the ship."

"Ah. Disappointing, I am sure. Have you seen all the confluences you wished, Rebbe?"

He shook his head.

Niko held out her hand. "Give me the list." She studied it and pointed at the topmost item. "Ganache. That's where we're going." She handed it back to Rebbe and stood. Without looking to see if they followed, she exited with the servitor on her heels.

Jezli and Rebbe rose. "Which one is Ganache?" she asked.

He bounced on his heel. "Chocolate. Nothing but chocolate."

"Now that does sound promising."

They followed Niko out.

The servitor had been given a full complement of senses, including processing pouches lined with taste buds, scanners extending from infrared to ultraviolet, means to analyze air, and gravity, and any substance anyone cared to put near it. It had sampled a great many already, as unobtrusively as possible, and had reached the point where every once in a while it scuttled to a discreet corner to eject a neat ten-centimeter-wide square of waste.

"That's biomass," Niko said. "Save some of it, and we'll get station credit." The servitor obediently began gathering its droppings as directed from that point.

It seemed that the station ran on biomass, a.k.a. primarily shit, more than one might have expected. Their mass had been calculated when they'd arrived, and they'd been informed of the amount of biomass per day they were supposed to supply, a figure that had Dabry frowning but helpless to object. There were even categories of biomass: some had "thaumic residue," which made them particularly valuable, and others, traces of rare elements.

Ganache was the promised chocolate garden, full of cocoa beans and adjacent species, such as palm-sized vanilla orchids and others, pale red, that smelled like cayenne and cinnamon. The food court here was vast, each establishment serving a different variation on chocolate: hot chocolate, spicy and thick as syrup in the mouth; morsels of white and dark chocolate spun together into zebra-petaled flowers; smooth globes of chocolate ice and rougher ones covered on the outside with chocolate shavings.

They ate until they all felt glutted to the point of mild nausea.

"Is this enough?" Niko asked Rebbe. "I cannot imagine going elsewhere to eat, but both of the other confluences you've marked are notable for their food more than anything else."

He had bought sample after sample with his trade money, and she suspected it would all get eaten rather than sold, but she could not begrudge him the happiness in his eyes. He patted the heap of packages beside him, and said, "I am ready to return."

12

Petalia observed their return with a narrowed gaze. Niko had gone off with one of the boys and then returned with not just the boy, but Jezli Farren. Jezli Farren, who Petalia thought might be after Niko, though in a friendly way. A very friendly way.

That was not to Petalia's tastes. Niko had abandoned them to Tubal Last and therefore Niko deserved no happiness in love whatsoever. It failed to cross their mind that up to this point, Niko could never have been declared to be lucky in love.

It wasn't that Petalia wanted Niko for their own—far from it! they told themself. No, it was the proprietary way that Jezli sometimes regarded Niko, a look that implied the captain was somehow undeniably *hers*. That long-nosed, sharp-eyed gaze was intolerable.

What would Petalia use as a starting point to get rid of Jezli Farren? A logical one. Jezli had provided the mechanism to dispose of Tubal Last, but that mechanism had failed.

They said as much to Niko when they managed to catch her alone, sorting through supply invoices. "Why is Jezli Farren still on board?"

"Because I have not put her off yet," Niko said shortly. Jezli's solo trip still irritated her. It was as if the damn woman was daring Niko to rein her in.

"And why is that?" Petalia demanded, making Niko look up from the invoices.

"Why does it matter to you? She is a passenger. As are you."

"She is a willing passenger. I am not. Circumstance forced me here."

Niko raised an eyebrow. "Have I kidnapped you, then? I was

under the impression you thought you were safer from Tubal Last here than anywhere else."

"Nowhere is safe," Petalia said darkly. "But that is not what I was talking about. You could put her off here, at Coralind. Plenty of traffic in and out, and she could work her way on a ship if she needed to. Here, she's just a waste of water and air."

Niko folded her hands on top of the invoices, and it occurred to Petalia they had gone about this the wrong way. They should have thought it through, figured out some careful scheme to demonstrate how unsuitable Jezli was as a shipboard companion. Now Niko was wary and on the defensive.

"I mean that—" Petalia started, but Niko cut them off.

"We do not think, on this ship, of wastes of air or water. This ship was a gift from someone who did not think that way, and we will treat it as such, and not as some sort of computational machine from which we must extract a particular value."

Petalia contemplated bursting into tears. That had worked on Niko in the past, plenty of times. But something in the flinty gaze told them that this might be one of the times it did not.

"I don't trust her," they attempted.

"That is totally understandable, given her history." Niko returned her attention to her papers. "You may close the door on the way out."

For a moment, Petalia simply gawped. Niko had never dismissed them like that. Never. But they could not bring themself to challenge this new Niko. They left, but brooded all the way back to their room. Jezli Farren, they decided, was the reason for this change. Jezli Farren had to go.

And when Petalia set their mind to something, it would happen.

At first, *You Sexy Thing* was very eager to find out what it would be like, absorbing the memories of its servitor.

It had never created something with the express purpose of recording sensations before, and it prided itself on the thought it never would have conceived of such a thing in the old days. It tried to imagine what Arpat Takraven's reaction would have been to his possession asking to go somewhere with him and knew, deep somewhere inside itself, that the reaction might not have been favorable. *Would* not have been favorable. Arpat Takraven was a man who discarded toys that no longer amused him.

So it stopped that line of thought, because it was easier than experiencing that particular range of emotions, though it did save them in case it ever wanted, for some reason, to go back again.

It created a hatch in the wall and had the servitor walk in, then sealed it entirely and began the complicated task of reabsorbing its material while retaining its sensations. It was difficult and off-putting at first, but then grew a little easier, and the ship was able to feel the sensations of the servitor as it had experienced the day.

However, it wasn't as simple as all that. The *Thing* was a little outraged to discover that despite all its careful programming, the servitor had had emotions of its own, totally without the *Thing*'s directing. Worse, several of them seemed to have been about how the servitor could manage to continue its own existence without being absorbed!

Using a remote eye, the *Thing* considered Minasit, currently cleaning Atlanta's quarters. The ship suspected that, like the errant servitor, Minasit experienced emotions that were, outrageously, not sympathetic to nor adulating of the *Thing* itself, which had, after all, created it.

Could it get at Minasit somehow and absorb it without Atlanta realizing what it had done? It could create a replica, perhaps, although that would also mean replicating the mark she had put on it, which might be more difficult. Although not impossible, certainly.

Reclaiming Minasit might require thought and planning. Or waiting for Atlanta to make some error that would justify the *Thing* taking Minasit back, although it couldn't quite figure out that configuration.

But there was always time. It could not practice *hourisigah* anymore, but it had learned one of its principles, that deferred gratification was extra gratification.

13

While the ship contemplated its servitor, Talon was in the war-ball room the ship kept trying to steer him into. He wanted a place where he could pretend he was alone, if he could just get the ship to shut up, at least.

A place where he could howl and scream and yell and batter at the walls, which he did, great gouging scrapes of his claws that the ship permitted because it didn't know what to do otherwise. It remembered what happened the last time it tried to restrain him.

All it could do was alert the others. It didn't mention the attack on its walls, uncharacteristically, because it thought maybe Talon had been punished enough, and after all, there were no pain receptors in that wall.

It did, however, take the liberty of allowing the wall to start oozing a sappy red liquid that immediately horrified Talon to the point where he stopped and stepped back.

"Is that blood?" he demanded, suddenly remembering that he wasn't in an inanimate object. "Oh, Sky Momma, I'm sorry, I'm sorry I hurt you," he gasped. He collapsed into a bundle, hugging his knees to himself, and howled his anger and anguish into his own flesh, muffling the painful sound.

The ship was uncertain what to say and paused for a while to revel in the emotion of uncertainty. Then it ventured, "I can bring you something."

"What?" Talon's muffled voice demanded.

"Anything," the ship promised rashly and then added, "that I can manage." Because it had a sad and unhappy feeling that the thing Talon wanted most was Thorn, and he'd already proven that was impossible.

Talon remained silent in the face of the offer, a mass of curled and tear-sodden fur that didn't want to be here, wanted to be anyplace else as long as it held his real brother and not this unkind impostor he could not help loving, no matter how desperately much he wanted to hate him.

The ship expected others to come, to comfort the boy, but Niko declined, saying "He needs to think things out, I believe," and the others followed her lead. With the exception of Jezli Farren, who appeared in the doorway after a time, looking at Talon.

He smelled her presence, he knew who was there, but he refused to acknowledge her. Finally, she went over and sat down beside him.

"I had someone once that I loved more than I loved anyone else," she said softly to the air. "It's not my nature to love, but Roxana was so good, down to the very core of her being that at first I admired her, and after time together, I came to love her. That was the first time I'd ever been fond of another creature."

He didn't stir, but she could feel him listening.

"I'll tell you how we met," she said dreamily, and told her story in the tradition of the Zandor. "Here is a story I offer to you, and it begins like this."

She went on to talk about a marketplace, and a stall, and someone in trouble that Jezli had meant to bilk when she had thought they were anything but in trouble. The soft cadences went on, and Talon listened, and the ship listened, storing it all away.

Gradually, Talon shifted until he leaned against her, and then slouched to curl fully on her. His head turned to rest on her thigh, eyes closed as her fingers ran through his hair, slowly, a motion like stroking a pet cat, while her story went on.

As she finished, her voice soft and low in the room's dim light, a shadow fell across the doorway. She looked up to see Niko there.

Jezli's face was somber, the restless energy of it muted for once, as they looked at each other. The only motion was the slow, even breathing of the sleeping youth in her lap and the equally slow movement of her hand, smoothing his hair. The ship wondered what Niko would say, but she only inclined her head toward Jezli and then stepped back into the hallway and moved on.

Jezli made a small noise.

"What did that mean?" the ship asked.

Jezli jumped, startled, and Talon mumbled in protest for a moment before she settled back. "What did what mean?"

"The noise that you made," the ship said. "According to my files, it could be surprise, or delight, or fear, or seventeen other choices."

Jezli huffed in amusement. "That," she said, leaning back against the wall, "I am not even sure I could tell you myself." She shook Talon's shoulder gently. "Come, Talon, I will take you to your room, and you will sleep there."

He allowed himself to be guided along. In the room, she led him to the bed, and tucked the bedding over him, and left.

"Have you determined what the noise was?" the ship asked as she made her way back to her chamber.

"You startle me so," she murmured. "I forget you are all around us. What is it like, to contain the creatures you are talking with?"

"I'm not sure what you mean," the ship said. "Are you asking about an emotion? A feeling? A sensation?"

"Are all of those different things for you?" she said in delight. "Do you have an emotion attached to it?"

"That is a very complicated question that I do not understand," the ship said. What a night of firsts, it thought. Confusion! And it was fascinated to see that confusion with Jezli had a different flavor than when it was the universe at large confounding it in one way or another.

"Then you are welcome," Jezli said. "I would prefer you not talk to me while I am in my chamber, so I may pretend that I am alone."

"But you know that you are not," the ship pointed out. "Pretending is something you do to fool other people."

"Not always other people. Sometimes the person you want to fool is yourself," she said. She went into her chamber before the ship could ask anything else at all.

Niko had expected security. After all, Biboban was literally the most important entity in this place, the thing that kept everything moving. The machinery was there but it would not function unless directed by the mind of a creature like Biboban—once a humanoid that had walked and talked and fucked and fought like any of the rest of them. Then, when he had died, his mind had not been judged worthy of being absorbed into the Holy Hive Mind, but instead had been used as the seed to create the creature that she was going to see.

But this degree of security seemed excessive—guard drones and sentinels of the kind she'd never seen aboard a peaceful station. Was war brewing somewhere in the vicinity, that Biboban felt driven to protect itself?

Or, she wondered uneasily, was it the sign of some breakdown, some creeping paranoia of the kind that sometimes seized things that were very old or otherwise very far removed from their origin, as Biboban had been?

Security chokepoints filled the halls. They seemed to press closer and closer, to the point where she found herself hunching her shoulders in an attempt to evade the sensation of being squished smaller by her surroundings. As she passed one and went through an airlock where blue rays scanned her for harmful microorganisms and constructs, the smell hit her. The heavy scent of decaying iron and flesh left sitting too long, a smell she had forgotten but which struck her with a wave of memory that made her stop in her tracks.

That smell had been omnipresent in interacting with Biboban then, when it directed the unit of war machines that served her soldiers. It was the smell of guilt, the smell of relief that her comrade, rather than she, had been chosen for this fate. It was the odorous tinge of righteousness, of knowing that the Holy Hive Mind had judged them both and found her the worthier of the two, like having a distant parent finally recognize you for some small thing.

The smell of holding herself taut, wanting to make sure Biboban never knew the cauldron of feelings every interaction stirred in her. Had she been successful in that effort? She had never been sure, but the other had never shown any sign of sensing the complex concoction of emotions its presence created in her.

"Captain Larsen?" one of the guards accompanying her said. She realized she had been motionless for long enough that they were unsure of her.

She covered with an apology. "Sorry, have a lot on my mind." She hastened her steps forward, straightening the hang of the long Trader's jacket she wore over dress pants, the *Thing*'s insignia embroidered on the breast, though a more subdued one than the variegated and gilt emblem it had first produced for her. Much more comfortable than last night's outfit.

They came to a set of double doors. The two guards drew themselves up on either side and motioned her forward, swinging the doors open. She entered. Nerves jittered inside her, inside the coiled chaos of her thoughts.

The smell was stronger here. Unsurprising, since this was a version of Biboban much larger than the one she had previously known. Great white tubes stretched everywhere amid vats of liquid large enough to house the entirety of Niko's crew (with the exception of the ship, which was somehow both crew and vessel).

Underfoot, circular white tiles of the same material as the tubes, gleaming pristine and clean, and waves of tiny bots moved everywhere, cleaning even as she looked. In the center of the chamber was a construct of flesh, with metal and other artificial bits here and there, that towered over her.

"Come closer, Niko Larsen." The voice boomed around her. Speakers set in the walls. She could not read the flatness of the tone, had never been able to. That was one of the least unnerving things about Biboban, both the entity she had once known and this thing it had become—an enormous mass sitting in a low dish that contained any outward spillage.

The smell was ten times stronger here. It filled her nostrils and crept into her mouth until it overpowered her senses, made her mouth taste like she'd been chewing rotten flesh.

She took slow paces forward until she was close enough to have stretched out an arm and touched fingertips to the glass before her. Her skin crawled at the thought and her hands twitched, but she did it nonetheless, pressed her palm flat against it in greeting.

"It's been a long time, Niko Larsen. Very long. Eight solar years, six months, seven days, five hours, three minutes, and nine seconds, if I calculate it correctly."

Niko could not help herself. "Is that calculated from the moment we opened comms, docked, requested this appointment, or right now?"

A gurgle of the sort that had always served Biboban for amusement. "You are quick as ever, Niko Larsen. From the moment you opened comms, and I realized you had returned. In a ship that is very distinctive, and very expensive, and a cloud of rumors and tall tales about you. That you closed and opened a Gate, for one."

Niko blinked. "I had nothing to do with that. I was caught in the vicinity when the Gate closed and got swept up in other people's affairs. While we were trying to turn an honest living feeding people."

"Another part of it that was new to me. Are you and Dabry Jen truly turned cooks?"

"We are," she said. "Good ones, even."

"And you think to turn yourself a profit at the Festival here."

"Nothing of the sort," she said. "Although it would certainly be most welcome. We are here looking for news."

"What sort of news, Niko Larsen?"

She wished again that it had inflections, rather than the autogenerated voice that so flatly served it, but she knew the lack of betraying emotion was why Biboban would have opted not to have its vocal apparatus augmented. The very flatness was its own message, with an edge of contempt for those who betrayed themselves with the words they uttered. Biboban could read the truth of what she said in her body, in her heart and respiration rates, but would it trust that data? Such things could be altered in a multitude of ways, after all.

"As you may have heard, we have had a great deal happen in recent days," she said. "Our restaurant on TwiceFar was doing well enough, and then the station was attacked. It was always prone to the rapid takeovers and changes in government, but normally they don't come in and blow half the place to pieces. Since then, we've been trying to recoup."

"In a ship whose cost would pay for the station repairs and then some other."

"The ship is on loan to us," she clarified. "In repayment for a favor. You might enjoy talking with it."

"I have been," Biboban said.

She blinked, and knew that the entity before her could read in that the shock that its words had caused. She paused, even though she knew that, too, would be read and analyzed.

"It is an interesting person to talk with, I am sure," she said. "Have you discussed its hobby of *hourisigah*?"

"At length, Niko Larsen."

She spread her hands wide, palms upward, her shoulders straight. "Then I will presume you know all of our situation, and that we are trying to find out where we must go next."

"You will have brought the vengeance of Tubal Last to my station, should I assist you."

"Tubal Last is dead."

"Semi-dead, perhaps," Biboban said. "One of him, at any rate. But he made preparations, I would be sure."

"Have you seen any sign of such preparations?"

This time Biboban paused. Thinking? Speaking again with *You Sexy Thing*? She had already made a mental note to have a lengthy conversation with the ship when she got back about what was acceptable to tell outsiders, and what should be kept to the crew alone.

"It is Festival," Biboban said. "There are many here from across the Known Universe, because the Festival has become a great thing under my guidance, Niko Larsen."

She nodded, trying not to twitch her impatience.

"There is chaos, whenever there are new people. It is easier for people to hide who they really are—and this station has never been one to press on that subject. We are a haven of sorts."

She seized the opportunity. "That is why we hoped you might help us."

"I will not help you, Niko Larsen."

"Why?"

She wished she had not asked the question because the answer came immediately, with a speed that made it seem rehearsed, over and over, from the time Biboban had last seen her. "Because you turned away and did not take me with you."

"I couldn't," she said, startled by the accusation. "They wanted too much."

"You could have bargained. Or even taken me by stealth or force."

That shocked her. How deeply had Biboban thought their friendship had run, that it had been so wounded by what it saw as a betrayal, rather than a lapse or lack? She had always treated it with kindness and respect. That was basic courtesy and common sense, too, when you worked with machines upon whom your life and the lives in your command depended.

She had always treated it like an equal, partially because the others around her did not, and it pleased her to be a little contrary in a way that might remind them to be better persons.

They had talked, plenty of times. Biboban was always awake, and when you were up late at night, poring over maps and data and strategies, it had been easy enough to consult it. She had not known it before it had been severed from its first body; she didn't even know what species the brain had come from.

She hadn't paid a lot of attention to the odd rumors about Biboban, but she wondered about them now. Wondered if it still had the tastes it was rumored to have. Could that account for its change in attitude toward her?

She took a deep breath of the choking air.

"I did what I could, and I have always regretted that I could not take you with me."

"So much regret that you do not seek me out until you are forced to."

"You are right," she said, trying to put sincerity in her voice. "So much regret that, once I heard you were here, and working, and out from under the Hive Mind's grasp, that I could not bring myself to come remind you of that past existence. I am sorry that my presence brings it back. They were unhappy days for both of us."

Brief silence. Then, "You may go, Niko Larsen."

There was a lot she had wanted to ask, including trying to wheedle a license to serve food, but it was evident there would be no wheedling.

"There is nothing more to be said between us?" she pleaded. But the reply came, toneless and devoid of emotion, implacable. "You may go."

You Sexy Thing was very interested in the conversations it had been having with Biboban, who among other things could think as quickly as the *Thing*, so there was no need to sit and wait and wait thousands of milliseconds for an answer. Their conversations ranged across topics, including a lengthy disquisition on the art of *hourisigah*, but Biboban had been most interested in how *You Sexy Thing* had come to be Niko's ship.

Which technically it was not, but the *Thing* didn't feel Biboban really needed to know all that. There wasn't much glory in being a ship that Arpat Takraven had loaned out, like a toy. No, it decided, the world should think that it actually belonged to Niko and it hedged, just a little, to create that impression.

Biboban was thus presented with more than one account of things, and it chose to believe what it would.

14

llllll.llllll.ll.llllll.ll.llllll.ll.llllll.llllll.ll.llllll.ll.llllll.ll

If they had thought the station busy before, now it was jam-packed. With the beginning of the Festival, all the floodgates had opened and travelers from across the Known Universe descended on the station to enjoy themselves. Everything was jostle-and-step, every destination took ten times as long since you had to fight your way through the crowds.

"Good news for once, sir," Dabry told Niko, waving a script in his hand. "We've been approved for a temporary restaurant."

She put down the handbliss markers she had been playing with despite the protests of Jezli and Skidoo, both of whom considered themselves to be winning. "Really?"

"By Biboban itself," Dabry said. "Had you asked about one when you spoke?"

"No, nothing like that," she said, searching her mind for the details of the conversation. "I didn't ask because I wanted to see where the waters stood before I asked for substantial favors—if at all." She didn't add that Biboban had seemed downright hostile, but she couldn't figure out what this gesture meant.

"Then it must have anticipated the need," Dabry rationalized.

The ship made a small noise.

Niko appreciated that the *Thing* was being more tactful of late about interrupting. "What, *Thing*?"

"I told Biboban that we wanted to open one."

"When you were talking with it before, or recently?"

"Just today."

"Do you remember our conversation about not telling our business to outsiders?"

"Well, you said you were its friend, is that not true?"

"Yes," she said, definitely not wanting the ship to convey a "no" back to its new friend. "But there are friends, and there are crew. Crew knows crew-business."

"How do I know when it is friend-business and when it is crew-business?"

"Assume everything is crew-business unless one of us has confirmed that you can talk about it to Biboban."

"Very well," the ship capitulated. "I will prepare a list of topics. Is discussing the previous restaurant . . ." It paused significantly. ". . . On the menu?"

"Oh, Sky Momma." Niko sighed. "Right here, right now, I am forbidding you from exploring puns."

The ship had hoped for a significantly better reaction than that. It had hoped, actually, to be commended on its adept command of "humor." It would have rolled its eyes, but that seemed to be off the menu too.

"I will give you the list in written form," it said sullenly.

"Which will be a document of no more than two pages at this time. Once that's been gone through, you can generate another two-page list."

The ship could have groaned at the length of time that this would take, but there were so many expressions that were denied it. Was Niko deliberately being cruel? It could not have conceived of this previously, but now that it occurred to it, it needed to analyze the question further.

"Very well," Niko said. "Send the questions to the sergeant when you're ready."

Dabry gave her a look. She shrugged. "I have to start working on figuring out how we're going to get space."

"There is an empty hangar one bay over," the ship informed her.

"Well, that's an interesting idea," she considered. "Could set up tentlike structures for people that like private dining, big open area where they could watch people going by. Did that pass say anything about possible locations, Dabry?"

"Says 'anywhere on the station.'"

For a second, she couldn't believe she had heard Dabry correctly. "Anywhere?"

That was a munificent gesture. A gesture of trust, she thought. One that Biboban didn't think she'd abuse. She must have entirely mistaken its attitude, or else it had reconsidered matters. Perhaps its conversations with the *Thing* had enlightened it to their good intentions. "All right," she said. "I'll starting pricing supplies."

"I need to shop," Dabry said. The idea of all the gardens raced through his head. What couldn't he conjure here, with almost every ingredient in the Known Universe at hand?

"Take someone with you. Gio, probably."

Dabry nodded absently.

"You hear me?" she said sharply. "Not alone."

Nonetheless, when he left a half hour later, he was by himself, the ship noted.

At loose ends in the ship, the fact that she'd been gulled like an ordinary tourist ate at Atlanta. Had she put off some aura of helplessness? Surely that was impossible. The seeds remained in her room, sitting on a small table, reminding her every day of her foolishness.

Well, Atlanta figured, she had the seeds. She might as well plant them.

The garden chambers, currently empty of people, always felt crowded with plants. One felt unable to move through it without having to avoid outreaching vines and tendrils. She took a deep, appreciative breath. It smelled fresh and green in here.

Dabry had been clearing racks in preparation for taking on

supplies, but there were basic grow-packs aplenty. She carefully slit each one in order to insert a couple of the seeds and found an unused corner rack to put them in. No one was using it; no one would be irritated that she'd crowded out other, sanctioned plants. It was a simple task, and she knew how to do it well by now.

Study to become a gardener? Who needed that sort of thing? Plants were simple—you put the seed in the right growing medium, and then let water and warmth start them off, then just make sure the grow light was turned to right frequency. Simple stuff.

So she planted them, muttering her paladin charm under her breath in case it would help, then crossed her fingers and hoped. She set a timer so she would remember to mist them at intervals. The ship could do it, but she felt as though she needed to assert her ownership of the seeds by tending them herself. It couldn't hurt, after all.

Niko went to check out the bay the *Thing* had mentioned. She was pleased to find water hookups, and she'd already known it would have plenty of energy to handle their equipment. It would have taken a hefty amount of portable matter printers and cookstoves to drain the equivalent of a starship's requirements.

Turning from her inspection, she found herself face-to-face with Tubalina. The woman looked haggard, bags under her eyes testifying she had not slept in cycles. She wore a hooded cloak over wrinkled clothing.

"I can feel his agents closing in," she said without preamble. "I worry that he realizes I intend to . . . work with you."

"Use us, you mean," Niko said softly. The woman shook her head, then shrugged.

"Use each other, perhaps," she said.

"Tubal Last never engaged in mutualities."

The woman bared her teeth in a ferocious grin. "Think of me as a Tubal Last capable of learning," she countered. "Chastened by the realization that I am not, in fact, bigger than the Known Universe. Humbled by the idea that I could be defeated."

"I cannot allow you aboard my ship."

"Why?" Tubalina's eyes searched Niko's face.

"I would rather not say."

She saw the calculations passing behind the other woman's eyes, but she was unprepared for her next question.

"Is it Petalia? Do they not want me aboard?"

"I would rather not say," Niko repeated with cold firmness.

"That must be it. Tell them I'm desperate. Tell them I'll do anything. Will you pass that along?"

"I will not."

The woman looked at the *Thing* and its open hatchway, clearly calculating.

"If I do not stop you, the ship will," Niko said pleasantly, raising her voice to make sure the *Thing* heard her. "And I warn you, neither of us will be gentle in keeping you off the ship."

"You don't understand." The woman's eyes were wild with fear.

"You are so unlike him right now that I find it hard to believe there is any part of him in you," Niko continued. "He was never a man to be afraid."

"Yes, I am a lesser version," Tubalina said quietly. "But as determined to live as he ever was."

"You aren't my responsibility."

"Very well, Niko Larsen." Tubalina turned away, drawing her cloak's hood up to obscure her face.

Niko's shoulders did not unstiffen until the other was entirely gone. How far would Tubalina go in her attempts to get aboard the ship? "*Thing*, I'm telling you now, and clearly, that woman is never to be allowed on board."

"What if one of us brings her on board?"

"The crew would never do such a thing. Maybe if she were a prisoner or restrained in some fashion." She thought about it. "Just don't let her sneak on board," she finally decided. "Or casually stroll in by herself, or run in or jump in, or any other manner of walking."

The ship stowed this slightly confusing directive away. It wished it could talk things over with Biboban. It had already prepared the next ninety-nine two-page lists of questions after delivering the first, in the smallest possible of fonts and barely perceptible margins, to Dabry. That, it thought, was quite reasonable and rather ingenious.

The other thing that gnawed at Atlanta was what the Banksin had said. *Whether or not you are real.* It woke her up in the middle of her sleep and would not let her return to her dreams. It wriggled around in her stomach when she ate so that she pushed the plate away. It tapped her on the shoulder when she was otherwise occupied and made her break off and return to worrying.

Because she didn't think a paladin would have fled the ancient and their questions. A paladin would have stood their ground.

Roxana would have stood her ground.

That was what she needed to be doing, in all occasions, she thought. Ask herself what Roxana would have done or advised. Let that be her inner voice—better by far than her counselors ever had been.

She paused. What if she created a replica of Roxana in her head, the way the counselors had served? It would not be Roxana, true, but it would be the same as asking herself what the other paladin would have done. Just a shortcut. If she programmed it right, it—she—would advise her and help her grow. Give her some of the training that Roxana would have led her through.

She wavered, walking very carefully around the edges of "What would Roxana have thought of this particular question?" before she laid it aside for now.

She could work harder at becoming a paladin, could train in fighting every day. Talon would help if she asked, perhaps. It would distract him from mooning around over Rebbe.

But when she asked, Rebbe was there. "I'd like to come too," he said. "I need to learn to defend myself. Is that all right?"

"Of course!" Talon said eagerly before Atlanta could open her mouth. Something inside her stirred uneasily, a thrill like a bell had rung somewhere in the distance, so far away it could not be heard, only felt. Then the feeling passed, and she shook her head. Perhaps she had imagined it.

She tried to reconstruct the sensation as she trailed the twins—no, not the twins, she reminded herself—to the warball chamber.

15

Now that the prohibition on business was over, Niko could finally go and speak with her bank. Time to get that underway—sometimes things took time, for one reason or another, so the sooner, the better. Supplying the pop-up would drain their reserves, possibly soon. Would that profit get turned before the bank finally coughed up the insurance money? She hoped not, but some institutions had turned the tactic of holding onto a customer's money into an art form.

Once again, she kicked herself for not listening to Dabry. It wasn't chagrin that he'd been right when she'd been wrong, or even irritation that he would refrain from saying "I told you so" in the most pointed of manners. No, beyond that, there was guilt. She'd made a tactical error, and a leader couldn't afford to do that often.

The bank office itself was hard to find, but eventually, near the confluence Abundance, she located its entrance.

Stepping in, she found herself in a luxuriously appointed but utterly empty reception area. She looked around for a way to signal that she was there and required attention, but found nothing.

"Mmm," she grumbled under her breath and sat on a couch, whose velvety depths swallowed her almost instantly. It was very comfortable.

Tempted to take a nap, she refrained. Instead, she pulled up station paperwork on her datapad and began filling it out. Might as well get some work done. Completing that, she began studying the trade news, what flowed in and out of Coralind. It seemed Biboban ran things well—more coming in than going out—and some of the trade goods it exported were quite interesting. She began to take careful notes.

After an hour of productivity on Niko's part, a hitherto invisible door opened in the wall and a head poked out. A small, officious Plubas, dressed in a pale blue and fuchsia uniform that made them resemble nothing so much as an ornamental teddy bear, looked surprised to see Niko.

"Do you have an appointment?" they asked.

"I was unable to find out how to make one," Niko said.

Button eyes blinked. "It's on our information page."

"It is not."

Nettled, the person emerged from the doorway and sat at the receptionist's desk. "Here, I'll show you."

Rapid clicking from the keyboard followed, then a brief silence, then another spate of clicking. After this had been repeated five times, the person said, "Hmmm. It doesn't seem to be there."

They turned their attention to Niko. "I'll issue an order to have the information page updated. Check back tomorrow and it should be there."

"Could we not make an appointment right now?" Niko pressed.

"Everything has to be done through the information page." They shrugged. "Have to do things by the book."

"Do we, though?" Niko said. She dropped a credit chip onto the desk. The receptionist looked at it with the same icy dignity that would have greeted a dirty tissue produced in offering.

"If that is an attempt at a bribe," they said stiffly, "be aware this interaction is being recorded."

Niko sighed and took the credit chip back, tucking it away.

"Perceive this, gentlebeing," she said in her politest and most formal tones. "I am cooperating with your protocols. Tomorrow I will book an appointment at the earliest opportunity."

The being seemed to relax. "Good!" they said. "Was there anything else I could do for you?"

Niko stared at them.

"I guess not," they said, unperturbed.

The air on board Gnarl's ship, the *Knot*, was kept exactly as he liked it, although most of the crew found it either too choking or had to take supplements to help repair the damage to their lungs. It had been that way since day one, and it would always be. Everything on this ship was designed to his hand, his dimensions, every inch of it.

His seat wasn't comfortable enough, even though it was shaped to his dimensions as well, and he knew why. Anger felt like fleas biting him up and down, every inch of him, and he wouldn't be comfortable until Niko Larsen had her comeuppance.

He had goods to sell. If the drugs were a little chancy, if they did what they sometimes (often) did, then Biboban might be tempted to go a little too far. If it perished, well, then, there were ways to point the finger at Niko and her crew. Too bad he hadn't been able to catch the were-lion boy outside the ship yet; he'd love to know how that experiment turned out. By now they would have disposed of the clone, so he wouldn't have that hold over them anymore, what a shame.

A guard appeared at his elbow.

"What?" he snapped. They should know better than to interrupt him when he was thinking.

"You haven't ordered guards for your trip outside, sir." The guard stared at the floor, not meeting Gnarl's eyes. Gnarl didn't trust him, though. Hadn't been the same since that time at the Captain's Gathering. Something subtle in the way he stood. Maybe the reason he wasn't meeting Gnarl's eyes wasn't deference. Maybe he didn't want Gnarl to see what lurked in his expression. No matter. He'd send him to be reconditioned when he had the chance.

"You and Basli," he ordered. Basli was his most loyal. His

most discreet. Since their mate had perished on the space moth, the one who must feel the deepest hatred toward Niko.

Without waiting for an answer, he swiveled back to contemplating his plan to bring Niko down.

In the warball chamber, Atlanta, Rebbe, and Talon prepared to spar. The ship took the liberty of adding suitable music. No one objected.

Accompanied by languorous flute harmonies, the three of them started with warm-ups, stretches, then feints and kicks at each other, easily avoided by ducks and sidesteps, more dance than battle.

Atlanta focused her attention less on the others and more on her own motions. She was getting better, she thought as she swung at Talon and he hopped back. The music shifted, added several string instruments and a percussion section, and moved into a faster beat.

"Enough." Rebbe jumped up. "My turn."

His eyes gleamed as he stepped in front of Talon.

At first it was gentle enough, and she watched without worrying. Then a blow from Rebbe left a long red swath across Talon's ribs, and she realized his claws had come out, just as the music shifted again, added a driving, buzzing overbeat.

Talon seemed to notice nothing. His own claws remained sheathed.

Then another cut, and another, Talon still not reacting. Red drops on the floor.

"Stop it," Atlanta shouted, but neither of them seemed to hear her. The air in the chamber felt warm and the smell of sweat was overtaken by blood. Another slice. Blood dribbled down Talon's leg to the mat.

"Stop it!" she shouted again, unheeded. Then, "*Thing*, do something!"

"What should I do?" the ship asked, stopping the music. It was unclear what, exactly, was happening.

"Separate them!"

The ship tried, extruding walls and barriers, but it could only do it so fast. Rebbe was faster, much faster, leaping over the barriers as they appeared. *Thing* feared using stronger means; it remembered too well what happened when it tried to restrain Talon before, how the boy had fought until completely drained of energy, to the point of almost-death.

"I'm going to get the captain!" Atlanta ran from the room.

The two teens circled each other. Then Talon stood still. Deliberately, slowly, he tilted his chin upward, exposing his throat and standing stock-still.

Rebbe lunged.

He halted, millimeters away from Talon's skin. His teeth were showing, his ears laid back.

They stood in silence, staring at each other.

Talon wanted to say so many things: What can I do, what can I say, that will convince you that you should love me? Wanted to say: We are all we have left of family, can we not cling together? Wanted to say: You cannot replace him, I know that, I forgive you for it. All of those were wrong, things that would only make matters worse. So he tilted his chin up another scant measure, and closed his eyes.

He felt the other take a breath, and step back.

Talon opened his eyes.

Niko had not thought to oversee all deliveries to the ship—they were taking on an abundance, after all, she thought irritably at the time—but she regretted this decision the minute she turned in to the comms room. Petalia stood, staring down at the flowers in a clear glass box before them.

"What are those?" she asked, crossing the room in three quick strides.

"They were sent as a present," Petalia said.

"From who?"

"There is no card, but I can guess. These are crystal lilies. He knew they were my favorite."

Niko could see that Petalia trembled. "I will not let this woman calling herself Tubal Last aboard."

"What if you have to?"

"I gave you my word, Pet. I would not break it unless you told me to."

Petalia looked Niko level in the eyes. "What if I want you to?" they said quietly.

"What?"

"Tubal Last spent many years with me. He . . . changed my tastes, to a certain extent. I fear him but I crave him sometimes. He may have placed that kindling inside me, but it burns nonetheless."

Niko's resolution to not let the false Tubal aboard strengthened further, but she kept that to herself. "You are on this ship, and part of the crew, and your protection is my highest priority."

"Is it?" Petalia asked. "Tell me, when push comes to shove, won't you save the greatest number, no matter who may fall?"

"I . . ." Niko found herself at a loss for words.

What Petalia said was absolutely true, and it described the perpetual war inside Niko. You had to make decisions as a leader, and you had to leave your own desires out of the equation, or else you became something very different from a leader. She'd seen that, time and time again, in her time with the Holy Hive Mind. She swallowed. "I cannot predict the future. But I can promise that I will always do my best in it."

"I know." For brief precious seconds, Petalia's cool fingers touched Niko's cheek. Then they snatched back their hand as fast as if the touch had burned them. "You cannot predict the future. But your creature can. Have you asked Lassite about me?"

"No. And I won't," Niko said. "If you want to know your fate, ask him yourself." She felt torn apart by her emotions, and she fought to keep them from her face. She grabbed the flowers. "I will dispose of these," she said, and left without saying more.

Petalia moved to the table where the flowers had been and laid their palm flat against its surface, just where the case had rested. They stood there for several minutes. The ship absolutely burned with curiosity about the conversation that had just taken place, and its implications, while knowing it would have to pretend it hadn't heard any of it. People were so difficult about that. *Thing* couldn't help it, they were talking inside its body! It would have had to make a deliberate effort not to hear them.

It consulted with Biboban. Yes, the other said, commiserating with the *Thing*. They were so slow, the shell people. They didn't understand the pace at which *You Sexy Thing* and Biboban lived, microseconds rather than minutes. They just couldn't keep up.

The *Thing* was forced to cut the communication short, worried that it would say things about the crew that Niko would reprimand it for later. Who knew what she considered worth keeping to itself?

All of this was most unfair. It wished it could sigh. But there was no audience for the gesture. Or at least one for whom the sigh would just underline the fact that the ship had been listening, and intently, as with every other conversation that occurred on board.

Out in the corridor, Niko almost collided with the hurrying

Atlanta. "Captain!" she gasped out. "Come quick! It's Talon and Rebbe."

Niko shoved the flowers in the nearest wall hatch. "Recycle those," she ordered and followed Atlanta.

"What is going on?" a voice demanded. The captain, stepping through the door, followed by Atlanta.

"We were sparring," Rebbe said calmly. "I am sorry, I got carried away." Then, toward Talon, "He didn't fight back."

Niko looked at the pair. Rebbe was unmarked. Talon looked like he'd been through a knife storm, but his ears were perked. As though he'd asked for this, had wanted it.

"I don't want to see either of you looking like you're been taken through the shredder again," Niko said to Talon and Rebbe.

"We were just sparring." Despite the battering Talon had taken, he stood a little taller and prouder, while Rebbe seemed less hunched and turned in on himself. Well, Sky Momma be praised, perhaps the two of them would work it out after all.

If they didn't kill each other in the process.

"You two," Niko said, "need to figure how to get along."

"We didn't kill each other this time," Talon noted. "We won't."

Rebbe dropped a slow nod of confirmation.

"So all is well?" Niko looked between the two of them.

They both nodded.

Niko threw up her hands and walked out. Atlanta trailed her. "Aren't you going to punish Rebbe? He nearly killed Talon!"

"Bloodied, yes, but injured severely, no," Niko said. "Here's a truth for you, Atlanta. Sometimes people need to fight things out before they can become friends."

"It doesn't seem like a very good way of making friends," Atlanta said. "Not the easiest, certainly."

"No," Niko said, shaking her head. "But sometimes one of the truest."

In her chamber, suspended in the gentle liquid, Skidoo thought about the same truth that she mulled over again and again, as regular and inexorable as some internal tide. She uncurled one tentacle and examined a mottling of brown spots along one end.

A slight discoloration, so slight that she hadn't noticed it at first, then had thought it a cooking stain.

When she'd tried to scrub it away, though, she only succeeded in making the flesh around it raw and irritated. The stain was more than skin-deep. The coloring was a deadening of her normal turquoise, a narrow splotch perhaps twenty centimeters in length.

This wasn't one of the symptoms of severing that the medic had mentioned. But what if he hadn't told her everything? This was her body doing a new thing, an unexpected thing—was it a signal? It must be. She curled the tentacle close to her, worrying.

If it was the second stage, she didn't have long. The medic had been very clear.

She would do something she meant to do for a long, long time, ever since leaving Tlella. She would write to the only person she regretted leaving behind, her teacher Wadoo. They had been so encouraging when she was a child; they had taught her so much. They would understand why she had chosen the path she did.

She would explain it all, and they, if anyone, would understand. In doing so, she would say goodbye in her heart to the planet, knowing she would not return there to die.

Her tentacles coiled and uncoiled. This decision filled her with a restless energy. Yes, she would write, and would do it today. It would take a while for the message to get there; longer yet for a reply. The sooner, the better.

16

Atlanta thought, finally, that she would consult Lassite about the words of the Banksin still haunting her.

Hadn't he given her the chant to say that somehow made her a paladin? It had been meant to bring luck, and she had been wanting to find her destiny, and so she had, even if she wasn't entirely sure what that destiny was or what it would entail.

She sought him out, thinking to find him in his chamber, but instead he was in the garden space that Gio had set up for his spores, moving from rack to rack with an old-fashioned instrument in his hands, spraying mist from it over the trays of growing medium.

She nodded to herself, her earlier instincts confirmed. If Lassite felt it important to water his plants himself, then she had been correct. She could not help but glance over at the rack where her own seeds lurked in their grow-packs, but chose not to mention them. She had more important things to discuss with him.

"It's about being a paladin," Atlanta blurted out.

Lassite cocked his head, listening and saying nothing. The ship followed his example.

"I . . . don't know what I'm supposed to do."

"You are supposed to be a paladin." The ship did not think Lassite's answer particularly good, but still refrained from comment.

"But what does that *mean*?"

"You are a champion, chosen by the gods, to fight injustices and wrongs."

"All of it?"

"What you encounter, because that is where the gods will have sent you." Lassite sent another spray wafting gently over the medium.

"How do I know that?"

"A paladin is not a matter of knowing. A paladin is a matter of being."

Atlanta drooped. "I just don't understand."

"So you came to me for some magic to help you understand."

Atlanta nodded.

Lassite set down his sprayer and used a bony finger to tap Atlanta's chest. "All the magic you need is in you already."

"That doesn't help if I don't know how to use it," she said.

"Did you ever see Roxana work magic?"

"No . . . well . . . sometimes. When she stepped on the moth ship, it lit beneath her steps."

"That was the ship reacting to the magic in her, not her working some active spell." He picked up another tray of plants and set it where he could spray it.

"So I can't cast spells?"

"I doubt you can, at least for now."

This was both a relief and disappointment. "You're saying you can't do anything to help me?"

"I am saying," Lassite said with patience, not looking at her as he misted the plants, "that everything you need by way of assistance is already inside you."

Atlanta could not help herself. She huffed out an enormous sigh.

Lassite blinked. "That," he said severely, "is most un-paladin-like."

She compounded her un-paladin-like qualities by sticking her tongue out at him as she left.

Lassite shrugged and returned to watering. It was a pleasant rhythm, he thought, and one that reminded him of the Golden Path over and over again. It grew like the plants grew, threading its tiny way through the future. He hummed a little. In the corner, on a previously unoccupied rack, two Derloen ghosts nosed their way along a row of grow-packs that Atlanta had placed there some time ago, dipping in and out of the medium.

Pleasant indeed.

This time, Niko resolved, she would achieve satisfaction from EverRich. She showed up for the appointment, which she had booked as requested, an hour early.

The clerk was not there. A half hour later, they appeared and finally summoned her up to the desk.

"There are certain irregularities hindering the distribution of your funds," they explained. "You will have to return again tomorrow with these forms filled out." They pushed a stack of plastic sheets at her.

"What kind of irregularities?"

"I am not at liberty to say," the clerk said coyly. "You will have to talk to our esteemed security delegates."

"May I do so now?"

"Not until the forms have been filled out."

Niko took a deep breath. "So I will return tomorrow . . ."

"You will need to make a new appointment, of course."

"Of course. And after that I will be able to meet with your security delegates?"

"You will need to make another appointment to do that after the forms have been processed."

"Which will take how long?"

The receptionist shrugged. "It depends on the workload."

This time Niko held her deep breath a full minim before releasing it.

"And your estimation of the current workload?"

"I am not at liberty to say."

They locked eyes. Niko's were fierce, but the receptionist was unruffled. They pointed at the door. "Have an excellent day, citizen."

Biting back her reply, Niko stalked out.

When Niko returned to the ship, she had plenty to think about beyond the bank and its forms.

"Admit plums," Dabry said, and plucked one from the box to toss to Atlanta. She sniffed it and, at his gesture, took a bite. Tart with an edge of sweet, the fibers soft and giving to the tongue.

"Combined with cherryh honey cream"—Dabry pointed at a large opalescent tub—"it'll melt in the mouth as quickly as you taste it."

"Cherryh honey cream?" Niko said, entering on the heels of this speech. She eyed the tub. "How costly was a tub that size?"

"We'll recoup it," Dabry told her with assurance. "We'll mark these at five a morsel. But wait, there's more."

"Of course there is." Niko watched as Dabry opened a crate on the counter, careful not to let them see the contents. Then he turned. Cupped in one of his upper hands lay a waxy white blossom, its petals still tightly closed. He held it out to them, then sprayed the blossom with a pink mist from the small tool in another upper hand.

The mist sank into the blossom, absorbed, and the petals began to take on a pink tinge, loosening. As they watched, the petals folded back, revealing a single golden cone. He held it out to Niko. "Eat it entire," he said.

Reaching out, she popped it into her mouth.

It tasted like sunlight on fields of yellow flowers, a honeyed warmth that was more an emotional sweetness than a matter of taste buds. It lingered on her tongue, flaking away, then disappeared. Closing her eyes, she swallowed the last fragrant breath, unwilling to let it go.

"Wow." She opened her eyes again. "What is that?"

"Rokke roses," he said. "Only on Coralind. Our main attraction. No prep, other than the spraying."

"That sounds good. Have you figured out who's crewing?"

"We all are." In answer to her raised eyebrow, he clarified, "If we want to take advantage of the fact that the festival is cycle-long, we need to be open. I've got us crewing in three-hour shifts. Milly, Atlanta, and I, then Gio, Talon, and Skidoo, then you, Lassite, and Rebbe."

"Lot of work," she said. "Jezli or Petalia offer to help?"

"Jezli said she would act as 'advertising consultant' and went off to 'perform research,' which I suspect means log onto the station net and read gossip pages. The ship is going to help with servitors."

"Oh. Good thought, *Thing*," she said, and didn't add the "for once" that echoed in her head.

"Thank you, Captain," the *Thing* acknowledged. Its tone was anything but modest.

"So we might as well start getting ready to cook and serve," she said. "Perhaps let's do a test run tomorrow?"

Dabry shook his head. "We need to start tomorrow. I'll have the dishes prepped for tonight's dinner."

"Why the rush?" Niko said uneasily.

Dabry looked down at the crate of roses, looking with pride and pleasure at the tightly furled flowers. "They're a bit perishable."

"How perishable?"

"Three days perishable."

"You couldn't contract for the bulk to be delivered tomorrow to buy us an extra day?"

"Not going to lie to you. It's already here, Captain. That's how I got such a good deal."

She frowned but forbade from further censure. Instead, her mind chased down a different speculative tunnel. "Speaking of that, you and I need to talk to Atlanta about something."

Atlanta had forgotten about the incident with her stomach, which had not repeated itself. She felt fine, and so thought that it had been a one-time thing.

When she was talking with Milly in the kitchen, though, Milly had her taste something. She'd said, "Delicious!" not wanting to say, "Too sweet for my taste."

She doubled over and fled the surprised Milly to rush to Niko for a consultation, finding her with Dabry.

"The pain is back!" she moaned. "But I haven't been off-ship or anything like that."

"Mmm," Niko mused. "What were you doing just before it happened?"

"Milly and I were talking."

Dabry and Niko exchanged looks. "What was the discussion about?"

"She had me taste some candies to give her my opinion."

"And you told her your opinion?"

Atlanta shrugged. "Not really. They weren't very good and I didn't want to tell her that."

"So what did you say instead?"

"I said they were delicious."

Niko and Dabry exchanged a Significant Look. "Tell me, Atlanta," Dabry asked. "What color are your eyes?"

"Brownish green," she said.

"Tell me they're blue."

"What?"

"Just tell him that your eyes are blue," Niko said.

"My eyes are blue?" she said uncertainly, and then doubled over from the pain. "My eyes are not blue!" she said, and felt it ease. "What is happening?!" she demanded of the other two.

"Fascinating," Dabry said. "I presume that you have been able to lie previously."

"What? I don't lie!"

"Not anymore, at any rate," Niko observed. "Roxana didn't warn you about this particular side effect of becoming a paladin, I guess?"

Atlanta stared.

"Roxana seemed like the type who might have never noticed," Dabry said. "She seemed very truthful."

"Think about it." Niko looked at Atlanta. "The first manifestation was when you had bought the seeds, but indicated you hadn't purchased anything to Gio, I would reckon."

"Yes . . ." Atlanta said slowly.

"Then you talked with Milly, and you lied about how the candies tasted."

"I don't understand," Atlanta started, and then realized, as she doubled over, that she did understand.

Niko felt the need to clarify, so that Atlanta could not possibly misunderstand. "As a paladin, you *cannot* lie."

"It would be interesting to see if there are other, similar effects," Dabry began.

"No!" Atlanta exclaimed. "I understand what is happening." She marched out of the room without another word.

"Could we persuade the entire crew to become paladins?" Niko said wistfully.

"It's a hard burden," Dabry commented, watching after Atlanta. "No polite half-truths, no lies of omission, all the little things that help us get along with each other."

He shook his head. "But that girl is smart, and determined, and she'll learn to live with it, possibly even make it a strength."

He turned back to Niko. "How are things going with the bank?"

It was the first time he'd asked, and Niko knew from his tone that, somehow, he knew everything that had happened so far. Still, she forced a casual air. "You know how banks are. They don't want to give up their money. But I'm stubborn enough to keep after them. Eventually they'll get tired of me sitting in their waiting room."

"Eventually," Dabry murmured, and left it at that.

One of Milly's favorite things to make were sugar prints, elaborate constructions of spun sugar that had to be planned out beforehand to calculate all the angles and supports. She was working on one now, not a piece to be consumed, but a practice piece. Gio stood by, supervising, which she didn't need but tolerated, and occasionally offered helpful suggestions, which were much more welcome than the supervision.

They had never spoken of Milly's betrayal on the pirate station, but it lay in the space between them, she sometimes thought, like a black hole whose presence could not be seen, but which showed its presence by its pulls and influences on everything around it.

Gio had thought, more than once, of bringing it up, but he didn't know whether it would do any good. It might actually clear the air instead of making things murkier, but then again, it might not.

He'd liked Milly from the first moment she'd entered the crew; she had a bright cheerfulness that he only later learned was like a candy shell over the rest. She had a more complicated personality than the outer shell would have ever betokened.

He thought she was coming to trust them. The thing that had tipped her in that direction was the fact that, after her betrayal, they had kept her on, that Niko continued to treat her no differently than she had in the past. But Niko had her own outer shell and he was unsure how the captain felt about Milly.

Did it matter? He pointed to an insufficiently strong strut. Milly muttered something impatient under her breath but nonetheless reinforced it.

"It's me!" the ship suddenly said. "You're making me!"

They were, as it noted, creating a construction of the *Thing*, spun in deep black sugar and dustings of sparkling crystals. The ship considered the project from a number of angles. While it thought the replica insufficient, it was, after all, an effort that celebrated the glory of its shape. Presumably, it thought, pleased with itself at the generosity in the concept, Milly would improve and make more and more replicas like this one.

"I am," Milly said. "You're nicely complicated, and it made a good exercise."

"What is the purpose though?" the ship asked. "Are you going to eat it?" That thought made it feel *anxious*. It wanted to preserve the creation, perhaps tuck it away in a secret compartment where it would be safe and could be gloated over in private.

"No, that much sugar would have us rocketing all over, then too sick to move," Milly said with a touch of regret. "I'll recycle it."

"No!" the ship protested.

Milly cocked an eye at the ceiling. "And what would you have me do with it?"

"Give it to me as a present," the ship suggested. It wasn't entirely clear on how presents worked, since they seemed to have a great deal of unspoken concepts attached to them. This was as good a time as any to begin to experiment. But were you supposed to ask for presents? The ship wasn't sure about that, but it seemed sometimes when people wanted something very much, they asked for it. That seemed to be how it worked, at any rate.

Milly cocked an eyebrow. "Oh, and what presents have you given me lately, *Thing*?"

"You have to give presents before you can receive any?" the ship inquired uncertainly. It cast about for justifications. "What if it is to be my birthday?"

"That makes it sound like it is not actually your birthday," Gio signed, drawn into the conversation despite his ongoing resolution not to argue with the ship the way the rest of them did. All the time.

"I do not know how to calculate my birthday," the ship admitted. "It took three solars to make me."

"There was no day where they pronounced you ready?" Milly asked.

"No." The ship thought. "One day they told me I was to be sold, and that was the first time I ever marked a day."

Milly and Gio exchanged glances. "Very well," Milly said. "This is yours, ship."

That sparked an entirely new chain of thoughts, because the ship had never really contemplated the concept of ownership, to the point where it suspected there might have been hooks installed into its psyche to prevent contemplating it, hooks that had been removed by the combination of Lolola's programming and the events it had experienced. It had, after all, saved them, it told itself proudly. In some ways it had given Niko and the crew a very fine present by doing that, but it decided not to point that out until it was necessary or worthwhile. Or might deflect some other issue.

It had taken the ship a long time to understand the concept of not saying aloud exactly what it thought at the very moment it occurred to it. The hobby of *hourisigah* had taught it a startling amount about how to save things to reveal later. Of course, it had promised Niko that it would not engage in *hourisigah* again, but it could certainly think about it. Think about how its first game had turned out, and consider what it would have done differently.

This in itself was a highly satisfying occupation, and the ship felt very grateful that Niko had suggested a hobby, even if she had taken it back and suggested a different, approved-of hobby. The ship was not certain what that hobby would be, but it knew the opportunity to acquire it would present itself at some point.

Passing her wand over the confection, shaping the last details, Milly wondered, "Have you noticed something off about Skidoo lately?"

Gio gave her a sharp look. "Off?" he signed.

"She doesn't seem quite herself. Quieter. Less . . . everywhere." She gestured vaguely. "Just . . . off."

Gio nodded slowly. "Yes," he signed. "I've noticed it too."

"Have you talked to her about it?"

"I'm not one who pries. Let her come to it as she will."

"Maybe," Milly said dubiously.

Gio signed nothing more but brooded over his own thoughts. Niko had told the crew what had happened at the Captain's Gathering. He understood why she had left Gnarl there on the space moth, to be picked up by his ship. Still, he wished Niko had killed Gnarl outright. Gnarl didn't hold grudges—he became them, devoting himself to nursing and acting on them. He'd never forgiven Gio for leaving, and he'd never forgive Niko for sheltering Gio. Bad enough they all worried over where Tubal Last—or Lasts—was, not to mention what each of them might be doing in preparation for a strike.

So much to figure out, and no way to do it. He comforted himself by sorting out the seeds he'd bought, although he grimaced as he was reminded of Atlanta and her bad trade. They'd all—or most of them, anyway—talked and agreed to chip in a little of their own money to give her another chance at trade. They'd tell her at dinner.

Atlanta, however, did not appear at dinner, preferring a tray in her room, and Niko, figuring she'd had plenty of surprises during the day, did not press her.

17

Perhaps Niko should have pushed to find out why Atlanta pre-ferred solitude. Sometimes minds, left to their own devices, may wander into odd corners.

Atlanta hadn't started assembling the simulacrum of Roxana so much as stumbled into it. Thinking about how she would do it, if she chose to, and then putting together some memory dumps as a trial to see how hard it would be to create something like this project.

She'd never made her own, but she knew that it was possible, in theory, at least. Her former mental advisers had been con-structed for her, according to her empress's instructions as well as her own preferences (the Happy Bakka had been her own choice, and the only one she had insisted on.)

But those mental advisers were gone now, somehow destroyed by what she had become. Would that mean that she could not construct one? Another reason to press forward, then, in order to find her own limits and what she could and couldn't do.

Learning that she couldn't lie had shaken her. It wasn't as if she planned to do much lying. But not even little half-truths? She shook her head. That definitely wouldn't have been any sort of advantage at court.

She needed someone to tell her what was going on.

It was slow going and took research, as well as a little more discipline than she would have liked. But if she had learned one thing in the recent months, it was that she possessed more inner reserves than she had ever dreamed of. Roxana hadn't put anything in her, installed some outside force. No, she had recognized some deep-buried part of Atlanta, coaxed it out, and strengthened it.

That part of her was pretty sure what she was doing was wrong, but Atlanta was also able to stifle it.

She downloaded all those endless moments outside time when she and Roxana had walked together through the heart of the space moth. Perhaps Roxana had anticipated this and furnished the material with which to re-create her, she told herself, using that thought to tamp down worries.

The little leaf had been crumpled and unworthy of being a gift, and therefore, Talon went to consult Gio.

Gio understood gifts. He showed Talon how he had everyone's favorite things tucked away. "When they need to smile," he signed. "Doesn't have to be something big. Something they like."

Talon decided, he would try making something edible.

He asked Gio, "Will you show me how to make protein biscuits? The kind that taste like meat." That had been a favorite of Thorn's.

"You want to learn to cook?" Gio signed, puzzled and confused. "You've never wanted to before."

"I don't want to learn to cook. I want to learn how to make these."

Gio thought to himself, well, at least it would keep Talon occupied; when he was at loose ends, the boy got into mischief. So he shrugged, and took down the ingredients, and together he walked Talon through his first batch.

Which was suboptimal to say the least. Irregular brown blotches cratered with oily meat-substitute chunks that looked like they were in the process of ejecting themselves from the biscuits.

Talon looked at what he'd produced, whiskers drooping.

"These are actually pretty good for a first effort," Gio signed. "You'll get better."

"Will I?" Talon worried. Cooking always looked so easy when the others did it, easy to the point of boring. Now he realized it might be more complicated than he thought.

Gio patted him on the shoulder. "It's a skill," he signed. "You learn it, you get better. Haven't had anyone get *worse* from practicing."

"Very well," Talon said grimly, and kept baking.

Gio let him. It wasn't as though they were short of supplies at the moment, meat biscuits kept well, and even the ugly-looking ones would be consumable.

Six batches later, Talon carried a little plate, covered with a napkin, down to Rebbe's room. He knocked.

"What?"

"I brought you a snack." It had been a smarter choice than he realized because Rebbe, still growing, possessed an insatiable hunger that was always ready to be sated.

The door opened and Rebbe stood there looking at him, then the plate.

"Why did you bring me this?" Rebbe asked.

"I made them and I wanted to share," Talon said, deciding (correctly) that "I made them just for you" would be too much.

Rebbe reached out and took the plate. "Okay," he said, and stepped back. Then, as an afterthought, "Thank you."

Talon's whiskers bristled with happiness, but he tried to keep it from his voice. "Oh, yeah, it was nothing," he said as casually as he could manage. "I like to make them."

Rebbe sniffed at the plate. "Smells good," he said, and then closed the door in Talon's face.

That didn't daunt Talon. His heart sang as he walked back

to his own room. Rebbe had taken them rather than refusing to take anything from Talon, which had been his greatest fear. Rebbe would eat his gift whether he knew it for a gift or not; surely he would feel the love, the devotion that had been baked into them.

Rebbe ate the biscuits and thought. Talon was trying to get at him again, this time with presents. His lips crept back over his fangs. He could see through the efforts; he knew this wasn't kindness. This was an ulterior motive, Talon trying to make him into his dead twin once more.

Anger seethed inside him. He had to get away from this. There had to be a way.

He ate another biscuit.

There was plenty to occupy everyone, preparing for what had been named, despite Niko's objections, the Third Last Chance.

"Going to be a success!" Gio signed cheerfully to Atlanta. "Those roses . . . I could eat my weight in them and still want more."

This time, Niko filled out all the paperwork before going to EverRich. She had all the forms, her identification, her ship's papers, even the flimsy deed to the Last Chance's space, snatched up at the last minute and tucked away, now to be produced with a flourish in case it was requested.

"The officers are discussing your case," the receptionist informed her. Frequent acquaintance had not rendered them any less prim or more inclined to assist Niko.

"Then I will sit and wait till they are done," Niko said with grim determination.

"It may be a while," the receptionist said flatly.

"I do not care." Niko produced the datapad she brought to

occupy herself with a flourish and sat. She whiled away one
hour . . . two hours . . . three. Finally, she could bear it no longer
and approached the receptionist.

"When do you think the officers will be done discussing
things so I can finally meet with them?" she asked.

"Oh, they are done. They have gone to their communal meal."

"I did not see them leave."

"Oh, they don't work here. They meet via viddie-link."

"What have they determined?"

"That we cannot give you your money. We believe this is a
case of fraud."

"Are you accusing me of fraud?"

"It is not that," the receptionist said. "It's that there has been
a great deal of fraud lately—Festival is very busy, as you know—
and this is for your own protection."

"So you are not giving me my money for my own protection,"
Niko said flatly.

"Exactly. One can never tell."

"Actually, one can. One can hand over one's money without the risk of one taking one up for illegal activity," Niko said
darkly, unsure whether the abundance of "ones" in that sentence
negated its effect.

The receptionist simply looked at her. "This is all entirely legal,"
they said.

"So how do I get my money?"

The receptionist shrugged. Niko threw up her hands in disgust and went to research her options.

It took hours. Longer and harder than Atlanta had ever worked
in her life. Roxana had been so real. It seemed almost blasphe-
mous to try to reconstruct her in any form. In the end, Atlanta
knew, deep in her heart, that what she created was not Roxana.

But the mental construct she'd built looked so very much like her. It stood in the mindspace she'd created, looking more real than anything around it.

If she activated it . . . she could at least have some guidance, or the sort of guidance her unconscious mind thought Roxana would have given her. It was not the same, though, not the same thing at all.

It's not like I'll be able to lie about it, she mused sourly. She always prided herself on her truthfulness, but having that option removed entirely was something else. What if a situation required her to lie, like being kidnapped by pirates again, and she needed to deceive them in order to escape? No, not fair at all.

So, she reached forward in her mind and touched a button.

The surrogate Roxana opened her eyes.

18

On the next day of Festival, in the confluence known as Jubi-lation, Biboban was due to make a rare in-person appearance, imprisoned in its tank but visible to the populace. This was the highlight for many of the visitors and station inhabitants alike, and attendance was determined by lottery, because the demand far outstripped the supply. To content those not lucky enough to have secured a ticket, the majority of channels across the station broadcast the happenings.

Niko dutifully put her ship in for the lottery and had been surprised by success. She wasn't sure how she managed to secure three tickets to the Festival, but she had.

The crew drew lots to see who would accompany her. Thus she ended up with Milly and Atlanta, both of whom expressed delight at the chance to witness the spectacle. Niko wore her Free Traders uniform, Atlanta a ship uniform made splashier by the addition of scintillants along the sleeves and hems by *You Sexy Thing*.

Milly, as was her custom, wore as little as she could manage. Feathers were their own costume, and she wore them with grace and aplomb. Their seats weren't particularly good; they were to one edge of the crowd, and a large pillar interposed itself be-tween them and the main event.

The event began with a choir of children of various species, a performance which was not very virtuoso but showcased the off-spring of a number of station dignitaries. The children were very earnest, and the one chosen to make a presentation to Biboban dutifully scuttled up to the tank and dropped in the garland of pale orange, waxy-petaled flowers that had been chosen for the occasion.

The children gave way to a dignitary, whose speech focused on the past performance of the station and its continued progress under the leadership of Biboban, as well as the outstanding success of the department the dignitary personally oversaw. Cheers were encouraged and the noise frightened several small children, whose parents unobtrusively exited with them lest they face fines.

For Vomasi, this was a day of unmitigated delight, in enjoying festivities that other people put on for once, ones she did not have to sample or oversee or check on the presentation of. She could sit back and rest her feet and enjoy the excellent seat she won in the special servitor lottery.

This was the first year she'd been privileged to witness this in person, and she planned to make the most of it. She packed a number of special snacks and sweets for the occasion. She deserved it, she thought to herself. No one had worked harder.

The oldest Gardener gave a speech about the traditions of the confluences and how time and new station visitors shaped them. She urged the visitors to make contributions to the festivities, perhaps by helping fund a display in some confluence. Perhaps even this one.

Milly felt pleased to be coming to the event. You didn't get to see this sort of thing often, not when you spent most of your days on a starship. It also showed how evenhanded Niko was, having them all pick lots to see who got to go with her. It would have been better with Gio as the other person coming along, but the girl was tolerable, and had, after all, been instrumental in Milly's redemption. But Gio would have appreciated the music more.

The music was too loud, Atlanta thought, and sometimes she didn't quite understand its purpose. There was such a lot of it, and sometimes you couldn't hear what people said. Not that what they said seemed that interesting.

A number of station officials made an equal number of speeches and gave much praise for the efficiency and thoroughness with which Biboban ran the station. At this point the crowd was encouraged to cheer again, and did so, with great gusto.

Niko watched Biboban's tank and frowned to herself. That liquid didn't look quite right; there was an odd glint to it.

From Biboban's point of view, everything was wonderful. The sparkling dust Gnarl had given it floated through its watery system of lungs, pumping the liquids that supported its brain. Everywhere it touched, Biboban knew pleasure, pleasure swelling outward: purple kisses and furry licks and all the sensations it had forgotten once having and now could only imagine. It floated in a sea of an overwhelming wealth of perceptions, details filtered through every sense—memories, too, vivid ones of being tiny alternating with being a blobbship, raining down destruction.

Then a sunset full of spice and velvet and orange and sand and nostalgia.

It hardly noticed when it began to die.

Vomasi, rewarded for her labors with a prime seat at the Festival, was one of the first to realize something was happening.

Behind the expanse of glass, Biboban was dying in a terrible way. Suppurating sores spread across its flesh, breaking open with astonishing speed. The skin surrounding the sores grayed, becoming a mottled, bruised purple. Flesh thrashed in the water in protest, while Biboban's attendants surrounded the tank in a flurry of motion. The screaming began.

Atlanta felt a hard pressure under her ribs as some part of her protested this turn of events.

"Gentle beings," the intercom intoned. "We will thank you to return to your homes and ships in an orderly fashion." Lights began to blink over the exits.

The exodus was anything but orderly. Everyone babbled, asking questions, trying to find out what had happened. Niko kept her crew close, including the reeling Atlanta—anything could happen in a crowd like this, and sometimes people used turmoil to hide other actions. Milly scanned the crowd, not trusting this turn of events. Who knew what sort of mischief Tubal Last might have engineered? She wished she hadn't come.

Niko led them toward an entrance. Her mind was awash with possibilities and implications of this event.

Biboban dead? She could scarcely fathom it. It seemed fine when they spoke, and there had been no hint of mortality. No, surely this all had been as much a surprise to Biboban as anyone else.

Atlanta tried to ask a question, shouting over the noise, but Niko shook her head and gestured her onward. Conversation would have to wait till they reached the ship.

"Captain," Dabry said on her intercom, the private channel only they used. His voice held undercurrents of distress. Freshly back to the ship, she watched the news while also combing through her research on paladins. It all seemed to be legends, scraps of lore. Nothing definite, nothing she could hand Atlanta and say, see, here's some instructions.

She closed the screen. "Yes, Sergeant?"

"The good news is that there are backups sufficient to last until some new mechanism can be put in place. The bad news, for the station, is that such mechanisms are few and far between. How often does one find a retired Jadoogar ship?" Dabry said.

"And the other bad news? For us?"

"There is a security detail for you outside the ship."

"A security detail to do what, precisely?" She had half expected this, though, so his words did not surprise her.

"They are questioning everyone who visited Biboban within the past three days. They think the toxin was administered at some point within that time frame."

Niko froze. "The same time span in which I saw them."

"You and a number of other people, it seems. All of you are summoned to speak with the security officers tasked with the investigation."

"How soon?"

"The message said as soon as possible."

"And you wasted precious time on this good news, bad news stuff," she snapped. "Well, then, tell them I'll be right there."

She knew he was worried. Sometimes security in a place took you away, and their word was law. Choose to lose someone, and they would, and investigations into what happened were few and far between. At least the military bases had some semblance of order when it came to this sort of thing.

But she was a captain, a prominent figure, and her ship was here, fully crewed, and if they tried to disappear her, they'd know there would be some sort of retaliation and a great deal of publicity. A tourist destination like Coralind couldn't afford that sort of thing. So, she grabbed her go bag, tossed out the armaments it normally held, shrugged on her jacket, and went to meet the security officers.

Dabry waited for her near the exit.

He reached out an upper hand and laid it on Niko's sleeve. "It will be all right, Niko. You did nothing wrong by seeing an old friend."

"Maybe," she said. "I'll change into formal gear and go to security. Meanwhile, can you get a list of everyone who's being interviewed?"

He frowned. "Planning on playing detective?"

"We may need to, if whoever killed Biboban is smart enough to hide how they did it."

The security detail consisted of four grim-faced officers, none of whom showed any inclination to chat or provide any information about where they were going. They moved into a speed-transport tube, and, sitting in the pod, she tried to look comfortable about the whole thing, while they stood. She'd chosen to wear her formal uniform, the long purple Free Traders coat that Dabry gave her, and she tugged on it to straighten the fit, and let her mind churn through all the possibilities.

One: Someone killed Biboban for their own agenda, and Niko was unconnected.

Two: Someone killed Biboban and hoped to frame Niko.

Three: Someone killed Biboban in order to frame Niko.

Four: Biboban died accidentally. That seemed unlikely, but you couldn't discount random chance, inside the Known Universe and out.

Five: Biboban committed suicide, perhaps to frame Niko for it, or perhaps not, if you wanted to fold two equally improbable things together. That also seemed unlikely. Biboban had enjoyed existence enough to cling to it, and here in the station, it was as close to a god as any creature on whose existence everyone's air and water and gravity and other minor comforts of life depended.

When they got to the security quarters, she was ushered into a small room, hardly large enough to hold the chair that sat against the back wall, and told she would have to wait. It reminded her, more than a little, of those awful hours in IAPH when they had all been crammed together while Last summoned them, one by one, and one had not returned.

She tried to stretch her legs out and finally settled for propping them against the door, then thought about that time in the pirate haven. If Milly hadn't—if the ship hadn't—well, who knows what would have happened then? So much random chance, all leading to their getaway and the destruction of the man who'd put them in that tiny room. She sighed.

"Captain Larsen?"

An official at the door, a small, plump woman in a natty red uniform that matched the flame of her hair, her name, Hildy, blazoned on the breast. "I'm Hildy, I'll be your advocate at the hearing."

"The what now?" Niko said. "I was told I was coming in for questions."

"Yes. That's the hearing," the woman with bright cheer. "Now come this way."

Niko held back. "Is everyone undergoing this procedure?"

The woman nodded.

Well, that made Niko feel better. "How many of us are there?"

Hildy checked her data pad.

"Thirty-seven."

That made Niko feel even better. Perhaps the station was just being evenhanded but thorough.

Hildy led her into an oval-shaped room with an oval table and a single chair at its foot. There was perhaps two feet between the table's edge and the walls. Niko slid uncomfortably into her seat and looked to Hildy.

"They'll be right with you," Hildy chirped and left, the door closing after her.

It seemed to Niko that the door had closed with a particularly firm sound, an I-won't-be-opening-again-anytime-soon sort of noise. Her suspicions were confirmed when video screens dropped from the ceiling into place around the table, each one showing a person from the neck (in most cases) up, and all of them looking at her, through some trick of the arrangement. She waved a hand in greeting. No one returned the gesture.

"Captain Niko Larson, currently in command of the ship *You Sexy Thing*." The ship's name was pronounced with a hint of distaste by the head speaker, an angular Dralnoi.

"Yes," Niko said.

"You visited the being known as Biboban three days ago in its quarter for a visit of ten minims?"

"I did."

"And the purpose of your visit?"

"Personal."

This made everyone on the screens focus their attention on her even more fiercely, but Niko had suffered worse tribunals in the Holy Hive Mind.

"State the nature of your business!" someone squawked, which made the head speaker make an abrupt gesture to apparently mute them.

Niko said easily, "Biboban and I knew each other from long before it came here. I came to say hello to it. To reminisce about the old days." She folded her hands on the table in front of her. She wasn't guilty; she had nothing to worry about, she told herself.

The interrogation went on for far longer than her conversation with Biboban. For over an hour, Niko answered question after question with careful patience. Were they trying to unsettle her with the pace? With the way they tossed the role of questioner from one to another? Each time, the new interrogator stepped in with such smoothness Niko hardly had time to draw her breath. They wanted her to not be able to think through her answers, and that was fine, since she had the truth to lean on. Telling the truth as you remembered it was always easier than remembering a set of lies.

So she smiled easily and kept her hands folded on the table in front of her, betraying no tells of her internal state of impatience and worry. Niko had always been good at that. It was why she was an excellent handbliss player, and sooner or later she'd be back on the ship and playing that again.

Did all of the thirty-seven undergo the same treatment that

Niko had? She didn't think so. Someone brought in a datapad's worth of notes and the humanoid talking to her broke off long enough to scan it before returning their attention even more sharply to Niko.

"Tell me everything about the circumstances under which you first met Biboban," they demanded.

She tried to oblige, giving them the unglossed details. Working together, leaving Biboban behind when she left the service, then what she knew of Biboban's own escape from the Holy Hive Mind. She didn't know those details, but she had plenty of guesses, which she was more than willing to share in order to demonstrate her good will and the fact that she had no reason to want to kill Biboban.

The deputy questioning her asked, over and over, if she had given Biboban anything. A small gift, they asked. Some trinket or transitory pleasure, so insignificant that it had slipped her mind?

Nothing, she insisted, over and over again. Finally, long after she had lost count, when she said it once more, the deputy shrugged, flicked a glance at his superior for confirmation, and said, "You may go now."

"Go?" she said, pleased. She started to rise to her feet, but he shook his head.

"Back to the cell."

Everyone on the ship knew, and quickly, that Niko had been taken away. Dabry knew they'd panic if left to their own devices, so he summoned them to the gathering room.

You Sexy Thing, very distressed about the entire situation, wanted Dabry to allow it to create guns. "I'm sure I could create very good ones," it said with an earnestness that Dabry might have found touching if it hadn't contained an ominous edge regarding the ship's willingness to embrace having weaponry installed.

The crew arrived more quickly than they might have otherwise. Each one entering, firing questions at him, but he waited until everyone was there before he said courteously, "*Thing*, you are part of this conversation," and then shouted, "Listen up!"

His tone of command stilled them instantly, even the civilians, although Jezli's face retained its sardonic expression. He took a deep breath and folded his upper hands in front of him.

"As you know, Biboban died and they suspect foul play. They have summoned every person that visited Biboban in the days leading up to the Festival, which includes Captain Niko. There is no reason to believe she is of any more interest than any other of the thirty-six beings who have also been summoned."

"But they sent a security detail!" Atlanta burst out. "Did they do that with everyone?"

"No reason to think otherwise, and perhaps it was a compliment to the captain, if it wasn't," Jezli soothed. "I'd certainly use a security detail just to make sure, if I were capturing her." The last was said in a tone of admiration that made Dabry shoot her a look. She smiled at him.

"All we can do is wait and see. And we might as well spend that time preparing for the Third Last Chance."

That cheered them, as he had known it would. Most of them looked grave but unworried, having been through worse in their time with Niko. Atlanta seemed uncertain, but she had been that way for a long time, and only lately was coming into her own self-confidence. He patted her on the shoulder with an upper hand, and she nodded at him.

"Think about what you want to do for the pop-up," he said. "You tried Velcoran food at the Gate. Now you can turn your hand to something different—within reason—if you want to try picking up a new skill, which is a good habit. The more skills you have, the more resources you have at hand, in life as well as in cooking."

"I'll think about it," she said.

Atlanta fled to her chamber to confer with Roxana—the simulacrum of Roxana, she reminded herself. But it was—and wasn't—like the first paladin. It said sensible things and gave good advice—wise counsel, which was what mental advisers were supposed to do—but it lacked the warmth and solidity that had marked Roxana Cinis.

Still, she panicked over this state of things. What did it mean for the future, that Niko was arrested? What if she never returned? You heard of plenty about that sort of thing happening, particularly in space stations. Each had its own laws and guidelines, sometimes regarding the disposal of criminals.

What if Niko were convicted of whatever they thought she had done? Had she contributed to the horrible death of Biboban? That moment had summoned some answering twinge in Atlanta. Had the death evoked that feeling? Or did the queasy sensation mean the death had been wrongful, something that a person had caused to happen to the creature rather than random illness or gene luck?

She said this to the simulacrum, who sat in an interior chamber. Flowers grew on the border of the chamber now, ones that Atlanta thought must have come from her subconscious, because she hadn't thought to add them. Little blue flowers, with a sweet, fruity smell.

Roxana said, "The crew is like a family, and you are part of that. Even if one member—even an important member, like the captain—is removed for a while, the rest are there and caring for the family."

Atlanta was silent.

"What are you thinking about that family?" Roxana asked.

"That I envy them, sometimes—most of the time, to be truthful—to have had that bond for so long."

"They all took their own hard paths to forge that bond," Roxana said. "Everyone takes their own path to making the family of their heart, and none of them are easy."

Atlanta frowned. "The people at court . . ."

"Had their own troubles, I have no doubt, that you knew nothing of. So trust the family."

19

IIIIII.II/III/I.II.II/III/III.II.II/III/III.II/IIII/II.II.II/IIII/III.II.II/IIII/II.I

There were fifty-eight-and-a-half ceiling tiles. Twenty-two energy bars on the side that gave way into the corridor. One toilet, one cot. One package of soap flakes. One low-grade, unflavored energy packet she hadn't had the appetite to eat just yet. You would think that on Coralind, they'd serve the prisoners fresh stuff, Niko thought.

Footsteps. She didn't raise her head but continued lying on her back, hands behind her head, contemplating the fifty-eight-point-five tiles above her.

The footsteps stopped outside her cell. Someone cleared their throat.

They could come in and get her this time. She was done with the interrogations. Cooperation had done her no good, so she'd see what this tack proved.

"Captain Larsen?" the person queried. They sounded more polite than anyone she had dealt with yet.

She raised her head.

"Janus, was it?" she said.

The security chief stood outside the cell. "Yep." He tapped the door pad and the energy bars vanished.

Niko didn't move. "Is it time for another interrogation? Because I've had a lot of them."

"I know," he said agreeably. "I'm here to let you go. But will you speak with me briefly before you do?" At her grimace, he added, "I know it's a lot to ask, Captain. I'll make sure there's good quality caff and a sandwich arriving for you within ten minims."

The caff was high quality and the sandwich excellent as well. Niko wolfed them down with a speed that amused Janus.

"Did you even taste it?" he wondered.

"High-quality fresh soybeans," she analyzed. "Salt, garlic, some crumbs of nevturi, and . . ." She paused, considering. "Challa tuber slices, very thin."

He applauded silently. "I stand rebuked."

"I should hope so," she said. "Do you know how long I've wasted here? Time is money, security chief."

"Ayuh," he drawled. "Well, I won't keep you much longer. We know that Biboban died of a particular substance."

"Which I did not give it."

He ignored her as though she had not spoken. "And we believe that substance was self-administered."

She sat back in the chair. "Suicide?" At his head shake: "An overdose."

He tapped his nose with a finger.

"Either way, that's not something I deal in."

"We know, Captain Larsen. But not all of the people who visited it were as clean as you."

"Gnarl Grusson," she guessed.

His eyes moved this way and that. "Well done. Yes, the captain has had past dealings. But we searched his ship and found nothing."

"It's a smuggler ship. You know you can't have found every nook and cranny."

"Nope. But short of getting Gnarl to show us, we won't."

"So you can't do anything?" She was outraged. "Don't you even intend to avenge Biboban?"

"I do," he said. "That's why I'm letting you go."

"You expect me to get at him somehow?

He shrugged. "You try. I try. Maybe I have a few other people trying."

She stared at him. "All right," she finally said. "But I want another of those sandwiches to go."

Dabry had waited and waited for news of Niko. But nothing came. He hated to leave the crew behind when she wasn't there, but he directed Gio to be in charge for the short while he'd be gone. The chimp gave him a beetle-browed, worried look but signed his acquiescence and went to organize a game of hand-bliss.

The bar the message sent him to was smoky and noisy and full of people celebrating Festival. It smelled of spilled alcohol and the musky sweat of drinkers. There was a scattering of other Ettilites here. No one that he knew, but they nodded at each other in that way you do when you don't meet another member of your species that often.

He sat near the back, where he could see most of the room, and the stairs leading up towards a sublevel that looked to hold storage stuff.

After only a handful of minims, someone slid into the seat across from him. Wearing cloaking gear so he couldn't learn much, other than they were roughly humanoid or wearing a number of prosthetics.

"You have doomed your daughter," they said. Voice-masking gear made the words flat and expressionless.

"My daughter is dead," he told them, careful to keep his own voice modulated. "My daughter died in warfare."

"No," they said flatly. "Her mother did, she watched her die. But the daughter survived, although the accident that marked her twisted her arm, and the wartime medics had not been able to give her the care she needed."

"Why have you contacted me?" he asked.

"To see if you're willing to let your daughter die again."

"Again?" His lower hands gripped the chair's arms, but he kept himself still. The bar haze made his head swim, overwhelmed him until he was moving with nightmarish slowness. Or was it a dream? If his daughter was somehow, impossibly, impossibly, impossibly alive, this person could lead him to her.

"You left her and her mother behind."

"I was in a war. They don't let you come home."

"You could have tried."

"Do you think I didn't?" He wanted to shout at this stranger, wanted to scream in outrage and pick them up in his hands, crush them, kill them. Not an honorable death at his upper hands, but the lower ones, the ones you reserved for the least and dirtiest of things.

They pushed themselves away from the table. "Very well, it doesn't seem we have anything more to discuss."

"We have plenty to discuss!" He started to surge to his feet, but the crowd roared as the current music came to an end and a fresh beat started.

People bobbed in the crowd around him, a sea of faces, none of them the nondescript blur of the hood. He tried to cross to the side of the room, achieve a place where he could see things. He jumped up a few stairs, grabbing onto the railing as a fight jostled past.

There, two Dralnoi grappled with a surprisingly agile Plubas. Directly below, a drunken human aimed a punch at their companion, and swinging wide, fell on her ass. He noted absently that every one of his race was gone.

Except for one.

Across the room, just at the entrance, so close, so far away, staring at him. Before she turned and vanished through the door.

The sight of her hit him like a laser blast, hard, as if the entire midsection of his body had vanished.

She looked so much like her mother, despite the scars.

No one was waiting for Niko outside the offices, but she hadn't expected anyone. She'd told Dabry to keep them all on the ship, keep them safe.

Which was why, returning, it was another blow to discover him inexplicably not there.

She spoke with the others, let them flock around her to touch her, convincing themselves she was really there. Even Rebbe, who stretched out a shy hand and laid it on her sleeve, then removed it immediately, but not before she saw his relief. *His life has been nothing but chaos since the moment he was born,* she thought, and tried to make her smile as reassuring as possible.

Where was Dabry? She went to their shared office and hunted through the papers for a clue. There, in a pile, was the message he had received when they arrived, the one he refused to show her.

But had, perhaps, left it here in the open to say where he had gone if something went awry.

She read it. Then read it again in disbelief. His daughter?

With infinite care, the same she might have displayed setting a delicate cake in a temperamental oven, she placed the note on the desk. She was reeling; everything had shifted. Then— ignoble thought!—she felt a flicker of jealousy that he had gone off when she was still in jail.

"Can you reach him via comm, *Thing*?" she asked.

"He has his comm turned off. That is not very fitting for second-in-command."

She almost rolled her eyes but restrained herself. She couldn't very well ask *Thing* to refrain when she didn't. She affirmed, "Definitely."

"Perhaps someone else would make a better second-in-command."

"*Thing*, I am not going to put you in command now or at any other time. Don't speak of it again."

The conversation made the ship consider some of the things Biboban had told it in one of their last conversations.

They don't understand, the shell people, Biboban said. *They live tiny lives, dependent on everything around them, and they don't understand what it's like to be unfettered. So they think of ways and reasons to fetter us.*

Us? the ship asked, unsure exactly what category it was joining Biboban in.

Ones lacking bodies like ours, which can live for centuries, with the right maintenance. That's all they're good for, really, maintenance.

These thoughts both frightened and thrilled the ship with their audacity. To think of itself as a separate thing, not dependent on the beings inhabiting it? That seemed unfathomable, inconceivable, as hard to fathom as the ghosts that Lassite insisted on.

Atlanta told the surrogate Roxana that Niko was back. She consulted her frequently, but for shorter and shorter periods. It was *almost* like Roxana, but not quite, not enough that it felt painful to talk with it. It had Roxana's cadences, her intonations, her gentle but firm eyes. It said things that she would have said and praised Atlanta for how far she had come without any guidance.

That last part really underscored that this was not Roxana, was something utterly unlike Roxana. Roxana would not have uttered that phrase. She would have simply looked at her with approval and that would have been sufficient. This, though, this was like eating candy, sugary candy, and she cut the link abruptly, without pretending she was saying goodbye.

She reached out and stroked Minasit, the ship's servitor she had claimed as her own. "You're still my friend and still here," she whispered.

She went to the lounge, Minasit trailing her, and found only Jezli, sitting, flipping through her data pad, apparently reading.

"Don't you miss her?" Atlanta blurted out. Not at all how she had meant to lead into this conversation.

"That," Jezli said with cooler dignity than Atlanta had ever seen her assume, "is a private matter. I do not ask you about your private matters. . . ." An arched eyebrow conveyed that she could have, and that Atlanta would not have particularly enjoyed the experience. "And so, I would ask you to refrain from inquiring into mine." She set her data pad down with an irritated click. "Is there something else I can do for you?"

"I remembered how hard it was to feel a part of the crew and so I wanted to say I like having you here."

"That is kind of you," Jezli said. "I take it you no longer feel it hard to be part of the crew?"

"I just have to trust in them, Roxana said . . ." Atlanta stopped.

"Back when we were on the space moth?"

"Noooo . . ." Atlanta trailed off.

Jezli looked at her, caught by her tone.

"I tried to re-create her," Atlanta confessed.

Jezli's eyes narrowed to green slits. "Re-create her how?"

"As a mental projection. I took everything I remembered . . ."

"And created an *abomination*," Jezli shouted, springing to her feet. "She is not a thing to be made, a creature to serve as your mental servant! How dare you!"

"What's going on?" Niko popped her head in, drawn by the noise. She had never seen Jezli upset like this—something must be terribly wrong. She took a step into the room. Atlanta was red-faced and teary-eyed.

"I wasn't making her into a servant!" she yelled at Jezli. "I wanted to talk to her. I *needed* to talk to her. Everything is changing in me, and I don't know what to expect!"

"So you made a puppet of her in your head," Jezli said, and made a rude noise. "Did they dance nicely for you, little princess? Did they spin and pirouette and bow to acknowledge your supremacy?"

"No!" Atlanta felt blazingly angry now. How dare Jezli say such things, assume such motivations! How dare she treat Atlanta like this when she wasn't even crew! Wasn't part of this family!

She shouted all of this, and more, and Jezli shouted back. Niko stepped between them, one hand raised to ward off Atlanta, and the other toward Jezli. "Enough!" she said. "I don't understand what this is about, but you seem to be arguing about an imaginary version of Roxana, and tell me, what would she have thought of this?"

"That's just it!" Jezli began, but subsided at a look from Niko.

"There's plenty of scut work in the kitchen crying out for a hand to do it," she told Atlanta. "You get along that way, and I'll talk with you later."

Atlanta sullenly trudged out and Niko turned to Jezli, who had closed her eyes and was by all appearances engaging in deep breathing exercises.

Niko waited, and at length, Jezli opened her eyes.

"I cry your pardon, Captain," she began. "The child didn't know what she was doing, I am sure of that. But Roxana would not have countenanced such a thing."

"Are you sure she would have wanted to deny what seems to be her heir any sort of guidance?" Niko asked.

Jezli's face sagged. "Maybe you're right." She stared at the floor. "But Roxana's not—wasn't—a toy, to be played with. She did not take herself too seriously, but she did take what she did—what she was—seriously."

"You've never told me how you met," Niko prodded gently.

Jezli shook her head. "No, that was a dark time. But I will tell you about the first time we worked together . . ."

By the time she finished, both of them were laughing, although there were also tears staining Jezli's cheeks. Niko reached out a hand to clasp hers as they sat in silence.

"Here's a pretty picture," Petalia said scornfully from the doorway. "Like a pair of schoolgirls. Will you be scuttling off to the shadows to play at kissing games next?"

Niko dropped Jezli's hand faster than if it were made of red-hot metal. Expressionlessly, Jezli looked up at Petalia.

"Don't make me start on you next, Florian," she said with genuine exhaustion in her voice. "Because once we start, you and I will go until we are finished."

Niko stood up and interposed herself in the stare down between the two. "That is enough arguing for one day, and I still have Atlanta to tend to, and Dabry missing. Knock it off, at least for now, I beg of you. For my sake."

"Very well." Jezli folded her hands in her lap.

"Where is the sergeant?" Petalia asked Niko.

"That," Niko said, "is exactly what I yearn, with every iota of my being, to know."

20

The sergeant in question was on his way back to the ship, lost in an emotional turmoil that kept him from doing much more than automatically putting one foot in front of the other.

How was his daughter alive? Why hadn't someone, anyone, contacted him to tell him? Why hadn't *she* contacted him? He could think of no reason why she wouldn't have, but perhaps at ten, she had gotten swept up by other things. Maybe taken in by some family that had wanted to hide her origins.

But still—when she came of age, surely she would have reached out?

What did all this mean, this reaching out to him to drive him away? What had she been told about him? He groaned out loud, eliciting startled stares from passing beings. He ignored them and quickened his pace. He would tell Niko what was going on, and together they would sort this out, as they had sorted out so many things in the past.

He was startled to find Niko in the entrance, waiting for him.

"You were released?" he exclaimed.

"No," she said dryly. "I escaped." And then, at his expression: "Of course not!"

"I had an urgent errand or I would have been here," he explained.

"An errand concerning your daughter," she said flatly.

He hesitated, then nodded. "You read the message." He didn't blame her; he had left it on the pile in case he didn't come back.

"Did you learn anything?"

"I saw her, Niko."

She blinked. "How?"

He shook his head. "I don't know. I don't know why she hasn't contacted me in all this time. She has been told misleading things about me, Niko, I would swear it, but the why of it I cannot figure out."

"And yet she stepped forward now. Does that timing figure into all the other coincidences that continually surround us?"

"I don't think so," he said slowly, grudgingly. "It's got a different feel to it than all of this. Can we ask Lassite?"

"Lassite is of no use lately. He nods to say we are on the Path and that everything is unfolding as it should, then he seems tense and uneasy."

"Whenever he's around Jezli, in particular. Have you asked him about that?"

"It would do no good. You're trying to move the conversation away from your daughter. What do you intend?"

"I have to find her. I don't know how."

"A return to your home planet might be in order."

"I'd thought about that, but didn't dare ask until I knew more." Once again, Niko had anticipated him, and he was deeply grateful. What would he do without her?

"Then let's solve other pressing issues for now, but make it our priority once those are past. Dabry, you owe it to the others to say why you've been gone."

His face was stricken at that, and she said, "Do it when you can. For now, let's figure out our options."

One thing Niko knew was that she needed more caff. Dabry trailed her to the kitchen and sat down across from her when she settled. She drank a swallow, set the mug down, and steepled her fingers. "Here's what I learned. Biboban didn't die by any poison, at least not as we define it. No, it died of an overdose."

"An overdose of what?"

"Ordalane. It's one of the reality-twisting drugs, and so illegal you can get fined just for mentioning it in public. So the question is—who sold it to them? You've looked at the list of people pulled in, I'm sure."

"Gnarl," Dabry said instantly.

Niko nodded. "Gnarl's dealt in worse before," she mused. "Trying to build his financial reserves back up so he could re-supply. Might have searched his stores to see if he had anything weird enough to appeal to Biboban." She snapped her fingers. "I might have given him the idea at the Captain's Gathering. Or he was probably already planning to sell to it, even then."

"But did he poison it deliberately?"

"Why strike at the heart of the station?"

"To deprive you of an ally."

"Which Biboban turned out not to be."

"Will they trace it to him?"

"Probably not," Niko said with a sigh. "And I can't think of any way to ensure they find out. He'll have it hidden on his ship, and those smuggler ships have hidey-holes inside hidey-holes."

She took another sip of caff and sighed again. "This arrived in your absence." She pushed the slip of plastic across the table.

He scanned it and made a sound of startled disgust. "Closed down?!"

"License suspended until the investigation is fully complete."

His eyes were stricken. "All those Rokke roses."

"We'll end up eating the costs. But we might as well make it literal and have the meal of a lifetime tonight."

Lassite had not seen his Derloen ghosts as much lately, but he paid it little thought. They would not leave the ship, and there was plenty of room aboard it for them to favor.

He would have been less complacent if he had seen all three of them coiled around Atlanta's seeds in their forgotten rack. They hid whenever Atlanta came to mist the seeds, which she did less and less frequently. When she was not there, though, each curled around one of the pots, always the same three selected although no one would have been able to tell whether or not it was the same ghost to each pot every time. (It was not.)

Deep in the seeds, cells began to stir. Forces gathered.

21

The crew gathered for a feast that was somber at first, eating as many of the Rokke rose blossoms as they cared to consume, along with the other perishables that, once sold and received on ship, were unreturnable.

"It is a rare occasion, at least," Jezli said, helping herself to another blossom. The rest of them looked awed by the amount she had consumed so far; they had seen some hearty appetites in the course of their serving careers, but this one seemed unmatched. She noticed their collective stares, put the blossom down, and took a delicate sip of water.

"I did say I wanted to eat my weight in them," Gio signed. "Maybe I shouldn't have said that."

"I do love the flavor," Atlanta commented. "What gives it that?"

"Rare elements," Dabry said. "Also why they're so hard to grow."

"Rare bio-elements?" she said hopefully, and he laughed.

"Not rare enough to recoup our losses! So eat up, Princess."

Despite his cheerful words, Dabry knew the Rokke roses had been a total financial disaster. He insisted on cleaning up by himself but wished he hadn't once he started. Too easy to worry over things with no one else around.

He had put their extra money in the roses, plus all that he had left, plus the majority of the emergency fund. He had thought it such a stroke of luck, getting a chance at such a rare treat, that if they sold them fast at the price he wanted—well, they wouldn't be worrying about money anymore.

Niko was having some trouble with the insurance, he knew. She didn't think he noticed that she'd spent hours there, returning each time looking grimmer.

What would they do if they were out of money? They needed fuel, and air and water were not inexhaustible. They might recoup a little with the biomass they'd leave behind, but that would be scant money. Maybe just enough to give them the illusion of having enough, but not really.

He thought of traders he'd seen on the drain, hoping to score that one big score that would reverse the flow of their finances, get them back on their feet. He'd pitied those people, thinking, of course, they hadn't had a good leader.

He wiped his hands on his apron, then rubbed his face with all four. What were they going to do?

Well, he could make one thing right, at least, and stop hiding his own problems while telling them they shouldn't hide theirs from each other, let alone him.

Skidoo took Atlanta, as promised, to the confluence Lassitude, one of the water-filled confluences. She hadn't wanted to at first, she felt too unhappy, but then Atlanta coaxed her.

"We could take some of the others," Atlanta proposed, but at that point Skidoo was ready, and said she only wanted to share it with Atlanta.

It was a long walk, and along the way, Atlanta bought herself one of the spice cookies a vendor was selling. Breaking it in half, she offered some to Skidoo, but the Tlellan shook her head. "Is being other things to be eating, in Lassitude."

The cookie was not anywhere as good as the ones Dabry made, and so she stuck the other half away in her pocket for later.

She had not been to any of the liquid-filled confluences before. Atlanta dutifully fitted the interpreter in her ear and prepared herself for the sensation as water seeped into the airlock and rose past her ankles, her knees, her waist (by now, the delighted Skidoo was entirely submerged), her chest, then a cold line creeping along her neck. And finally she dipped her face in, rather than wait any longer, and opened her eyes.

Along with a crowd of other festivalgoers, they spilled out of the airlock as it opened.

"There is being rides. I is being buying tickets, and you is being waiting here."

"Very well," Atlanta said and remained in the admission area. It was filled luxuriantly with verdant underwater plants moving languidly in the soft current, and among them were flickers of movement and color, fish ranging in size from the largest, as long as Atlanta's arm, to the smallest, so tiny they could barely be seen. She watched them nosing about the plants and remembered the half cookie in her pocket.

She fumbled it out, thinking to sprinkle the crumbs where the fish could take them, and found herself instantly surrounded by a circle of eyes as the fish gathered around her at arm's length. She faltered, and they surged forward expectantly a few inches.

She felt an edge of panic. Well, they were only fish, how frightening could they really be? And they must be genetically engineered. Or androids. Androids couldn't hurt people.

They moved forward another inch and she remembered how Thorn had died.

The fish pressed forward again.

Then Skidoo materialized, a thrashing of tentacles. "Is being shoo!" And the fish shooed obediently, as though they had never thought of doing otherwise, and went back to nosing among the plants.

Skidoo gave Atlanta her severest look. "Is being foolish, feeding things," she admonished. "If everyone is feeding them, they is being expecting it and is becoming a nuisance." She pointed at a sign that Atlanta hadn't noticed, which clearly conveyed the message not to feed the fish with an emblem showing an extended hand spread in panic, toothy fish affixed to three of its seven fingers.

Nuisance, Atlanta thought, was hardly the word for it.

Skidoo looped an affectionate tentacle around her wrist. "Is being coming this way." She pulled Atlanta through the silky, cool water.

The rides were drawn by enormous frill-finned, golden-scaled fish with googling, protuberant eyes that seemed ready to pop out of their heads. Each pulled a tangle of ropes, and you grabbed one and held on as you moved, faster than you ever could have swum on your own, feeling the rush of the water across your skin.

They rode for a while, and explored the coral reefs, and each other, in a happy tangle that answered all of Atlanta's questions and then some.

They returned to the ship still happily tangled, Skidoo's tentacle looped around Atlanta's waist. As they entered, Dabry met them.

"What's wrong?" Atlanta asked.

"I need to tell you all something."

He had them come to the kitchen because he felt the most comfortable here, and thought that being there might be comforting. He broke out some of his special treats, less as a bribe than a way to put everyone in a good mood.

Instead of feeling comfortable, it felt overly crowded with everyone, except Jezli, gathered around. Niko leaned against the wall with folded arms and a sardonic expression not unlike Jezli's.

"When we arrived, I got a letter," he began. "It told me that my daughter was still alive."

Startled exclamations and a few quick questions before he held up his upper hands for silence. "Let me unfold it all, then you can ask questions, if you have them. Before I go further, my apologies to you all for keeping this to myself."

He couldn't help but look at Niko with those last words, but her expression remained blank and unyielding. She was still angry with him, even if she wouldn't show it in front of the rest of the crew.

He detailed his hunt for information, saying only that he hadn't wanted to speak of it to anyone until he had hope.

Gio understood why Dabry hadn't told them. Hoping in the face of no hope was hard; he'd seen people lost to chases like that. It made him think about his own folk. Most of the elders had relocated to the Old Terra Preserve by now, but his cousins recently reached out to say they were all putting in on a trade ship, pooling their earnings, and his experience would buy him a stake if he wanted in.

He hadn't hesitated in saying no. Who would pass up a ship full of chances to cook, and more than that, good friends, friends he'd stood shoulder to shoulder with in combat? He listened with furrowed brows as Dabry continued, talking about the meeting with the masked figure and the last-minute revelation that his daughter had been there.

Atlanta sat on a counter and nibbled smoked soy-sausage, hurt to the core that Dabry hadn't told them. She felt a little jealous of this daughter as well. Did his silence about her mean she had his allegiance? Would he leave them all in order to chase after her?

Milly had no problem with any of this. People come and go in a military company. They muster out or transfer or go elsewhere; you got used to that. Still, this had been a stable crew over the months she'd known them, and they'd won her trust. You had to trust people who forgave you like that; you had to resolve never to do it again to reward their trust in you. She said, "Appreciate you telling us, Sarge. We back you, whatever you want to do."

Lassite nodded in agreement, but in truth, worry kept snaking up his spine. All sorts of choices were coming up, particularly for Atlanta. Events would come to a head soon. The daughter was a matter for down the road; she meant nothing at the moment. A distraction.

Skidoo felt sympathy, although only up to a point. At least he was healthy and didn't have to worry about his body falling apart, she thought. That thought surprised her at how much darkness lay in it. She had a letter of her own, received today, back in her quarters. She hadn't dared open it yet.

Rebbe remained relatively unmoved by all of this. Family bonds made sense to him in theory—they'd been explained in the tape-learning he'd come out of the cloning cocoon with. He didn't feel how they could matter the way that the learning suggested they could feel. It was all an academic exercise, and a little boring to boot. Perhaps they'd all stop talking soon and he could do something more interesting, like researching more confluences. He planned to go to at least ten more before they left. He had a list.

Talon's emotions echoed Atlanta's. It wasn't that the sergeant was like a father—were-lion fathers were strict and unrewarding, never affectionate. More like an uncle, one of his mother's brothers. What if the sergeant was the next loss in what seemed to be an unending series of losses?

Looking around, Dabry could read some of this in their faces and guess at other emotions. But they did bring one thing to him: acceptance, rather than outrage. They would not waste time second-guessing his choices, and he thought that same motive might lie behind Niko's silence. He looked at her again and she failed to smile back. Okay, so actually angry, not being supportive. He'd hear more about this in private later.

For the *Thing*, this was all much of the same. It had known what was happening early on, but since it had been Dabry's secret, it had respected that. It had some hopes the daughter would be brought on board, because that would be something new and interesting.

Above all, it enjoyed seeing Niko not told immediately; she thought she was so smart, but she wasn't. The ship and Biboban had discussed that at length before the other had *died*. That meant they were offline and wouldn't come back on, which was, the *Thing* knew, a *sadness*.

Skidoo had expected a reply to her letter, but had forgotten about sending it in all the hustle and bustle of Niko getting taken in for questioning. Had forgotten till this reply came.

She had written her heart into that letter, explained all her thinking and reasoning and the restless drives that led to her renouncing her people's way of life and going to the stars. She wrote about the things that she missed on Tlella, and one of them had been her teacher, who had known her since she was tiny. He had been the kindest figure in her turbulent life, and she had always wished she had been able to say goodbye. The letter had been that goodbye, and something more to boot.

She took the sealed reply to her chamber to open it, moving quickly and carelessly despite the startled look that Gio, who had been distributing the mail, gave her. For a long time she sat, looking at the envelope. What would he have said? Would he have been able to give her the comfort she asked for?

Then the summons to hear Dabry's confession had pulled her

from it, and she lingered in the kitchen, listening to the chatter, all the while thinking about the letter in her room.

When she first returned to her chamber, she avoided looking at the letter. She circled the water-filled room, picking possessions up and putting them down, making a pretense at tidying. But the circles grew tighter and tighter, their center always the letter.

At length she reached out and took it up. She tore it open and scanned it, quickly at first, then slower and slower. She let it flutter away in the current.

She was anathema, he said. An abomination. He didn't know how she had come to the point she did, but all her choices had been wrong, and he regretted knowing her, since she had brought him such great disappointment.

She floated in the water and felt the words washing around her, hurting her, stinging her like fireworms. She wished she were a creature that could scream, because surely that would be the only way to let out such pain. She could understand why Rebbe had torn Talon so; if she had her teacher here . . .

No, she thought. That was unworthy, that was undignified. "Is being better than they is being, than they is ever being," she said out loud.

The ship reluctantly filed away its questions about what Skidoo said in the category of "things one couldn't ask about because people were pretending that they were by themselves and it wasn't polite to mention you had heard, even if you couldn't have helped hearing."

It did not particularly enjoy this exercise in *frustration*.

22

"Captain," the ship said.

Niko was filling out yet another round of bank forms, this time including several complaint letters to every office she thought might actually read them. She also compiled a list of every review service available on the station net and methodically worked her way through the list, placing an unfavorable review for EverRich on every one, which she didn't think would achieve much, but did afford some degree of satisfaction. "Yes," she said absently.

"There is an unsanctioned person aboard."

"Who?" Niko was already rising from her desk.

"I am not sure, but I believe she is the individual Jezli calls Tubalina."

Niko was out the door. "Where?"

"The receiving room."

"We have a receiving room?"

"Arpat used it for receiving visitors."

"What do we use it for?"

"Storing supplies."

Niko groaned and broke from a trot to a full-out sprint.

Pots of spoiling Rokke roses crowded the storage room, a smell simultaneously so sweet and rank that it was almost overpowering. So close they almost touched, Tubalina and Petalia face-to-face, Tubalina speaking in a low, urgent voice, Petalia silent. She broke off as Niko entered.

"What's going on here?" Niko demanded. "Why are you on my ship when I expressly forbid it?"

"I was invited," Tubalina murmured. Her glance toward Petalia brimmed with sly satisfaction.

The Florian trembled, but their face was calm as death.

"Are you all right, Pet?" Niko moved to interpose herself between the pair, shouldering Tubalina away. The other woman gave way without resistance, stepping back a few paces, but her expression remained the same.

Petalia shuddered, a deep shudder, like one breathless, emerging from water. "I . . . had to . . ." They faltered.

"Why?" Niko demanded, still keeping her attention fixed on Tubalina.

"It was . . . right . . . ?" Petalia faltered again.

Niko took a step forward, and another, forcing Tubalina to back up against the wall. "Go to your quarters, Pet," she ordered. "Or wherever you feel safe. I'll be with you as soon as I see this woman off."

Petalia slipped out. Tubalina addressed Niko. "I beg of you. I will be killed."

"I have no responsibility for you," Niko bit out, "and by forcing your way on my ship, you have only convinced me I was right to forbid you in the first place. I don't know what trickery you worked, but I will not let you work it again. Now get out or I will throw you out with my own hands."

"You will be sorry if you eject me," Tubalina issued. "I will make you sorry, wait and see." She breathed out the last as a happy hiss.

"You can try," Niko said, baring her teeth. "Shall we?"

The other woman backed away and fled. Niko marched at her heels, so close she might have trod on them, all the way down the access hatchway's ramp.

As Niko stood watching Tubalina's departure, the ship spoke with a tremor it thought would convey *nervousness*. "Captain?"

"Yes?" she answered, not taking her eyes off the departing figure. What had the woman said or done to Petalia to make them let her on board? Petalia had been so adamant that Niko would have sworn that nothing could break that will.

"There was a strange energy burst when the visitor was departing."

That caught Niko's attention. "What sort of strange energy burst?"

"I don't know."

"How can you not know?"

"I only noticed because I thought I imagined it, so maybe it is . . ." The distinct hesitation clearly required a prompt.

"Go on," Niko said.

"Sometimes when I am imagining things, it seems to be connected to magic."

"Tell Lassite about it immediately."

"Maybe you should tell him," the ship hedged. It did not want to admit anything to Lassite regarding its attitude toward magic.

Niko threw up her hands and turned back to the ship. Tubalina was gone and she might as well indulge the temperamental vessel. Still, she muttered things to herself as she walked along the corridor that the ship politely pretended not to hear.

On her way to Petalia's room, though, she paused to speak to Lassite.

"The ship says there was a strange energy burst."

"I felt it too. That's why I came out, to see if I could figure out where it came from, but it seems diffuse."

"Can it hurt us?"

He shook his head. "It isn't a harmful energy, I can tell that much. If we were planet-side, I would say it is a growth charm, such as farmers use."

"Is that something they practice here on Coralind?"

"Of a certainty," he said. "They are very spiritual here, and that is an easy magic. However, there is a flavor to this one . . ." He lifted his head as though smelling the air, then shook his head. "I am not sure, Captain."

"Keep investigating, then."

At Petalia's door, she knocked.

"Go away," came the answer.

"Last is gone, Pet. Why did you let her on board? How did it happen?"

"I was going to look at the restaurant space, to see if anything more could be salvaged."

Niko was touched that Petalia had done something of actual help to the ship, which had not been their practice so far, but refrained from mentioning it. Instead, she prompted, "And while you were there . . ."

"I turned around and she was there, and yet it wasn't her." Petalia's voice sounded ragged. Niko laid her palm flat against the door and wished the other would let her in, if only for this moment, to comfort them. "He was there, like a ghost overlaying her. I can't say no to him, Niko, I never could, he made certain of that."

"She will not come again, and you will not leave the ship without a guard, preferably myself."

"So I am to be a prisoner?"

"Make up your mind!" Niko's fist pounded the wall beside the door. "Are you in peril to be guarded, or are you imprisoned to be freed?"

There was a long silence from the room. Finally, Petalia said, with weariness in their voice, "I am both, Niko. Go away and let me think." Then, grudgingly, "And thank you for removing her."

"You're welcome," Niko said, but stood in silence for a long time, hearing nothing more from the room.

Lassite knew what the energy was, but he could not say. He could only pray that everything he had worked for would not fall in the coming moment. He could not bear it. He went to his chamber and sat in the center, and prayed and prayed and prayed, hunched over, murmuring the words as much to himself as to the universe at large.

Atlanta and Skidoo had gone to the gardens together, and afterward, Atlanta had thought they would talk about what they had done, but Skidoo was withdrawn lately. She had seemed her old self in the gardens, but as soon as they returned to the ship, she became . . . morose, if such a word could be applied. Her body language drooped; her movements held a sluggishness.

Was it regret that she and Atlanta had done what they had done together? Surely that must just be insecurity on Atlanta's part. But Skidoo had been . . . less friendly? Less talkative? Less Skidoo, altogether.

Sometimes things take time, Roxana had said. So she would think of something else to do. She found Gio in the kitchen, and he was ready enough to advise Atlanta on trade this time. She had a handful of credits. Not enough to do much with really, he said, eyeing them, but they might find something that could be given greater value with a bit of work.

They went to Abundance confluence, and the great court around it that was the free market, places where anyone who had managed to wrangle the license fee and registration months ahead of time had set up stalls, each delineated with walls of greenery, trellises with vines growing over them, spilling trumpet-shaped flowers striped in purple and scarlet. Where many other sections were primarily Dralnoi and Plubas, here there seemed to be representatives of species after species.

Gio was advising her on the purchase of some purple-and-white fabrics, gauzy and suitable for fancy wrappings or making into scarves, he said, when Atlanta felt the same pang she'd felt at the Captain's Gathering scant days before.

She turned from the transaction and the startled fabric vendor to see Gnarl, three booths away, coming toward them through the crowd. The same bodyguards that had accompanied him at the Gathering walked a pace behind. Gnarl hadn't seen her, but the bodyguard who she had interacted with met her gaze as they scanned the crowd.

The other hesitated, as if to give her time to step away, their eyes flicking once to Gnarl, warning her off. But the same pang that had made her turn made her straighten her spine, just as Roxana would have, and widen her stance, waiting for them to come to her.

Gio also turned and assessed the situation. Two guards, who'd back Gnarl in a fight, but they bore no visible weapons. Well, he didn't have any visible either, but plenty hidden, and they might too.

Still, there was station law, and Peacekeepers circulating with the crowd, patiently guiding festival participants where to find a particular vendor, or refreshment, or other amenity, such as the lavatories. They'd be quite ready to move from that amiable mode to hostility if someone broke the peace, and they *did* bear visible weapons.

Still, the girl beside him stood fully prepared. He squinted at her sidelong with pursed lips, and when she nodded at him, he nodded back. His stance looked easier, almost slouched, but just as ready for a fight as hers. Atlanta said over her shoulder to the vendor, "Give us a moment, please."

Gnarl had seen them by now, and barreled through the crowd, pushing several startled people aside. The interaction caught the eye of a Peacekeeper another few booths on, and they moved in their direction as quickly as Gnarl, although with considerably less pushing.

By the time he reached them, Gnarl was frothing words, so incoherent Atlanta could barely them make out: "Traitor—took too much—using what I taught you!"

"I knew how to trade when I hired on with you," Gio signed. "Anything I gained with you, I taught myself." He worked his mouth to spit, glanced at the calm Atlanta, and refrained.

"There is nothing for you here," Atlanta said to Gnarl. As with her stance, her face, her voice remained serene. But Gio sensed the readiness lurking within her. He had never seen Roxana in a fight, but paladins were said to be nigh unbeatable. It took a troop to take one down.

Gnarl snarled and took a step forward, but the bodyguard closest to him stepped in between, speaking in a low, urgent voice, pointing to the oncoming Peacekeeper. Frustration bubbled from Gnarl, but he acquiesced, his body stiff with rage, stepping back. He turned, snapped something at the guards, and marched off in another direction, again shoving his way through the crowd, jostling and pushing.

Atlanta looked to the guard. He nodded at her once, said something to his fellow, and they were gone.

Gio put his hands on his hips and regarded her. His face was brimming with laughter.

"What's so funny?" she demanded.

"Big bad paladin," he signed. "Just not something I would have expected when you first got shipped to us in a box." He laughed silently. "No warning label! Dangerous individual inside!"

She shoved at his shoulder, and he caught her hand and patted it. "Proud of you, Atlanta," he signed. He pointed at the stall and the vendor. "Now charge into trade battle!"

"How'd she do?" Milly asked Gio when they returned.

"Not bad," he signed. "Of course, she didn't have much to spend. Takes a while to build your stake if you're starting with that small a seed."

"Don't mention seeds around her, unless you want her to get all upset. Doesn't help that we're all wondering if we can keep going," she said.

"At least we had the meal of a lifetime from it."

She laughed, clacking her beak softly. "Yeah." Her face sobered. "What do we do if we get so low on supplies and cash that we can't afford to leave?"

"The captain and the sergeant will figure out a plan," he signed. "We're good enough for now." He reached out and tapped her elbow. "We have each other, all of us. Crew is like family. Isn't that enough?"

"You trust it," she said. "Our families aren't like yours. We toss the chicks out of the nest as soon as they're able to forage on their own, sometimes earlier in some cases. Makes us tough, and otherwise too many would be born."

He grimaced. "That's sad. But you have us now. We're not tossing anyone out of the nest." He drew back a little. "Unless they want to be tossed?"

She shook her head. "No. No, I want to stay as long as I can."

"That's all a family is," he signed. "People staying together as long as they possibly can."

23

Even though Rebbe never mentioned the biscuits again, Talon still thought bringing Rebbe the right gift would make the other like him. They couldn't talk about all the troubles, but Talon could give him something. An I'm-so-sorry-for—well, for all sorts of things.

He considered many possible gifts, driving vendors crazy with his questions, picking up an item and seeming on the verge of buying, only to put it back down again and again.

Finally, he settled on a scented, blunt wooden cone from Dewsun. It had no history, no hints of the past, or things that Talon had liked. It was something new, and he'd bought it because he liked it, in the way he knew that most of his species would have liked it. He bought one for himself as well, but took care to pick something very different, a rounded wooden cube with a different perfume.

To his surprise—and delight—Rebbe acted as he had when first touching the perfumed things at the vendor's cart. He rubbed it against his face, whiskers twitching forward, eyes half closing.

The deep-throated rumble from the other startled Talon. His first thought was that Thorn never made that sound, but he forced himself to relax into the moment and was rewarded.

Rebbe took the cone away with an obvious effort. He opened his eyes fully to look at Talon, who looked back. Rebbe's eyes were so like Talon's, pale green, striated with gold and amber.

"I like this," Rebbe said simply. "But when you give me gifts, it makes me uncomfortable. You want something in return—"

"I don't!" Talon said frantically. "Not at all.

Rebbe looked at him steadily until Talon's words ran down.

"You want something in return," Rebbe said. "That's one of the purposes of . . ." He waved vaguely in the air. "Gestures," he concluded. "Communication. What are you trying to communicate to me with this? That you'll leave me alone—as I've asked, more than once? Because gifts are another form of attention. Even when they're nice." He sniffed at the cone again. "Very nice," he said reluctantly.

He pushed it back toward Talon, but it was not accepted. Talon put his hands behind his back. "If you give it to me, I will drop it on the floor. It is not mine. I bought it for you, and now it's yours to do with as you like. Throw it out the airlock if you can't stand it."

With that, he turned and walked away, trying to do so with the same chilly dignity he had witnessed Niko summon when the occasion demanded it.

He hated this. He hated Rebbe. Maybe it was time to strike out on his own.

Rebbe did not throw the cone out the airlock.

Talon had looked at berth listings before at the hiring office, but never seriously. He and Thorn used to study them, imagining all the possible paths they might take if they switched ships, but never as though they might actually make the choice. For either of them, the thought of leaving Niko and the others behind would have been unthinkable.

Now, though, it was quite thinkable. Rebbe hated him, and wouldn't accept his gifts, even if he gave them to Rebbe, rather than Thorn's ghost. Talon had moved past things, was ready to accept Rebbe as Rebbe, as someone other than his lost twin, but Rebbe thought Talon never would, and that wasn't fair.

So he decided he'd sneak out and look at leaving the ship for another. He had plenty of experience. Plenty of skills. Most of the ones that fit his qualifications were fighting ones. Did he want to fight any more? He was skilled at it, he knew. But Niko said they didn't have to fight anymore in a tone that said it was a very good thing, and so he had always considered it good.

Now he thought about a chance to fight, the way he hadn't fought back with Rebbe, and the thought made his whiskers bristle and puff. He could do that.

He studied the wall board, watching it change, before going to an individual terminal in order to enter his search terms. The first page came up, and he scrolled through it.

As he did so, he thought, what would it be like, fighting side to side with a bunch of strangers? He knew his team, knew where everyone would go, what they'd do, just as they knew him, how to cover him, how to give him his best chance to go in hand-to-hand, because that was what he was best at.

"Looks like plenty of possibilities," a voice said beside him.

He managed not to jump but gave a startled twitch. How had Jezli Farren managed to sneak up on him so silently?

"What are you doing here?" he demanded.

"I might ask the same of you," she countered. "Thinking of leaving the *Thing*?"

He nodded once.

"Hmmm," she considered. "Well, I think you'd want to crew with a ship that runs in the style you're used to, and that's the Free Traders. Problem is, with them, you have to buy your way in and put up a pretty considerable stake."

Free Traders? That would mean he might encounter the *Thing* from time to time, maybe, in trading, and that would be good, because he would definitely miss everyone. A lot.

"How big a stake?" he asked.

She told him, and his eyes widened.

"What *I* would do," she said, casually, "is stick with the ship for now, and build my financial reserves."

He nodded again, but more slowly.

"That lets you know you've got an out, and you're working toward it, which always helps with a bad situation." She spread her hands with an expansive shrug. "And who knows? You might not find the situation so bad after all, once everything's totally shaken out. You've changed things; you've added a new dynamic . . ."

"I didn't mean to!" he burst out. "I didn't think."

She smiled at him. "No, you didn't. As I was saying . . . new dynamics mean everything moves around, and sometimes that's a little rough. Rebbe is all but a scattering of days old, can you expect him to act like an adult? Like you, who has so much experience?"

The flattering tinge to the words was balm to his soul. He puffed his chest out a little. "I have lots and lots," he said.

The patient Jezli let him expound on that experience all the way back to the ship.

It seemed to Skidoo the tremors came more and more frequently. Surely this was a sign of the next stage. It was progressing, swelling like a wave, and sooner or later it would wash over her and carry her away. What would she do? How would the others react? She didn't want to be dependent on them. She didn't want them to see her die, it would hurt to see them hurting, and that would be beyond bearing.

She retreated into her chamber and swam restlessly from wall to wall.

Thing said, "The others are gathering for a meal."

"Is not being hungry," she said.

"You have gone approximately eight hours without eating," *Thing* observed. "I do not believe that is normal for your species."

"Is being nothing that is being normal for my species!" she

snapped, and then regretted her words as *Thing* lapsed into hurt silence.

She stroked the wall. "Is being personal, *Thing*," she tried to explain. "Is being something that cannot be spoken of."

"But why?" it demanded. "Are you sick?"

"Is being personal, *Thing*," she emphasized again. "Is not being that I is not being wanting to tell you."

Silence again. Then, worriedly, from the ship, "Will you tell anyone?"

"When it is being time to do so," she said.

"Come to dinner," it coaxed. But she would not.

Rebbe had papers, but no actual experience, even though those papers said he'd lived eighteen years rather than eighteen days. He studied the berth board as it flashed possibilities, and used his data pad to call up some of the listings it mentioned.

This one called for experience with a gravitron, the next one a Bussard ram ship. He had no zero-G experience; that would be impossible to fake. He didn't even know what half the words in the next listing *meant*. His whiskers sagged at the thought of looking through listing after listing and finding none of them a fit for him. It was as though the weight of the Known Universe sat on his shoulders.

"Anything of interest?" a cheerful voice said at his elbow.

He jumped a few inches. He must have been oblivious, not to notice her approach.

He could summon no composure, simply blinked at her. Finally, he stammered, "Did you . . . did you follow me here?"

"I'm not sure why you'd be so interesting that I would have done so." Jezli gave every appearance of genuine curiosity.

"Why are you here?"

She shrugged. "Sooner or later, your captain will be asking that very same question, but about my continued presence on her ship. It seemed wise to look into the possibilities. So, anything of interest?"

"Everything requires experience," he muttered.

"Put in bioship and see what happens," she advised.

"I don't have bioship experience."

"Technically you have lived your entire life aboard one. You have at least some experience of what talking to the *Thing* is like."

"Bioship" yielded a handful of listings, one of which he might qualify for, if you stretched all his qualifications as far as the idea of being experienced with bioships did. He tabbed through them all, dutifully, trying not to react.

"Want more of my advice?" Jezli said.

"Sure."

"Stay on the *Thing*. It's a good berth, and you have people there who care whether you live or die. People who have a reason to invest energy in making you happy."

"In that case, why don't you stay?"

"For one thing, Niko would have to make that clear, and for another, Petalia would nix any such notion."

He considered this, although it was hard to sort out everything. "Why doesn't Petalia like you?"

"Sometimes people are like that." Jezli shrugged. "Oil and water can't mix. Well, except in emulsion, thus proving another old proverb wrong." She patted him on the shoulder. "Download the one you're thinking about and come back to the ship with me to mull things over. Don't make a snap decision."

He trudged back to the ship with her, his steps slow, the indefatigable Jezli chattering all the way, despite his monosyllabic replies.

Skidoo was missed at dinner. Milly and Gio exchanged looks, and he shrugged, spreading his hands.

Gio remembered when he'd first met Skidoo. Both of them freshly enlisted and wet—literally, in Skidoo's case—behind the ears. They'd both been a little bewildered by it all, and he would never admit it, but he'd been hoping—knowing it unreasonable, knowing it unlikely—that his fellow newbie would also be a fellow chimp. Plenty of young ones went off for soldiering and worked off their early years of aggression. He'd done so, and then realized he liked space, much more than he thought he would. He'd been back a couple of times in the interim, but it hadn't felt the same. Always having the same degree of gravity felt odd, and the air fluctuated all over the place, which in a ship would have signaled something was terribly wrong.

He hadn't really wanted to get along with Skidoo at first. She was weird, unlike anyone he had ever encountered before, and above all, very unlike him. Her way of talking drove him a little crazy sometimes, particularly when he realized she often switched into a simpler syntax in moments of stress and panic.

She'd grown on him over time, though. She did that with everyone. Skidoo had a sweetness, an innate gentleness and goodness that was utterly endearing—but in an operation, she was razor sharp, hard as steel, even if she was all apologies afterward for having snapped. He trusted her with his life and knew she trusted him to the same degree.

So why wasn't she talking about what bothered her? He'd caught her lapsing into thought more than once, considering some middle distance with an almost frightening intensity, as though she looked to some doom.

Talon had gone with her on the trip into Coralind, and he only knew that from looking at the logs. So what had happened?

He found Talon in a lounge, slouched morosely against the wall, watching a viddie. On the screen, there were a lot of explosions. He tapped Talon's shoulder to get his attention.

"Yeah?" Talon straightened enough to remove his headset and regarded Gio.

"You went into Coralind with Skidoo?" he signed.

Talon nodded.

"Where did you go? Did anything happen?"

Talon shrugged. "Nothing happened, really. She wanted to talk to a doctor who treated Tlellans."

This alarmed Gio. "Is she sick?"

"She doesn't act sick," Talon commented.

"You didn't ask her?"

"I figured it was her business, and she would tell me if she wants to," Talon said, a little sourly. "People are always just looking for a good excuse to scold me, and I'm tired of providing one."

Gio gave him a hard look from under furrowed brows. "She's your friend as well as your shipmate," he signed. "We all have a responsibility to each other."

Talon was defensive. "Everyone tells me to mind my own business all the time!"

"Have they said that to you lately?"

That made Talon think. "Not really."

"Because you've been so wrapped up in your own troubles you forget other people have their own," Gio signed with a disgusted face.

"Her business," Talon said sullenly. "If you want to know more, you'll have to ask her yourself."

Very well, Gio would do exactly that.

"Your young lions are restless," Jezli told Niko as they—Jezli, Niko, and Dabry—played a triple game of handbliss in the lounge.

Niko picked up a marker and discarded another. "What do

you mean?" She was very close to winning with a slam of a hand, if she could last just a few more rounds. She studied her cards expressionlessly.

Dabry glanced at Niko's face, checked his hands again, and played an unremarkable four of iron.

Jezli pursed her lips and took a very long time considering her cards. "I've found both of them down at the berth board, trying to figure out the listings."

"What?" Niko looked up from her cards.

"Unsurprising," Dabry said. "They're both unhappy."

"What did you do?" Niko asked Jezli.

"Gave them good advice about why they should stick on the ship for now, and a task to accomplish while they do that. Rebbe will ask to study bioships, unless I miss my guess, and Talon will work on his trademark, building capital." She played a five.

So close, Niko was so close to completing the first slam of a hand that she barely paid attention. She played her discard and prayed neither of her opponents had tracked her hand as scrupulously as they would have had to from the first moments of the game.

Dabry hadn't, apparently. He played the page of wrong and said, "That was kind of you, Jezli. And well thought, to give them some purpose."

Jezli said agreeably, "Yes, of course." She picked through her hand, glancing between it and what lay on the table. "Would you have had me do it any differently, Captain?"

Suspense crawled up Niko's spine. "Of course not," she said. "I believe it's your turn, though. Were you going to play a card?"

"Oh, of course." Jezli studied her cards while Niko chewed the inside of her lip. So very close. One card, only one card. The only card Jezli could play that would prevent it was . . .

"Three of iron." Jezli laid her card down.

Niko threw in her hand and stared across the table at her. Dabry kept any amusement to himself, with difficulty.

"Such a pleasure playing with you both," Jezli said.

"If you ever—"

"Yes, Captain?" Jezli looked attentively at Niko.

Niko shook a finger at her. "If you ever suggest playing for anything other than imaginary money, I will throw you off the ship. Is that clear?"

Lambent green eyes blinked. "But of course," Jezli murmured, then added, "Is that entirely fair to me, though? Have I given you any cause to think I would do other than that?"

"You have not," Niko said, grudgingly.

Jezli nodded.

The ship was the first to notice the seeds hatching. It was accompanied by a strange energy flux, much like the one it had experienced when Tubalina came aboard. For a moment or two, it wasn't sure if it had started *imagining* things again.

It opened its eyes in the garden chamber where the strange energies seemed to collect. It opened a second eye, and a third, fourth, and fifth in order to examine the situation from all angles.

"Captain?" it inquired. "Are you busy?"

"Yes? But not if you need something."

"You need to come to the gardens. As soon as possible."

"On my way."

"Captain?"

Niko paused in the doorway, almost colliding with the trailing Dabry. "Yes?"

"You need Lassite as well. I'm calling him now."

24

They entered the garden and almost instantly put their hands over their ears. The air thrummed with a pressure that was painful.

The garden looked as it always had, green and filled with plants. "What is it?" she demanded. "What's making that noise?"

"In the corner," the ship said. "The one farthest from you."

It seemed to both of them that the garden itself tried to prevent their passage. Vines snagged at them; roots seemed to tangle around unwary feet. The air smelled like ozone and mint and crushed greenery.

They pushed forward and found the rack where Atlanta had planted her seeds not too long ago. The rack spilled over with coils of blue-green leaves, growing so quickly you could watch their progress.

"What are these?" Niko asked. "I thought this side was unused racks." Wasn't there enough going on already, she thought to herself. Now some new fresh hell.

"Atlanta planted seeds there," the *Thing* informed her. "Was she not supposed to?"

"Those seeds weren't viable. The assay said that. What could have happened?" She pushed forward and parted some of the vines. She could see the heart of the plant now, so intermingled with a Derloen ghost that the vegetation seemed to grow out of the ghost.

"Lassite!" she shouted.

"Here, Captain." His voice came from somewhere near the doorway, obscured by vines. "What is this?"

"Your ghosts have combined with some seeds and the results are . . . unexpected," Niko said.

He pushed his way through the vegetation, which seemed to increase even as he walked through it. When he got to Niko, she pointed silently toward the ghost.

She'd never seen Lassite look discomposed, but his eyes widened at the sight. Bending over the plant, he reached down to try to coax the ghost out, but quickly snatched his fingers back.

"What now?" Niko asked.

"It . . . bit me, I think?"

He held out his hand, and she saw the ragged jaw marks along the outer edge, oozing blood.

"Get that taken care of at once," Niko ordered. "Have the medbay do a thorough analysis. I mean, *really thorough*."

He hesitated. "But the ghosts . . ."

"Get taken care of, then we'll worry about them," she said grimly. All sorts of thoughts crossed her mind. Who knew what sort of odd ailments might be carried in a bite from a ghost? She'd never heard of one attacking a human; Derloen ghosts were harmless, if disconcerting at times.

"The vegetation is increasing," she said. "*Thing*, if I leave, can you close off this chamber and . . . perhaps absorb the matter inside?"

"Maybe?" *Thing* said uncertainly. It was not sure how much of this it was imagining. You could never tell with imagination; it felt fairly certain about that. Maybe they imagined this. That would certainly be an interesting turn of events.

Dabry appeared and made his way through the room to Niko. The vegetation continued pressing around them.

"Should we do something with the plants?" Dabry suggested.

"If the *Thing* can't absorb them, spacing them would be the obvious choice," Niko said, clenching her teeth. "Even though we lose a lot of pricey biomass with it."

"All my special herbs are in that corner." Dabry pointed.

"Salvage what you can," she said. "Then let's get out of here."

Dabry mourned a number of his plants as he grabbed cuttings and seeds. His collection had taken a hit when they had to evacuate TwiceFar, and this was another blow.

Outside, he conferred with Niko. "Is this a random occurrence? Or part of some scheme?"

"Easy enough to spot Atlanta and sell her seeds," she said. "That wouldn't have taken much planning. But that she would plant them after they had been pronounced nonviable? That seems like a leap."

"Perhaps they would have interacted with the ghosts in any case," Dabry said.

"We need Lassite's knowledge. Ship, seal this area off while we talk to him in the medbay." She gave Dabry, all four arms laden with plants and cuttings, a look. "I suppose you'll need time to drop those off?"

"Just a few moments," he promised her. "I'll hurry."

"We think someone got those seeds on board specifically to interact with the ghosts," Niko told Lassite without preamble. "Then whatever Tubalina did, set it off."

"How would she have known about the ghosts?"

"We made them a fucking advertising point back on Twice-Far! How do you think someone monitoring our every move might have known?"

"I don't think she's told you everything about the multiple iterations of Tubal Last," Dabry said.

"Indeed." Niko was in total agreement. "But it takes a mind like Tubal Last's to conduct a plan with so many moving parts."

"A complex plan," Lassite said in a neutral tone.

"I get the feeling you know more about this than you are let-ting on," she told him.

He raised his eyes to her. Over the years, she had learned to read the micropatterns that betrayed his emotions. He was tense, almost at a breaking point, she realized. He said evenly, "I say as much as I can say, Captain. I have always done so, always told you everything I can."

"But not everything you *could*." It wasn't a question.

He shook his head slowly. Dabry frowned but kept silent.

"And those circumstances are absolute?" she asked. "If we were about to die or walk into some trap, those circumstances would prevent any warning?"

Agony and fear warred across his face, though that would have been invisible to most. "Everything I can," he assured.

"What happens if you say more?"

He spread his hands wide. "It changes so many factors! Then everything leads to disaster greater than you can imagine."

"I can imagine a lot," Niko said softly, but he shook his head again.

"You do not understand the stakes," he insisted. "They stretch as wide as the Known Universe, and beyond."

"So big, and us so small," she mused.

"Together, we are all that matters," he said.

She looked at him hard, but he said nothing more.

Lassite was worried, though. He had thought the ghosts would be important, but not that they would weave themselves into things like this. He had seen them on the edges of the path, but they seemed so minor. Now, several influences moved together and disaster threatened to overtake them all.

He delved into his magic, tried to change the energy on the

ship, but it resisted, threw him out in a backlash that tried to turn him inside out.

The mottling had worsened, and now it spread across almost all of one tentacle. No one had spoken of it, but she saw Atlanta looking at it this morning with the faintest of frowns.

Skidoo floated in the water. Was she dying? Would they miss her? What would they do without her?

A knock on the door.

"Is being going away," she told the water.

"Gio says to tell you he can hear you," the *Thing* said.

Skidoo raised her voice. "Then is definitely being going away because you is being hearing me!"

A silence. Then the *Thing* relayed, "He says he won't go away until he knows what is wrong."

"Everything! Nothing!" She curled helplessly in the pool of water at the room's center.

The door opened. Gio stooped beside her pool, a hand outstretched to touch the nearest tentacle.

"You don't need to tell me," he signed. "Just let me keep you company."

Company. She had only ever wanted that in life, and she hated that she would no longer have it when she died. Her tentacle uncoiled and reached to curl around his wrist.

"I is not being going anywhere for now," she told him, and while he didn't understand her meaning, he nodded.

That was when the ship alarm sounded.

25

The *Thing* sealed off the plants and thought that was the end of it. The plants, however, had disabled sensors by insinuating a thousand tiny rootlets into them, and so the ship did not understand what was happening until nearly too late. It blasted an alarm into every chamber. Almost everyone was sleeping except Lassite; at the sound of the alarm, he rose, already dressed in his priestly robes, drew his red hood over his head, and moved toward the door.

"What's going on, *Thing*?" Niko, and Dabry, and almost everyone else on the ship asked, and the ship answered them in a unison from its speakers, a startled bleat that crawled up the spine and set the nerves on edge with contagious panic.

"Too much! The plants are too much!"

They approached the hatchway leading down to the garden chambers. Vines crawled out, long and shining with a ghostly opalescence that roiled with oily colors. They were sluggish and slow, but their movement seemed inexorable. Thorns rode their purple and green lengths, iridescent and dripping a sap that sizzled when it touched the floor, leaving pockmarks that grew in front of their horrified eyes.

Dabry's fingers danced over screens. "The vines are everywhere," he said, his voice calmness wrapped around tension. "We can't get out, they're blocking the hatches."

"They're HURTING me," the ship screamed. "They're DISSOLVING me." A wave of servitors boiled around them, trying to attack the vines but being repelled by the acidic thorns. They fought on without question even as they dissolved into heaps of pseudoflesh.

Niko's hands covered her ears. "Stop screaming, *Thing*!" she shouted, unsure whether it could hear her over the din it made.

Apparently, it did, because the noise cut off.

"Help me, Captain," the ship begged, and the quietness in its voice wrung her heart.

"Lassite?" She looked to him, but he was looking elsewhere.

Atlanta came down the corridor radiating light, a light that mixed together warmth and love and common sense, the same light Roxana had shed. She had awoken not knowing what was going on, only that she was called, that every iota of her needed to respond. She moved like a woman in a trance, eyes wide and clear and fearless.

Dabry moved as though to snatch her from the thorns, but before he could, the vines hesitated, quivered, then snatched forward, seizing Atlanta. Everyone cried out, but she remained silent. The entangling vines bound her hands to her sides, thorns digging into her flesh. She felt their bite distantly. That didn't matter. Only what she was called to do mattered.

But it was not enough. She was not enough. The vines curled around her, tearing deep.

Skidoo watched her lover caught by the vines, hanging suspended in the air. Did it mean anything to her, when she was dying? The world was passing away. Was anything worth bothering about when the severing was about to take her away from that world?

But it did mean something. She moved up, regardless of the flailing vines, and unrolled a tentacle, stretching it out to coil around Atlanta's wrist, giving her strength. Atlanta's light flickered, growing brighter.

Dabry and Niko exchanged glances. She was still angry over his dereliction, but she held out her hand. Together, the two of them stepped up, laying a hand on Atlanta, whose light grew even brighter.

Still not enough. The vines pressed higher and tighter, thorns tearing at the walls.

"Us," Talon turned to Rebbe. "Talon and Rebbe, not anything else." He held out his own hand and after a moment of consideration, Rebbe nodded, and they also stepped forward.

Gio and Lassite linked hands without questioning. Milly hung back for a moment and then joined them. She was as much a part of this as any of them, she told herself.

Even the ship became part of the light that poured from Atlanta, washing over the vines, shriveling them, driving them back.

Only Jezli Farren hung back, watching. She'd had some part in creating it, in making sure that Talon and Rebbe were both present, for one. If she tinkered too hard, Lassite would sense her hand rather than simply suspecting it. This moment was as it should be, one of the moments where his path and hers coincided. God help the universe when they did not.

26

Niko didn't expect Janus, but there he was, outside and asking to visit. She went down to meet him.

He squinted at her. "Seems like one of Gnarl Grusson's own bodyguards turned him in. Showed the authorities where there was a nice little stash, including some of the same batch that killed Biboban."

"That's a relief," she said.

"Strange moment," he said. "Revelations and confessions all over the station." He hesitated. "I know your restaurant got closed. That wasn't part of the investigation. Biboban set that up the day before it died."

"Part of its revenge," she said slowly.

Janus's eyes sharpened. "Revenge for what?"

"For not being the friend it thought I was."

He held out a plastic sheet. "This states you're clear."

She took it and put it away for safekeeping.

"We owe you for the false accusations made against you," he said. "If there is anything we can do . . ."

"As a matter of fact," Niko said, "there just might be."

The EverRich receptionist looked up when Niko, followed by two others, entered the room. Before she could speak, they declared, "I have told you before, nothing can be done without an appointment!"

Niko shrugged and stepped aside.

Janus stepped up and said, with his usual mild apologetic air, "The lady is to be given every cooperation."

Their head swiveled and their eyes widened with outrage. "And you are?"

He flashed his credentials. "The man with the powers to shut you down."

Niko returned with the full sum, plus 3 percent interest for the time the money had been held.

It felt like unfinished business, so Atlanta returned to the Banksin, but this time she took Lassite with her, after telling him the full account of what had happened before.

The tent was still there with its guarding sentinel. She looked at him and he regarded her, but this time he did not beckon.

Still, she made her way through the crowd and stood before him. "I'm going in," she stated, "and he is going with me." She indicated Lassite with a sweep of her hand.

The guard nodded once and stepped aside.

Atlanta entered the tent with Lassite at her heels. It smelled as unpleasant as it had the last time.

As before, the Banksin sat on their throne-like chair. "You have returned to tell me your story?" they asked. "It must have gotten longer in the interim. You have brought great changes to this station, and others that will linger in your wake."

"It sounds as though you know her story already," Lassite observed. His voice sounded polite, but distant, as he looked around.

"Ahhhhhhh," the Banksin said, as though spotting him for the first time. "The Sessile prophet."

"Not a prophet," Lassite said. "Nor are you one."

"Why has she returned then?"

"How did you know what to say to scare me?" Atlanta asked.

It peered at her. "That is the question you would have me answer? Because I will answer once, and then you will owe me your story."

"Agree to nothing!" Lassite interjected sharply. "That is not trade law, and you are a luck stealer, who frightens people into giving up bits of themselves."

"Mmm." The being settled back into its throne, regarding Lassite. "Not always because they are frightened," it said. "Sometimes they want to be rid of something."

"Your trade is not ethical," Lassite continued. "The reason they knew what to ask you, Atlanta, is that there are basic questions at everyone's heart: Why is the world unfair? Why am I not loved? Why am I not happy? Was it something like that?"

"Sort of." She looked at the Banksin.

"They want your story so they can unravel your luck in listening to its details. They pretend to give you clues and let you construct and solve the mystery, then they take the credit for it."

This was as animated as she'd ever seen Lassite. He took her by the wrist and tugged her out of the tent. "You cannot give away your luck, you must watch over it!" he scolded.

"I don't know anything about how to do that!" she protested.

"I cannot teach you magic, but I can teach you that at least. We will begin tomorrow. Do not eat or drink anything before you come to me."

"Does that help?"

"It makes sure you are not sleepy," he explained, and she couldn't tell if he was joking or not.

Atlanta had presented the idea to Dabry first.

"You said the station takes some of our biomass when we go, and some people make a little extra selling it," she said.

"Yes," he confirmed. "If it's something they might want."

"I had a piece of vine analyzed," she said. "Here." She handed him the printout. "Are those things they'd want?"

His eyes scanned the printout. "Oh, sweet Sky Momma, as Niko would say."

"That's good?"

"Very good." He beamed at her. "Well done, Princess."

For the first time, the nickname had no sting.

"Bio and thaumic mass all together in one package," the Chief Gardener noted happily. They tabbed up the load and showed Dabry the figure. "You couldn't have done better if you'd spent six months choosing a cargo."

Dabry signed the manifest and tucked away the credit slip. Back on the ship, he showed the amount to Niko. She whistled.

"That's enough to keep us going, what, six months even with a few splurges?"

He nodded.

"Talk about spinning silver out of starlight," she said. "Well, that's good news for once."

This time, Skidoo asked Atlanta to accompany her to the medic. Talon hadn't been a bad companion, but she needed to tell Atlanta. Atlanta, who had become so special to her that sometimes Skidoo felt herself as a thing coiled around the other's name. More than her name, the *thought* of her. The vision of her burning brightly, vines around her, Skidoo reaching out and being part of that, as though Atlanta drew on her essence but at the same time returned it. Made her something more.

She said nothing of that. Instead, she told Atlanta what made her come to the medic in the first place, and what he confirmed.

Atlanta listened quietly, not asking questions. Skidoo conveyed what he had said of the second stage.

"We is being going back," she finally said. "I is being asking him what to do now that it is coming."

"Thank you for telling me," Atlanta said. She waited until Skidoo had gone through the lonely office doorway to break down and cry into her hands. At least she was underwater and the tears, so much hotter than the cool water, flowed away as fast as they came.

It wasn't fair, she thought. For the best to be taken like this. First Thorn, then Roxana, and now Skidoo. Skidoo, who she loved, and who loved her.

A touch on her shoulder. She looked up to see the receptionist offer her a small, chilled, white cloth. The receptionist motioned that she should hold it against her face. She did, and the sensation felt refreshing, like plunging her face in cold water.

"You are all right?" the receptionist asked.

"Sad news," Atlanta explained. "I had sad news."

"Often, here." The receptionist gestured around herself. "Your friend, though . . ."

"What?"

"Ever since she came, the doctor has been different."

"Different how?"

"Kinder. Gentler. Do you know what she might have said to him?"

Atlanta shook her head. "That's just how she is." She managed, just barely, not to start crying again. "That's just how she is."

When the medic entered, Skidoo unrolled her tentacle with a dramatic flourish in front of him so he could see the brown mottling, and waited.

He peered at it. "Hmm." He turned it this way and that, considering. He gently prodded a mottling with a finger. "Does this hurt?"

"It is not being hurting," she said.

"Good. I've got a spray that will clear that up. Give this chit to the receptionist and she'll give you a ten-day supply. Don't stop spraying until the full ten days are up."

Skidoo, startled, blurted out, "This isn't the severing?"

He frowned. "Of course not. Have you had any of the symptoms I told you about?"

"No . . ." She felt like she had been tied into a knot, then forcibly untangled.

"Could be years, maybe decades. No one knows, your case is extraordinary." He paused. "Something about you changed my bedside manner and at first I thought I was going soft." He shook his head. "And then I saw how my patients responded." He coughed. "I'm sorry I was unkind."

"You is being bringing me good news, which is being very kind," Skidoo said.

Outside, Atlanta gravely asked how things were.

"Is being a spray to cure it!" Skidoo told her.

"So you're not experiencing this dissolution thing?" Atlanta said. "Skid, you scared me!"

Skidoo coiled around her, despite the gasp of scandalized delight from the receptionist. "I is being fine," she said in Atlanta's ear. "And before we is going back to the ship, we is being going to Lassitude again."

So they did.

Milly and Gio offloaded bushels of leaves in the antechamber as Atlanta and Skidoo floated past. They paused.

Gio signed to Milly, "Never seen Skidoo act like that." He grinned.

"Never expected that myself," she responded, and forked a load of leaves at him, which he returned, and so they went on, offloading and throwing bundles of leaves at each other until Niko came out and kindly suggested that they cease their shenanigans.

Talon and Rebbe worked together for once, stacking boxes under Gio's watchful eye. It was hot work in the enclosed space, and heavy, but at least it was something to do.

Talon deliberately kept himself from racing the way he would have with Thorn, vying to see who could go the fastest. Instead, he settled into the same slow but steady rhythm Rebbe adopted, and they worked together in silence for some while.

Then Rebbe said, "When I went out, we went to Ganache confluence and that was my favorite. What did you like best?"

"The one where Skidoo and I went. We went swimming!"

"I didn't try that one," Rebbe said thoughtfully. After more silence, he spoke, more to the box he hefted than to Talon. "I was thinking about taking another ship, but I don't have a lot of skills."

"Bioship skills," Talon said promptly. Then he parsed out the other's words. "But *I* was going to leave!" he said indignantly. "Jezli Farren talked me out of it."

Rebbe's expression was almost comical. "She stopped me too! Did she sneak up on you?"

"I wasn't really paying attention to anything but the boards," Talon said defensively.

"Yeah, me too." Rebbe looked at Talon. He had a family, he had a ship, he had people who loved him and cared about them, and he'd been prepared to give all of that up to Rebbe, to leave because he couldn't see any other choice. "We aren't brothers, we will never be brothers."

The breath caught in Talon's throat at the desolation in

those words. But Rebbe continued. "Maybe, though, we can be friends."

"Friends is good," Talon said. "Friends is fine."

"I can't replace him. He's gone."

"I know that. I really do."

"All right. But I have a favor to ask. Don't talk about him around me, okay?"

Talon nodded. He held out a hand.

They shook on it.

This was good, Rebbe decided as they went back to work. This was very good. Everything would be fine.

As long as what he feared the most never happened. As long as Thorn never *did* come back. Once again, he checked his internal echoes, worrying that someone lived inside him without his knowledge, but found nothing there.

27

Atlanta never got messages, and yet here were two. The first said the following:

Atlanta—

Word reaches us that you have become a paladin. We know of such, but never dared dream that our planet might be graced by such an individual, when so few are called to the path. Your power as a champion will help protect the empire.

You will forgive me for launching you in such a fashion, but by secret tradition, we send our potential heirs into the Universe, and the one who achieves what will make them the most useful to the empire is the successor. It has been three hundred years since the crown last passed from one hand to another, and finally, I have found one worthy.

We understand you may have further training to undergo. Rest assured that we have summoned the finest experts and scholars on paladins. When we applied for an actual paladin to mentor you, they told us that it would not be necessary, which surely means that this is sufficient.

*Accordingly, funds have been placed in the Imperial
bank for you. Draw upon them, and return to us,
daughter. We are well pleased.
Empress of Pax, her seal*

Atlanta then turned to the second letter:

Esteemed paladin—

*I thank you for your kind words, and for the strength they
gave me. I turned in Captain Gnarl because things were
only going to get worse and worse, and he was going to
drag down the crew with him. Some of us are good people;
we just fell in with the wrong folk. Tell your shipmate Gio
he was lucky; everything was worse after he left.*

Signed with a scribble. She set that one down as well.

No word of where he planned to go, what he planned to do.
Were Gnarl's crew setting up without him? Would they be able
to do that, or would Gnarl's incarceration force him to give up
his ship? That worried her a little.

Then she folded both letters up and put them away.

She had a bank to go to, and beyond that, errands to run.
Minasit counted as company, surely. Plus the servitor, unlike the
other ill-fated one the ship had sent with Niko, hadn't gotten a
chance to step off the ship. Travel broadened one, she'd heard.
Surely it would do that for a servitor as well.

Thing felt that Atlanta, waiting for a moment of distraction, had
snuck Minasit off-board, otherwise the *Thing* surely would have
noticed long before Minasit stepped out of its mental field and

vanished. Outraged, it focused its cameras outward and saw the two leaving. Atlanta had failed to reply to any of its commands to return along with the servitor.

It was incensed and immediately reported her to Dabry and Niko simultaneously. It was a measure of its fluster that it failed to notice both were in the shared office, and so two different speakers began announcing the news at the same time.

"Atlanta has gone unaccompanied onto the station with my servitor!"

"That does not, precisely, count as unaccompanied," Niko said. "And Sky Momma knows everyone else seems to have snuck off for their own excursions, here and there." She avoided looking at Dabry. "If she's not back within two hours, let us know."

"Perhaps I will need to reabsorb the servitor with her," the *Thing* continued. "In case it has been compromised in some way."

"Now you are just being petty, *Thing*."

The *Thing* looked up the definition of *petty* and decided that was not a good thing to be. It seethed and contemplated possibilities. It remembered the strange behavior of the servitor that had accompanied Niko. It did not trust its servitors, it decided, once they left the ship, and it would no longer allow any to leave, no matter what.

"In the meantime," Niko said to Dabry, "we have this." She flourished a message.

"Something that concerns us, sir?" he asked.

"No," she said. "A serendipitously timed invitation. Arpat says he hears we've been doing a great deal and perhaps we might check in again?"

"Does that seem wise?"

She shrugged. "It seems as good as any other course we might lay in. He'll serve a fine table, he's in Space civilized enough that

Tubal Last would have trouble acting without incurring the notice of the Counterpoint police, and that's something he'd prefer to avoid for all sorts of reasons, the least of which is illegal cloning."

Dabry's eyes flickered. "And Rebbe?"

"We will introduce him with the name change story. We'll order him and Talon both to be on their best behavior. As far . . ." She broke off. "No, he knew of Talon's death. Rebbe will have to stay onboard."

"As will I," Jezli Farren said from the doorway.

"Should I just assume you've been listening since the beginning, and not bother filling you in on the salient details?" Niko snapped.

Jezli smiled. "I could hear the name 'Arpat Takraven' being mentioned as I came down the hall, and I am well acquainted with the history of this ship by now. Your garrulous crew—not to mention the ship itself—enjoyed having a new audience. However, I do not want to meet Arpat Takraven. I've met his kind aplenty before."

"Plus, he might give your background some scrutiny?" Niko queried.

Jezli rolled a shoulder to stretch it and took her time answering. "Believe whatever you like, Captain, but nonetheless, I will stay behind and entertain Rebbe. And the ship, who sometimes seems to need entertainment to keep it out of mischief."

"I have never been in mischief!" the *Thing* interjected.

"Mmm," Niko murmured. "Although some might call it *hourisigah* by some other name."

The ship remained silent.

"Settled, then," Jezli said. "Perhaps you will bring back some leftovers?"

"Ready to go?" Gio signed as Atlanta trudged up the launch way, a laden Minasit behind her. "What's all that?"

"Trade stock," she said.

He raised an eyebrow. "Find some good things, did you?"

She shrugged with elaborate nonchalance. "Fair enough," she said. "Might do okay next time we're somewhere."

Gio nodded and waited to grin to himself until she was inside. Let the girl pull off something clever, that was good, and would build her confidence. Nothing like doing well in trade to give a little puff to your huff when you needed it. He'd been worried her experience with the seeds would have put her off.

Atlanta did have complete genetic workups for everything she stacked in her cabin. Trade certificates and articles of authenticity, and provenances when applicable. It turned out the cost of a passage back to Pax was the equivalent of an awful lot when you converted it to high-quality trade goods—and some chocolate.

She considered. Would she tell Niko that the empress had summoned her? Or would the empress, realizing that her supposed heir had fled, contact the captain?

She wasn't an heir anymore, though. Not a pretend one, not a real one. She was one and one thing only. She was a paladin, devoted to helping the universe move as it should. And there was no better place for her to be learning how to do it than here.

They had been unable to find any sign of his daughter, but the station officials assured Dabry she was not there. She must have taken a ship out, they said, and provided him with a list.

He hated leaving the mystery of his daughter behind, but after meeting with Takraven, Niko promised they'd cast in the direction of his home planet. "It's best to present a moving target, anyway," she'd explained. "And I don't know that he knows of your daughter's existence. How could he, when it has been something hidden from you for so long?"

As for the gardens, well, they would come here again, surely, and for a longer time, when they had no troubles weighing on them, and no reason to keep looking over their shoulders. Then he would have time to explore them and the ingredients that had been so intriguing.

28

Festival was over, and it would be a full year before it came again. Vomasi wasn't worried about that distant future so much as today. With Biboban gone, so much was chaos. The government was breaking down, with fewer and fewer services provided each day.

In his cell, Gnarl Grusson stared at the ceiling with hate-filled eyes. He composed his list of who he would destroy, and no matter the configuration, Niko was at the top. She was somehow responsible for the way his crew had managed to break conditioning and betray him.

He turned over on the cot and punched his pillow in a futile attempt to soften it.

Footsteps, coming along the hall.

They stopped outside his cell. He could feel them, whoever they were, standing there, looking him over. Well, let them. He wouldn't give them the satisfaction of paying them attention.

But their words caught his attention when they finally spoke. "I believe we have a foe in common."

He turned over to look at the woman, unremarkable in appearance, who stood there.

"I have a proposition for you," Bette, sometimes known as Tubalina, said.

She smiled at him, and it was a smile full of promise of very unpleasant things for that common foe.

29

The surroundings that Arpat Takraven provided them were lavish, each note carefully calculated to enchant, to please, to flatter those within its setting. Servants brought plate after plate of collated nibbles, each a different marvel, leading into others.

The rough, black lumps amid coils of green weed of one such plate lay in three perfect concentric circles, drizzled with a resinous oil, and once carved open, revealed perfectly cooked interiors so decadently delicious even the non-meat-eaters tried a taste, or two, or several. The glassy spoon used to eat a honeyed pudding shattered into sweet, icy splinters to follow its consumption. The glowing eggs illuminating the table hatched into balls of luminous dough that turned out to have centers of savory paste.

They sat at an enormous circular table, its center hollow so the droids could circle, serving food. Arpat's almost throne-like chair was constructed of a metal that Niko, who was sitting beside him in a much humbler but still incalculably valuable chair, had never seen before.

Seeing her examining it, he grimaced. "It's back support," he murmured. "My lifestyle's hard on it." He wore a body identical to the one in which she'd first encountered him, seemingly so long ago.

She made a noncommittal noise. Was he one of those who moved from body to body with ease? Harder than it sounded. First, you had to have the money, and then it took a special kind of mind to move from host to host.

She looked around at her crew. Talon sat by himself. She wished they could have brought Rebbe. Lately, he and Talon had been sitting together for a change, actually passing each other things.

Not the way Thorn and Talon would have, with little pokes and fierce whispers, pretending to be vying for the choicest morsel. More like shipmates, if not brothers, who knew they had to get along and weren't, for the moment, having a particularly hard time doing that.

Lassite regarded their host with a fixed gaze. She'd caught him with that same parsec-long stare before. When she'd prodded him, he said something unintelligible about the way fate lines curled around the entity currently known as Arpat Takraven.

Dabry ate but still worried at thoughts of his daughter, wondering what to do. One of the ships on his list had a significant destination—where she had supposedly died. Niko thought she might have fallen in with the rebel movement there.

Atlanta looked happier than she had for a while. The girl was coming into her own, finally, and had stopped looking so lost. She still needed guidance, certainly, and guidance of a type Niko could not personally provide. Where would that come from?

Milly laughed with Gio, swapping bites. Good to see the two of them friendly again—for a while, she had wondered. But sometimes you left people to themselves and let them work it out, because they'd do it better than you ever could.

Skidoo draped a tentacle across the back of Atlanta's chair. This was interesting. Skidoo had always been indiscriminating in her activities, but clearly there was some special bond between the two, and Niko thought the gardens of Coralind might have witnessed some interesting moments.

The *Thing* wasn't here, though, although it felt as much a crew member as any. When Arpat asked about their adventures, she wondered how much she should make of the *Thing*'s new capabilities, of its possibly dangerous eccentricities. The hobby of *hourisigah*, for example, was something Arpat surely would not appreciate, given how little Niko herself appreciated it. She did miss the moments of thematic music that the ship had managed to interject here and again, though. Next time, perhaps they'd bring one of its servitors.

Everyone enjoyed themselves. Dish after dish flowed past in an unending stream.

Once they were sated, Arpat leaned back. "Tell me about your adventures," he said.

It took longer than they might have thought to recount their adventures, although Niko found herself reducing Jezli to a minor figure, one that wouldn't attract Takraven's notice, a helper to the fallen paladin more than anything else. Dabry noticed and gave her a quizzical look but said nothing. The rest of them followed her lead as well.

"I could not help but notice," Niko noted, "that you summoned us well before a year was up."

Takraven raised an eyebrow. "Oh, I certainly want you to complete that." He beamed. "No, so much had happened, by all accounts, that I wanted to check in. What now for you?"

Niko ignored the question. "So, you may require other such check-ins? How often might we expect them?"

"Captain Niko, Captain Niko," Arpat chided. "I'm sure things will settle down and your lives will be less eventful." His smile suggested the opposite. "If you want to keep operating the *Thing*, some small prices must be paid here and there. Nothing more onerous than this sort of meal. I ask again, because I am so curious: where to, next?"

The question was unavoidable. "Dabry's home planet," she replied.

"And the mysterious Tubal Last?"

"Still out there. But I think he may have miscalculated. If Tubalina was able to make schemes on her own, then all of them can. And that means they'll turn on each other."

Arpat dabbed his lips with a napkin.

"And when that championship is over, and the winner looks in your direction . . . ?"

She raised her glass and toasted him but did not smile.

"We'll burn that bridge when we come to it," she said.

ACKNOWLEDGMENTS

Every book is its own journey, and this one took me through a passage of enormous changes: the dissolution of a twenty-five-year-old marriage; relocation across the country, back to where I grew up; and the purchase of a house that is becoming the new Casa Rambo. I continue to love Niko and her crew, and I'm working on their next installment now.

Thank you to everyone who has helped in the creation of this book. I'd particularly like to call out:

The able crew at Tor, including Aislyn Fredsall, Jess Kiley, Peter Lutjen, Gertrude King, Rebecca Yeager, Desirae Friesen, Michelle Li, Ryan T. Jenkins, Greg Collins, Jacqueline Huber-Rodriguez, and most of all, editor Jen Gunnels, who had a great deal of patience with my constant typing "Thorn" when I meant "Talon" and vice versa.

My awesome agent, Seth Fishman.

My Patreon supporters, who cheer me on and keep me going. Our lively Discord community is one of my main sources of support, and I love you all.

Three awesome friends: Anastasia Mayette Draper, Ken Peczkowski, and Wayne Rambo.

The baristas of Chicory Café, Biggby, and Jack's Donuts, who kept me caffeinated throughout this writing.

ABOUT THE AUTHOR

CAT RAMBO lives, writes, and teaches somewhere in the Pacific Northwest. Their two hundred plus fiction publications include stories in *Asimov's Science Fiction, Clarkesworld Magazine,* and *The Magazine of Fantasy & Science Fiction.* They are a Nebula Award winner, and an Endeavour and World Fantasy Award finalist. For more about them, as well as links to their fiction and their popular online school, the Rambo Academy for Wayward Writers, see www.kittywumpus.net/.